'Niamh Mulvey's w[...]
prose offer great ple[...]
is sharp, and the be[...]

Joseph O'Connor, author of *My Father's House*
and *Star of the Sea*

'A smart, subtle, engrossing and moving novel that gives voice to so much that's unspoken about Ireland and about youth'

Emma Donoghue, author of *Room*

'An extraordinary achievement. *The Amendments* is about a lot of things – love, family, girlhood, growing up, sex, legacy, compassion – all blended into a moving plot, expertly handled. Wonderful'

Jessie Burton, author of *The Miniaturist*

'I loved *The Amendments*. Rare is the novel that is as significant as it is enjoyable: her characters glimmer with heart and soul, her writing is beautiful and her themes profound. It's a book about mothers and daughters, friendship, hope, bravery and what it means to believe in something. A fantastic and important achievement'

Emma Stonex, author of *The Lamplighters*

'Rarely has a book moved me as *The Amendments* has: it cuts to the heart of what it means to be human, to want, to love, to be a mother or a daughter or a woman moving through the world. It's a triumph of a book, and a vital one too'

Elizabeth Macneal,
author of *The Doll Factory*

'I genuinely loved *The Amendments*. I found it such a tender, compassionate, deeply believable novel. I'd defy any Irish woman, in particular, to read this and not feel that sense of innate recognition that all the best writing elicits'

Niamh Hargan, author of *Twelve Days in May*

'Intriguing . . . Abortion, the Church, teenage pregnancy, the Celtic Tiger – Mulvey has covered plenty of ground'

Irish Independent

'Niamh Mulvey has written a deft and deeply moving fiction about cross-generational secrets and longings, because such is the stuff of our everyday, dramatic, secretive lives. This is a work of beauty and insight'

Ed O'Loughlin, author of *Not Untrue & Not Unkind*

'*The Amendments* is a compelling, beautifully observed novel about the long reach of shame in the lives of Irish women across generations'

Sarah Gilmartin, author of *Dinner Party*

'An engaging debut novel'

Irish Examiner

'A questing first novel of significant prowess'

The Observer

'Compelling . . . smart, perceptive . . . *The Amendments* is an opening salvo from a novelist of grit and power'

The Irish Times

'Elegant prose and an earnest engagement with emotional integrity are the hallmarks of this engrossing coming-of-age tale . . . The novel brims with drama and dilemmas as Nell and her mother together tackle the thorny issues of faith, freedom and feminism in a cloistered society'

The Mail on Sunday

THE AMENDMENTS

Niamh Mulvey is the author of the short story collection *Hearts and Bones,* which was shortlisted for the John McGahern Prize. Her writing has been published in *The Stinging Fly, Banshee, Southword* and *The Irish Times* and has been shortlisted for the Seán O'Faoláin Prize. She lives in Kilkenny, Ireland. *The Amendments* is her first novel.

ALSO BY NIAMH MULVEY

Hearts and Bones

NIAMH MULVEY

The Amendments

PICADOR

First published 2024 by Picador

This paperback edition first published 2025 by Picador
an imprint of Pan Macmillan
The Smithson, 6 Briset Street, London EC1M 5NR
EU representative: Macmillan Publishers Ireland Ltd, 1st Floor,
The Liffey Trust Centre, 117–126 Sheriff Street Upper,
Dublin 1, D01 YC43
Associated companies throughout the world
www.panmacmillan.com

ISBN 978-1-5290-7987-6

Copyright © Niamh Mulvey 2024

The right of Niamh Mulvey to be identified as the
author of this work has been asserted by her in accordance
with the Copyright, Designs and Patents Act 1988.

All rights reserved. No part of this publication may be reproduced,
stored in a retrieval system, or transmitted, in any form, or by any means
(electronic, mechanical, photocopying, recording or otherwise)
without the prior written permission of the publisher.

Pan Macmillan does not have any control over, or any responsibility for,
any author or third-party websites referred to in or on this book.

1 3 5 7 9 8 6 4 2

A CIP catalogue record for this book is available from the British Library.

Typeset by Palimpsest Book Production Limited, Falkirk, Stirlingshire
Printed and bound by CPI Group (UK) Ltd, Croydon, CR0 4YY

This book is sold subject to the condition that it shall not, by way of
trade or otherwise, be lent, hired out, or otherwise circulated without
the publisher's prior consent in any form of binding or cover other than
that in which it is published and without a similar condition including
this condition being imposed on the subsequent purchaser.

Visit **www.picador.com** to read more about all our books
and to buy them. You will also find features, author interviews and
news of any author events, and you can sign up for e-newsletters
so that you're always first to hear about our new releases.

For Rose and Ger Mulvey

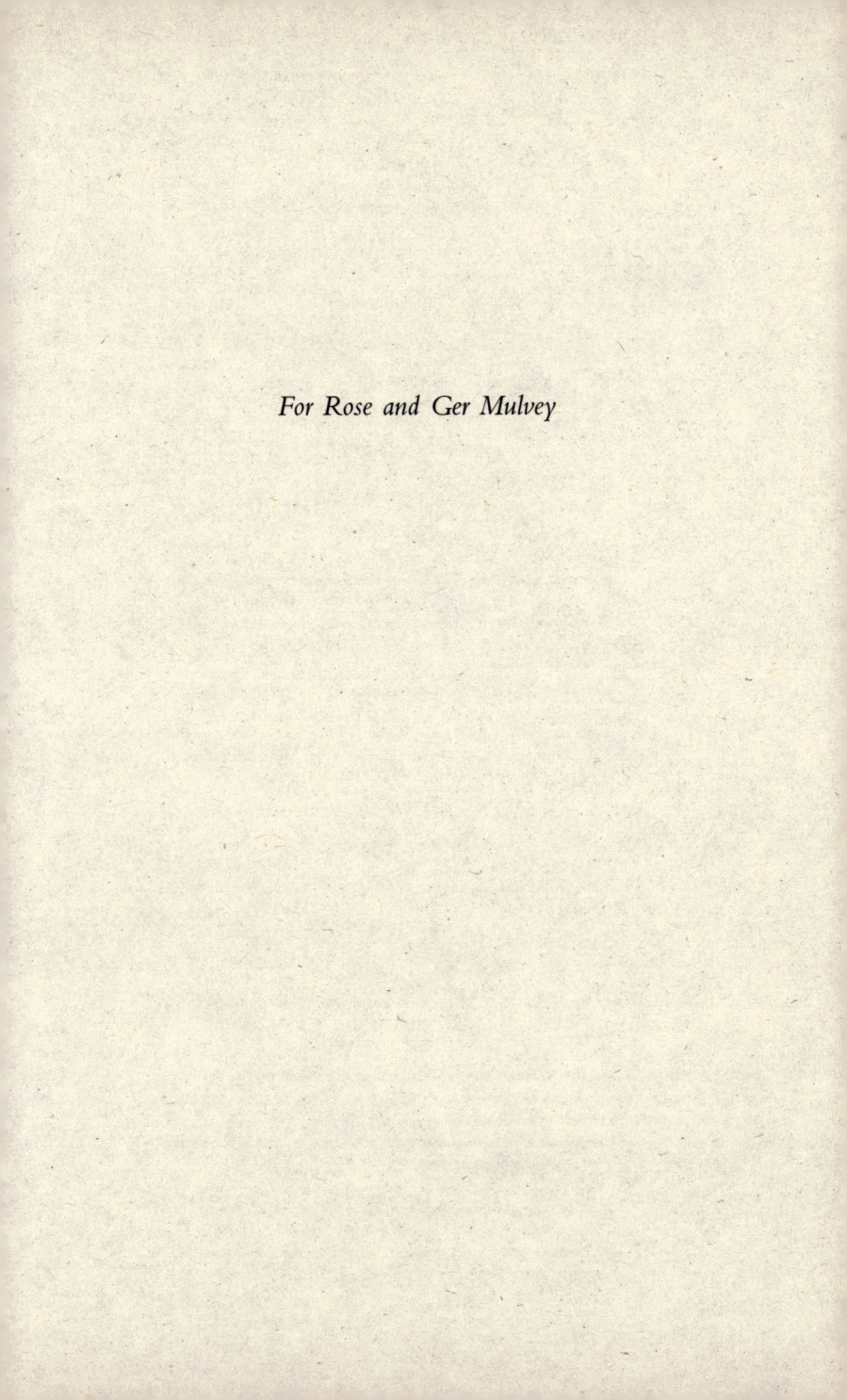

'It is not night when I do see your face'

William Shakespeare,
A Midsummer Night's Dream

I

London, January 2018

The atmosphere in the room is deeply familiar. Nell tries not to notice what it reminds her of.

Madeleine, the therapist, a well-preserved forty-five or so, looks at them both with an expression of contained but intense curiosity, rather like a cat before it pounces. Her nails are pink, but pointed, her thin hair neatly combed but a little crackly at the edges as if alive with static.

They have been talking for a while, or Adrienne has been talking for a while. She sketches out the basics of their predicament, she puts words on the situation. It amazes Nell to hear her do that – part of the reason to be in love with someone was to have them explain you, she reckons. She didn't know that, before Adrienne.

'Mothering,' Madeleine says. She says it a little grandly, a little luxuriously. 'You are both going to be mothers to this child. You both have different experiences of being mothered. And you, Nell, have been a mother.'

Madeleine turns her attention to Nell, her eyes are certain and blue. Nell feels irritated. It's one thing for Adrienne to sum up her life, it's quite another for a stranger to do so. She looks away, she feels Madeleine's eyes on her cheek. But looking away brings her face to face with Adrienne, who is more terrifying than Madeleine is irritating. So she turns back again.

'I never thought of myself as a mother,' Nell says. She hears herself speak tersely, she feels bad about it. But these things are being pulled out of her and it hurts.

'It's what you were,' Madeleine says. 'You carried a child in your body. It's textbook.'

'Yes,' Nell says. 'But I never looked after it. So it doesn't feel right. To use that word.'

What she wants to say is: she didn't want to use that word then, now or ever. That's the unsayable truth here, the thing that makes a mockery of this entire process. If Adrienne finds out the full extent of Nell's not wanting, then she will leave her. And Nell has no doubt that Adrienne will do that because Adrienne is the kind of person who always, ultimately, does the right thing.

Madeleine smiles, her attention now straight ahead, her chin slightly tilted up. She has a professorial, somewhat dramatic air, as if overcome by the grand complexity of human affairs but prepared, all the same, to keep on keeping on. Her voice is deeper than one would think just looking at her, the authority her voice imparts heightened somehow by this unexpectedness. Nell imagines that Madeleine enjoys the disorientating effect this must have on people, she also wonders what it must be like – to be so sure about things.

'I appreciate that, Nell,' Madeleine says. 'It's the looking after that counts, in mothering. It's about the relationship. If it helps, I won't use that word to refer to you during that time.'

Nell shrugs. She doesn't care what this woman calls her. She feels herself being managed. She resents it, but only a little. What's important is that Adrienne is smiling, in her fierce way. What's important is that Adrienne feels like this is working.

Adrienne is just about pregnant. It happened easily, shockingly easily. The sperm is that of Adrienne's childhood friend Jacob. It is, to Nell, an unsettling, almost panic-inducing situation – except when she talks to Jacob about it. His seriousness calms her. He is gay too, but also quite a serious Christian. His family are Anglicans, the kind of ones who are almost Catholic, the kind of ones, Jacob says, who yearn to be Catholic. Such things make Nell's head spin. She didn't know you were allowed to be a Catholic, or almost Catholic, and to be gay and to assist other gay people to have children. She isn't really sure if you should be allowed, but here they are, anyway. A neighbour who had her baby with a donor egg says that once the baby comes, everything makes sense. The neighbour knows they are trying to conceive, the neighbour rejoices in her curly-haired one-year-old and looks forward to the day she has a playmate next door.

Nell smiles at the neighbour when she says this but deep down she feels something like bitterness, something even like contempt.

But this is unfair. So she works at it. After that first session with Madeleine, she takes the one little scrap of something she can use, something she can build on. And that is to think of all she gained when she met Adrienne. And of all she stands to lose.

Because before, she avoided proximity, closeness, anything approaching intimacy the way a tongue avoids a rotten tooth. She sometimes saw rats by the railway track as she cycled to work in the early mornings, or around the back of various restaurants she worked in, and they didn't scare her, rather they reminded her of herself, the way she skittered around the edges of things, the edges of the city, the edges of life itself.

Because before, she sometimes saw in a flash of disquieting insight quite precisely the way in which she would go mad, if she were to go mad. It was right there, as if preordained, all she had to do was follow that particular path, it would be so easy, there would be such relief in it. This is how things stood, before Adrienne.

Before, she would spend hours alone, smoking cigarettes, feeling wretched, and feeling wretched for feeling wretched (*they fucked you up so badly, that's why you're like this; you only think you need love because they told you what to think; you only hate everything about your life because they told you you would*), on and on her thoughts would churn – before Adrienne.

And then when they first met, at the photo shoot, watching her boss people around, feeling compelled by her but terrified also, terrified that despite the girlie dress and the flirty look at the young male intern, she knew that this new person was into women, was into women as Nell was only then allowing herself to be. And the absolute terror, or not quite terror, more like hunger that rose within her then, but for the first time she did not immediately reach for cynicism but for hope.

What was life before there was that? Now that she knew what life was – *love* – she realized she had also known the total absence of love which was to say, death, a kind of living death. She felt she had spent a long time not really living at all, without realizing it (*you don't know you are living a lie until you find the truth*, this thought came to her, carried from some place she'd been to long ago). And now she *was* living and it was all because of Adrienne, and it was wonderful, but Adrienne, unfortunately, was not just an object, not just a saviour, not just a happy ending. Adrienne, it turned out, was a person with her *own* dreams and needs and desires. And those were: *more* life, more love, which was to say, which is to say – a baby.

And despite this – despite this almost unthinkable fact – Nell is not going back to the way things were before for the simple reason that she knows she won't survive it. And, notwithstanding her grumpiness, her irritation, her fear, after the first session with Madeleine, she finds she is able to admit to herself that she *wants* to survive. The baldness of this thought startles her, her heart thumps as she thinks it, it seems audacious to think it. She looks at herself in the mirror and she reflects that all living things want to survive. And it is such a relief to include herself in that humble category of all living things.

And so, after the first session, she decides to tell Adi about the movement, to *give* Adi the movement. It seems to explain a lot, doesn't it? And it costs a lot to go there, it really does. She sits at the kitchen table, she'd bought a notebook and a pen, it felt excruciating to do even that. The therapy sessions are on Tuesday afternoons – her days off are typically Mondays and Tuesdays, and Adrienne, who works office hours, takes a long lunch break for the session. Adrienne is working as an in-house social media manager for an agency that represents people who became famous through the internet and now want to get more famous through selling books or TV ideas or creative endeavours the shape of which do not quite exist yet. Nell shudders at the very idea and even Adrienne kind of hates it – she has always been freelance and does not cope well with having to work nine to five or do what she is told, but they need the money and the maternity leave which the company has been shamed into providing after making a big deal out of a pregnancy influencer. That's what prompted Adrienne to get a job there in the first place. It amuses Nell to watch Adrienne go after things, get them and then get what she wants from them.

Nell sits at the Formica table in their flat, that Monday, the day before their second session with Madeleine. The flat is rented, it occupies part of the middle floor of a large four-storey flat-faced Georgian house in Kennington. The flat has two bedrooms. Nell has lived there for years, previously with a flatmate and now with Adrienne. Adrienne transformed it from student grotto to Insta-friendly within a few months – the Formica is duck-egg blue, there are plants and battered cookbooks and bottle-green coffee cups without any handles on them. Nell loves to sit at the table alone in the quiet and observe how the objects around her glow with serenity, the right things in the right place, even the shelving, mere Ikea, is carefully installed and full of tact. Adrienne knows how to arrange things, in fact it seems to Nell that things simply arrange themselves in her presence. She shuts her eyes as she feels this thought, it shudders through her, how precious this is, this life they share.

The notebook she got that morning at a big stationery store on Tottenham Court Road. She had walked around it feeling panicked, she saw a lot of fluffy pens and shiny diaries, it was all very wrong. She found a plain black thing, it was cheap and unimportant, and then some plastic pens and then she fled. Back home, these objects took on the serenity of the flat and the pens it turns out are exactly the kind she loved to use as a schoolgirl, pleasingly scratchy; she forgot how much she liked the feeling of a pen moving across the page. She remembers how furiously she used to write and she feels a deep throb of sadness when she notices on the side of the middle finger on her right hand that she still has a tiny little tender bump, a bump that had once been a great big glorious deformity born out of her incessant note-taking and essay-writing and idea-scribbling.

Because Nell had been a good girl, a really, *really* good girl. She had studied, she had won prizes and she had loved it. She looks at the bump now, a woman, a really, really *bad* woman, and she feels a glimmer of fondness towards the person she had once been.

That old Nell, the good Nell, would start the essay, the story, the explanation, the excuse, probably with outlining the rules of the movement. People like rules, they like to inhabit worlds with clearly delineated ways of existing, boarding-school stories never go out of style. Nell loved boarding-school stories and maybe that's what she had been looking for, back then, a place in which everyone knew their place, a place in which chaos was contained. Nell feels ashamed by the degree to which she is compelled by rules – and then confused by the way she always ends up breaking them. The chaos in her longs for order, but then whatever order she finds can't contain the chaos. So she can't flatter herself by thinking herself some kind of renegade – and it would be extremely easy to see it all like that. She is, after all, a lesbian; she had, after all, grown up in (ugh) Ireland; she then (of course) brought herself to (hurray!) London where all the misfits come to shine and dazzle and prosper. That's the story she could so easily tell, that's the one the world would reward.

It's just not true, though, is it. And Nell does care about the truth. And so, here she is with a pen and a notebook and a desire to write it all down.

No, *no* desire to write it all down, she can think of almost nothing she wants to do less. It's a *duty* she has, a duty to write it all down. Nell sits up a little straighter in her chair – designer, some Scandi she can't remember the name of, Adrienne found it on eBay. She stiffens her spine at that word *duty*. Now there is a word that works for her.

2

Ireland, 1998

The convent was not a boarding school, but it felt like one. It was strict and orderly and it took bad girls and made them good and it took good girls and made them excellent. It was carpeted throughout, noises were muffled and the windows were clean. You had to stand up when a teacher entered the room, some of the teachers had them mutter a quick, furtive Hail Mary before class commenced, some of them didn't. There were almost no nuns left by the time Nell started but their influence emanated from the very walls.

Nell loved it. Her primary school years had been fragmented by several house moves, her family only settled in the town permanently when she was eleven years old. Her only real friend was her younger sister Jenny, who was so temperamentally unlike her – Jenny being chilled out, dreamy, and uninterested in schoolwork – that they got along very well. But Nell still yearned for the intimate, all-encompassing soul-sisterhood she encountered in the books she read. Her final year of primary education was spent as the shy new girl in a mixed school with a new headteacher who was going through an experimental phase: the boys were wild and aggressive, the girls cliquey and sardonic. Nell was scared every day. She wore a bra to hide the fact she didn't need one; the boys pinged it, the girls laughed at her. She read more and more intensely, this did not garner her much in the way of social approval. She liked *Chalet School*, Maeve Binchy, *Little Women*, *Emily of New Moon* and sad children's novels about the Famine. She thought about becoming a nun. Her mother, Dolores, told her everyone feels like that sometimes.

On her first day in First Year at the convent, September 1998, Fiona Quinn – a name Nell did not yet know – absent-mindedly left her key in her locker and then strode across the hall towards her classroom. Fiona was small for her age and she also had a short pageboy haircut and glasses and a very determined affect, she reminded Nell of a little mole peering ahead and burrowing forward. Nell was already sitting in the classroom, right up at the front so she had a front seat to Fiona's inaugural humiliation: her locker key was attached to a keyring that constituted a coiled spring device which, when unravelled, stretched far enough to allow Fiona to almost reach the classroom door before she was suddenly jerked backwards by the weight of the locker pulling on the elastic spring that unfurled from her person like a taut fluorescent tail. Nell gasped and burst out laughing and then the rest of the girls saw and then the entire room was rolling on the floor as Fiona turned around to angrily interrogate whatever had impeded her progress. Nell saw her realize what had happened – that it had all been her own error – and she never forgot the way the girl straightened herself up, walked back to the locker to remove her key and then marched into the classroom with her head held high. And yes, she was blushing and yes, Nell could see the tiniest glint of a tear in her eye but mostly she saw someone who was full of grace and poise and vigour – someone that she wanted to get to know.

Fiona was initially wary – Nell had been the one to kick off the laughter that crowned her humiliation – but that was soon forgotten and on the way home, they chatted madly about what subjects they were taking and what the teachers were like and who they knew from before. Fiona, Nell was a little intimidated to realize, knew a lot of people and she was popular, even with some of the bad girls, due to the fact of her older sisters and the various permutations of friend groups in the housing estate she lived in. On the way out of school that day, Nell recalls a girl in Third Year picking Fiona up and swinging her around as if she were a toddler and Fiona squealed and swore at her and it was very amicable and Nell was envious.

She remembers the first time she went to her house after school, she remembers her mother. Ita didn't work, she kept the house nice – Fiona was the middle of five, there was a lot of activity. Everyone played sport, there were many photos of family on the wall. Her cousins lived across the road. Nell had cousins too, and aunties and uncles plenty, they just did not live locally, they just did not see them very often. There was something in Nell's family that felt very small and unified – though they were not solitary, they were not antisocial, her mother Dolores had a broad and unusual net of friends, women from all over would come to visit her and drink tea in the kitchen and tell all sorts of things to her. But Nell's family, the Larkins, they did not feel embedded. They were not from the town. They had no family there.

In her notebook, Nell writes, in very small letters, *Fiona*. Next to her name, she draws an arrow, it loops down the page.

The movement was called, grandly, gorgeously, La Obra de los Hogareños – the Work of the Homemakers. But no one called it that, they called it La Obra or sometimes, La Ob. And the idea was that when people from the movement gathered together anywhere in the world, they were at home; that between and within them, they created a sense of home, and this sense came from the presence of Jesus, or *Jesus in the midst* which was one of the catchphrases they had. The hogareños – the people at the heart of the movement, the ones who kept it all going – were lay-people who dedicated their lives to God. They were a bit like nuns or priests in the sense that they were celibate and lived in houses with other hogareños but they were unlike nuns or priests in that they had normal jobs in normal places and they didn't say Mass or wear robes or habits, and their whole vibe was a lot more funky and post-Vatican II – guitars, peace, love and universal brotherhood.

Then there were the married hogareños: people who lived normal lives with their (usually large) families – it was Catholic, this thing, even if it didn't quite feel like it was – but who also dedicated their lives to God/the movement and showed this devotion in various ways, such as attending spiritual meetings, getting their kids to attend spiritual meetings, and quietly pushing back against the secularizing ethos of whatever country they happened to live in.

Nell did not know enough of the world back then to wonder if the movement genuinely wanted the whole world to be part of the Church, for the boundary between Church and state to cease to exist, for everyone in the world to know the joy of Christ, and all of that. She assumes now that they did, that they must have, but she feels they didn't, not really. She sensed even then that most of the people involved in La Obra enjoyed the fact that they had found a space that was separate from the rest of the world. They were not particularly evangelical. It felt cosy, and almost exclusive. It often felt like somewhere for people who could not find a place in the ordinary world. *To love, to be the first to love, to love always.* This was another of the catchphrases, this tended to attract people who struggled to find love elsewhere.

Then there were the youth groups– the hermanos and the hermanas. These were mostly comprised of the children of the married hogareños and whatever friends they could persuade to come along to events and meetings, before said friends (or the children of the married hogareños themselves) drifted away due to the off-putting earnestness (the movement was founded in Spain and it was permeated therefore by a Continental directness that most people in Nell's culture found alarming), the tedium of the meetings, and/or the dawning realization that despite all of the nice songs and guitars and universal brotherhood, these people were really serious about all the Catholic Stuff (no sex before marriage, no contraception, no gays) that they tended to gloss over in the earlier years.

She remembers Rebecca, two years ahead of her and Fiona at the convent. She remembers her hair. It was long and luxurious and glossy, and she was always tossing it over her shoulders, it was like the hair was something that anointed her, she looked a bit like a saint. She did not act like one at all, however. Rebecca was powerfully contemptuous of everything; she was very into Jesus. It was a dazzling, intoxicating combination, and she knew it.

Nell met her first at Fiona's, one day after school, probably later that September or early that October. She remembers the bite in the blue air, the crisp white-page feel of the new school year, sharp and alive amid the decay of autumn. She and Fiona were in the kitchen, Rebecca came in the front door, she didn't knock or ring the bell. Fiona's mother Ita smiled at her, Rebecca nodded and looked around and saw Fiona and Nell. They were wearing their new school uniforms, Nell recalls how pristine they were – the long skirt with its pleats still hard-edged and distinct, the green jumper with its cuffs still neat. Rebecca's uniform, by contrast, was grubby and ragged. Fiona loosened her tie at the sight of her, Nell pushed up her sleeves.

'And who's this?' Rebecca said to Ita, as if she were on the same level as the mothers, as if she were as studiously amused by everything as they were.

'That's Nell,' Ita said. 'Fiona's new friend.'

This Ita said as if Nell's presence were a joke, although she did not intend to be hurtful. Nell recalls that people back there mostly announced things humorously, particularly new facts or information.

'Is she now?' Rebecca said.

They went out to the garden. Rebecca sat on one of the swings, it was a green-and-orange plastic set, the grass underneath rubbed away by many years of young eager feet. Fiona took the other swing and Nell leaned uncertainly against the frame. Rebecca interrogated them both as to their first days at school, what teachers, what subjects, what friends. Rebecca was in Third Year, her knowledge vast, her insight sharp and unforgiving. She said mean things about the appearance and weight of several of the teachers, she advised who was a pushover and who was strict.

'Is she brainy?' Rebecca asked Fiona, looking at Nell.

'Yeah,' Fiona said. Fiona was brainy too but she seemed to know already that Nell was brainier.

'I thought so,' Rebecca said. She continued to look at Nell. 'Did you tell her about the meetings? She might come.'

'You tell her,' Fiona said. She sounded weary. Rebecca and Fiona had known each other since early childhood; they were both intense, hot-headed, competitive. They could not have been friends – there would have been murder – were it not for the moderating influence of Ursula, another friend from the street. Ursula was a free spirit, she took Ordinary Level in most subjects, Nell was yet to meet her, things made more sense when she did.

'I can't, I have to go home now,' Rebecca said. 'It'll take ages to do my homework. I'm *not* brainy, you see.'

'What meetings?' Nell said, although she didn't really want to ask. She felt like she was being set up and this annoyed her. But she didn't yet know how to handle Rebecca, she couldn't help but walk straight into her traps.

'They're about God and things,' Rebecca said with a smirk as she walked towards the back door. Ita was standing at the sink inside the kitchen window looking out at them and smiling with a benign vagueness.

'Oh,' Nell said.

She went along the first time out of curiosity. She went along the first time out of a desire to maintain and develop her friendship with Fiona. She went along because she did think it strange that they – her family, her community, her country – called themselves Catholic but she herself knew next to nothing about what that meant. She saw depictions of Ireland in films and on TV – sheep, cows, priests like idiots, nuns like demons – and it looked nothing like the Ireland she lived in.

She made her Communion at seven, she did her Confirmation at twelve, she remembers asking a girl in her class, 'Do you think we'll feel the Holy Spirit coming down upon us on Confirmation day?' The girl looked at her like she was insane and Nell was mortified. She didn't know what things you were supposed to take literally – and it was right there in their religion textbook, the gifts and fruits of the Holy Spirit, they came down upon you on your Confirmation day, the Bishop himself came to oversee it all. If it was all a ruse, then it was a very elaborate one. And if everyone knew it was a ruse, then why were they going along with it?

She was learning that to do well in this life meant you had to become proficient in managing what things you really believed in and what things you only pretended to believe in. And she also knew that you had to pretend to believe in such a way that made it clear the belief was only a pretence: to be thought earnest about something you were only supposed to *pretend* to be earnest about – this could lead to social ruin.

Her parents were not much help: her father went diligently to Mass, as most people still did, but told her not to take it too seriously; her mother went occasionally but seemed uncomfortable about it.

Nell felt she needed more information. And she thought maybe this meeting, this meeting about God and things, might help.

La Obra meant 'work' but in the sense of 'good works' or 'artwork' rather than 'labour'. Martina, the hogareña who guided Rebecca and Fiona's hermana group, explained this to the girls at the first meeting Nell attended. It took place in the Clerys' house, the home of Rebecca's rich uncle and holy aunt, the ones who brought the movement to the town in the first place.

'I think of *obra* as anything that is done well, anything that is done to serve others,' Martina said. 'It reminds me that no task is too small or too menial to do with love.'

'It's like *obair*,' Nell said. '*Obra* is like *obair*, isn't it?' As she spoke, she felt the coarseness of the word in Irish; its contrast with this smokier, sexier Spanish incarnation. She shivered. She liked this new language, these new words.

'That's right, Nell,' Martina said. 'The cultures of Europe are connected through language, and through faith.'

Nell, an incorrigible teacher's pet back then, glowed happily.

Rebecca rolled her eyes, and looked at Ursula, who dutifully giggled. It was only the four of them that day, Nell thinks: Rebecca, Fiona, Ursula and her. Other girls came and went over the years, but they didn't last long.

'Words are how we make sense of God,' Martina said. 'And paying close attention to words, to language, is a way of paying close attention to God.'

She looked at them then, as if she was really interested in how they would take this idea. She was small and nimble, with short hair and a face that wasn't exactly pretty, but wasn't unpleasant either, it was a smooth face, easy to look at, easy to look through – as if she were clear, like water, or a mirror. There was something very calming in the way she paid attention to them. Ursula stopped giggling. The silence went on a little while and Martina then laughed. 'You are all so serious looking,' she said. 'There's no need for us to be so serious.'

Her accent was local and yet Nell sensed something foreign about her. This was exciting. Nell didn't know anyone who came from anywhere else.

The next thing they did in the meeting was speak of their 'experiences'. This meant describing a difficulty encountered in the course of school or home life, and an elaboration on how the difficulty was overcome with reference to the guiding principles of the movement. Among these principles were the concepts *creating unity; Jesus forsaken* and *to go against the current*. There were others, but those were the main ones. They were to do with love, suffering and courage, respectively. That day, Rebecca discussed how she dealt with her older sisters teasing her about her membership of La Obra. Nell tried and failed to imagine girls older and more contemptuous than Rebecca herself. She felt thrilled by this unexpected access into the interior life of this powerful girl.

She smiles as she thinks about this, the Kennington Nell does. She is beginning to see now, what the attraction was. To understand love, to understand suffering, to understand courage. These were useful things to grasp. And then she shivers at the irony of it all.

Everything was beautiful in the Clery home, dark red curtains hung by windows of stained glass, green wool blankets were folded over plush sofas, the coffee table was faded but large and sturdy, the bookshelves in the alcoves wide and deep. Mrs Clery – Rebecca's aunt, from Malta – served excellent snacks: spiced biscuits and walnut cake, hot chocolate with cinnamon and nutmeg, a pastry roll made with dates and almonds. These things thrilled Nell, as did the fact that the Clery house was located on a hill on one of the old main roads into town, behind a high stone wall, and the house was old, and huge. The neighbours were doctors and solicitors; their gardens long, and wild and tangled at the back.

Old things were just better than new things, Nell felt – and you knew that because it was only rich people who had old things, who cared about old things. Her own house was new, or had been new when her family moved into it, and it was uninteresting to look at, it was boring to live in. She imagined the kind of girl she'd be if she lived in a house like this, the kind of conversations she'd have, the way she would walk out the gate and into town, casual and elegant and upright.

Kennington Nell remembers this and thinks maybe it was all just about the material things, that gorgeous house, that delicious food. She had been the greediest among the girls, they often joked about how much she ate at the hermana meetings, how excited she got about new types of snacks they discovered at the bigger events. She almost died and went to heaven itself the day she first tasted ceviche made by a homesick Peruvian hogareña called Milagros at the movement's national centre one afternoon early in Nell's time as a hermana. The piercing bitterness of the lime, the fat tender flesh of the fish. She hadn't known that food could taste like that, how come no one had told her that food could taste like that?

Dolores, her mother, worked with food, she made sandwiches in her own kitchen and drove up to Nell's convent school and sold them there, every school day for at least twenty years. But this did not interest Nell back then. Nell feels a sudden thump of shame when she remembers her scorning of Dolores in those years, for being what she thought of as provincial, as ignorant, as – horror of horrors – content.

She blinks that feeling away and returns to the memory of the ceviche, she feels her mouth water as she remembers it. She remembers telling Martina about it, that day at the national centre, she remembers Martina laughing. She remembers how Martina seemed to enjoy her delight. Martina already knew about ceviche, she remembers realizing that and thinking that Martina seemed to already know about everything.

At the therapy session the next day, Nell feels therefore equipped. She thinks all of the information about the movement, about Fiona, about the rules of the movement – she thinks talking all of that through will take up her part of the session. She thinks Adrienne will be happy, she thinks it will all go well. During the session, she talks about all of that, and she talks about the food too. She mentions that she had never connected these two parts of her life before: the fact that she discovered her love of food through the movement, the fact that this interest in food gave her the livelihood, the freedom she now enjoys. She talks a lot, she talks quickly. She has a sense of clearing things up, of getting things straight. She feels she is sending a version of herself into the world, a new version and it is improved, it is wiser than the previous one, more honest, more willing to be honest. Madeleine looks pleased, and Adrienne too.

After the session, Nell and Adrienne walk down Denmark Street and across Charing Cross Road towards Soho Square, Nell recites the names of these places in her mind as they go, it is a thing she does in this city, it's a comfort. It's cold but not raining. The streets are quiet, the day feels hard and buttoned up, deliveries arrive at restaurants, waiting staff smoke cigarettes on corners as they wait for the day to properly begin. It's Nell's day off but she feels tense and weary. She wonders how many more years of kitchen work she can get out of her body. She knows she's tough, she knows she's built for endurance. But sometimes she feels herself hardening, becoming brittle and then shattering. She senses that in her future, she feels it, in the bones that long – she sometimes thinks, she sometimes feels – to become dust.

They get coffees and sandwiches and sit on the benches in the square, the mud is hard, a small brown bird pecks bleakly at it.

'*Hogar*,' Adrienne says in an excellent accent. '*Hogareña*.'

Nell blushes. 'It's so silly,' she says. 'So weird.'

'*No*,' Adrienne says, in Spanish, maybe. Her mother's family are Italian, her father's Greek. But your name's French, Nell said, one morning in the early days, and Adrienne shrugged, as if to say, *and so?*

'I don't think it's weird at all,' Adrienne says now. 'I like it. It sounds safe. Is that what you wanted? Something safe?'

Nell feels her heart close over. Her meditation app tells her to pay close attention to her feelings, to register them as just that, to create space between the thing that she is and the feeling that she is feeling.

Nell doesn't like her meditation app.

She doesn't answer Adi's question. Adi puts her head on her shoulder.

3

Ireland, 1982

May's third daughter was Dolores's favourite. She was just one year old but there was a brightness about her, a directness, people said she'd been here before. When Dolores watched her curl into her mother's lap – the child loved May the most even though she, Aunt Dolores, spent far more time with her – she felt a little scared. There was such exclusivity in that embrace, such smugness. She could sense how you could be trapped for ever by love like that. She saw May shut her eyes as the child's arms tightened around her neck, she watched her eyelids flicker as if in response to a drug.

Brigid, Dolores's mother, didn't want Dolores to get too caught up in other people's lives. There was not much she could do to prevent this happening – Dolores was the youngest of the seven children of the Reidy family, she was dependable, she was sensible, she was smart, and so the family could not help but draw from her like a resource, the family was its own organism, it had to sustain itself in whatever way it could. This was something Brigid regretted even while facilitating it. So when, at twenty, Dolores said she thought she might go to Dublin to do a secretarial course, Brigid saw this as her chance to be supportive, even if it caused practical challenges in the short term: as well as the childminding she did for May, Dolores worked evenings in the family pub and her labour was cheap and excellent.

Dolores felt a little ashamed that she wasn't going further. Lots of people were on their way to England, some even to America. But Dolores felt something in her, keeping her there. Her father was a nationalist, and the sight of young people leaving broke his heart, so he said. He grew angry when rebel songs started in the pub – it was all very well to sing about Ireland, he said, all very well to *die* for Ireland, how about you work for her, stay around, do your best, start a business, like he had.

She was almost three years after her Leaving Certificate, at which she underperformed. She didn't get the marks to go to college and no one had expected her to, not because she wasn't clever, but because she'd had to work so much in the pub there had been no time for her to study. Working there had offered its own education, of course – mostly in what kind of woman she didn't want to be and what kind of man she didn't want to be with. She didn't know what it was that she wanted but she felt it, she sensed it, and it wasn't standing behind the bar at home until someone decided to marry her.

Until Liam decided to marry her. She was trying to escape him too, and the fact that he was also going to Dublin that autumn, he had a job waiting for him in his uncle's garage up there – well, that was just a coincidence, she was in no way following him. They weren't even properly *going out*, there was nothing more to their relationship then than a few sneaky smiles, a kiss the previous New Year's Eve and a walk, one autumn evening, along the old road, the horse chestnut trees brimming over with conkers, he picked one up and rolled it in his hands, she marvelled at how smooth and polished it was, like something man-made rather than something out of nature. She always remembered that, the prickling spikes of the soft green cask, the hard, inedible fruit inside. He only walked with her for a while that day, he was nineteen, he had other stuff to do. She remembers the pull on her heart as he bounded away from her.

She had to keep that in check. Women felt too much – she saw it in the way some of the older women would drink at the bar, sodden and beleaguered and full of incomprehensible muttering. So when she decided she was going to go to Dublin too, she was stern with herself. Not too much Liam. Maybe a little bit of Liam, but not all Liam.

So maybe she was looking for Annie, without even realizing it.

Annie was likewise twenty, studying law and French at Trinity, and her father was a professor and her mother an artist and she had grown up in Rathgar. Dolores wondered did Annie recount herself to herself like that, and if so, did it thrill and delight her, like it had thrilled and delighted Dolores to tell these details to her mother? Brigid had laughed when she heard, and said she'd better not bring her to visit, she'd never get the place clean enough, and Dolores cringed to hear her mother talk like a peasant.

Annie was the one who let her know they were peasants, but it was fine, because when Annie said it, it was a matter of self-flattery, a strategy she employed to downplay the other stuff (Rathgar, Trinity, professor). Annie would refer to her own mother's family as good peasant stock from Kerry, though Dolores caught vague references to such exotica as said mother's French boyfriend from a post-university year in Paris, and childhood trips to post-war London. Dolores had never left the country, something Annie found very exciting. She said she was jealous, that the first time she went it was going to be so *meaningful*. This comment rendered Dolores speechless – as many of Annie's comments did – and quietly thrilled, because the way Annie spotted the things of which Dolores was most ashamed and dredged them up and exclaimed over them as if they were treasures gave her a dizzying vertigo. She was not who she thought she was with Annie, and she wanted to keep on finding out more.

Dolores first met Annie at the cafe where she worked during the day – the secretarial course ran three evenings a week and it cost money, and the savings she had from her years working at home would only go so far, would only last so long. Annie had come into the cafe with some friends of hers, they were students, and Dolores felt a throb of envy looking at them, the same age as her, from the same country, but they may as well have been from a different species. Mrs McGrath, the cafe owner, was only ever nice to Dolores when the students came in, a solidarity of sorts, Dolores supposed, one she could have done without.

Annie was talking about the amendment that day and none of the girls she was with wanted to hear about it. Dolores does not remember what she was saying because she didn't know anything about all of that yet, but she remembers sensing that the girl with the curly hair didn't quite fit in with the others. She was talking too much, she was a little wild-eyed, a little eager.

She does remember that one of the others said, at one point, Annie, you are such a *women's libber*. And the other girls all giggled. Annie, Dolores noticed, didn't blush. Rather she sat up a little straighter and didn't say anything, but her affect, her posture, said, *you bet I am*.

Dolores smiled at her. She couldn't help it. And Annie grasped on to that smile like it was a life raft. She beamed back at Dolores, really, she did.

It was an act of fundamental misunderstanding then. Annie thought Dolores smiled at her because she believed in the cause. Dolores actually smiled at Annie because she felt sorry for her.

Annie came in a lot, after that smile. She looked meaningfully at Dolores and Dolores nodded back. She saw herself in Annie's eyes; she saw that Annie saw that they were the same age. She saw Annie notice that Dolores was good at her job, that she didn't prattle on like some of the other staff, that she held herself well. Dolores knew that she was classy – she wasn't sure where she'd got it from, but she knew it. So she wasn't all that surprised when Annie started to try to be her friend.

'Are you from here?' Annie asked her, one day. It was grim, deepest January, the evening outside black as soot.

'No,' Dolores said. 'From down the country.' She heard her voice, it sounded flat and rural. The rest of the staff were all inner-city Dubliners, they sometimes couldn't understand her, they called her the Farmer, they thought everyone from outside the city was a farmer. Annie's voice was different again, soft and clear, like a child's.

'Oh,' Annie said. 'What are you doing here then?' After she said that, she blushed. 'Sorry, you don't have to tell me. That's extremely rude of me.'

Dolores felt bad for her. She understood Annie's desire to know. She felt it too – she wanted to know everything too. Some people just did.

'Just working,' Dolores said. She didn't mention the secretarial course, she didn't quite know why. She felt this new person was being quite presumptuous, she also sensed that she could maintain the respect she seemed to be inspiring in her by denying involvement with education – the very thing this girl's life revolved around. It was better, Dolores felt in that second, to deny any effort to improve herself than to admit to be so doing in such a meagre way. She thought of Miss Lacey, the evening tutor at the secretarial college, and her look of gentle despair when she spoke to the assembled girls about how to speak with delicacy on the telephone in jobs that did not exist – in their own country, at that moment, anyway.

'Oh,' Annie said again.

They were standing facing each other across the glass-fronted cabinet that displayed cream cakes and sandwiches and quiches and coleslaw and plastic boxes of various gloopy-looking salads. Customers sometimes complained that the cakes acquired the oniony taste of their savoury neighbours but Mrs McGrath refused to do anything about that, such comments just made her even more belligerent and chaotic. She had flaming red hair with white roots and broad yellow teeth. She was standing behind Dolores as she spoke to Annie, gazing out the window into the darkening street. She didn't like to let on that she noticed anything of interest happening to anyone else. She never, as a point of principle, talked about anything except her own affairs – which were admittedly quite dramatic, possessed as she was of several tumultuous daughters.

'Are you interested in the amendment?' Annie said, boldly. Her voice had a slight tremor. Dolores could tell it was really important to her that she answer yes to that question.

'Kind of,' Dolores said. She didn't want to let this girl down but equally she feared any questions that would follow an affirmative response. The truth was she didn't know anything about it. She was not interested in the news, she didn't read newspapers. She liked pop music, pop magazines and big old novels. She had heard some stuff in the air, some stuff to do with babies, some stuff to do with sex, but she didn't pay attention. It was too embarrassing, to have to think or talk about things like that. She knew the priests were angry but that was nothing new.

'I knew that you would,' Annie said, beaming. 'I could just tell. You're really clever, aren't you?'

This felt oddly like an accusation to Dolores, and for a moment she felt she had to explain what she was doing there, standing alongside Mrs McGrath in this grotty cafe, if she were indeed so clever.

'I suppose,' she said.

'Then, come,' Annie said, handing her a flyer. 'We need girls like you.'

She left, and Dolores looked at the leaflet. Mrs McGrath shook herself out of her reverie.

'She's trouble, that one,' she said, and Dolores was surprised – both by what she said and by the fact that she was deigning to acknowledge the occurrence of an interaction that did not involve her. Mrs McGrath snatched the leaflet out of Dolores's hand and looked at it. On it was a picture of a cross made out of various words. Mrs McGrath had taken the leaflet too quickly for Dolores to be able to read those words – she just got 'No' several times in large letters and then, at the bottom of the page underneath the cross, the words 'Hands Off the Constitution' followed by several exclamation marks. Underneath that, scrawled in pen, the time and location of some sort of gathering, she assumed, some sort of meeting.

Mrs McGrath crumpled up the leaflet and put it in the bin.

'That's what comes of educating women,' she said, shaking her head, jowls burning, eyes flickering. 'You stay away from girls like that.'

Dolores blinked at her, startled by her ferocity. Mrs McGrath then disappeared into the small room behind the counter and Dolores took the opportunity to fish the leaflet out of the bin and stick it in the front pocket of her apron. Mrs McGrath came back with a filthy old mop and bucket and thrust them at Dolores.

'What would your poor mother say?' she said. Dolores shrugged and took the mop and reflected that Brigid would have plenty to say about the state of this place.

4

Liam came to her home on Sunday afternoons and they did the things that they wanted to do. She felt proud of herself. She had her own money, her own place to live. She was different, here in Dublin, she felt different in herself, she felt herself appear differently in his eyes.

It was terrifying – they had no protection, they had to be extraordinarily careful – but it was also wonderful. She understood that it happened in a realm that everyone knew about but no one spoke of, and that felt right. To speak of these things – of love, of desire, of intimacy, of risk – in ordinary neutral language, the only language she had, would be to destroy them.

She thought, however, that the women at Annie's meeting would behave differently. She thought they would say what others could not. She thinks that's why she went. For years afterwards she told herself it was Annie – she needed her friendship, she was lonely, she didn't want to become too dependent on Liam. But it wasn't just that. She felt drawn to the things that were not to be said, she wondered how that all got decided. She felt it likely that she was missing some essential understanding. The people who got things done in the world were motivated by certainty, she knew that. And she wanted to find out how they got to be so certain. Her own ignorance dazzled her, amazed her. Responding to this invitation to meet this group seemed potentially like a way of penetrating it, just a little.

The meeting was held in a small room on the grounds of a university located across the road from the cafe in which Dolores worked. She did not know very much about it. She had never been inside it. As she approached the front gate, she stopped, wondering for a moment if she required a ticket to get in. She continued walking, through a large wooden gate and then through a short passage into a cobbled square. No one stopped her; she felt like someone should have. It didn't seem right, that she could just walk in.

The room, when she found it, was draughty and unpleasantly lit. A group of women sat on plastic chairs, in a circle. They mostly wore jeans and jumpers, one or two were more formally clad in skirts and see-through black tights.

There were about ten of them. They smiled at Dolores as she came in; she was a little late, it had taken a while to find the room. Annie beamed when she saw her. She seemed to be the youngest in attendance, most of the other women looked to be over thirty. The woman who was addressing them stopped speaking and she turned to Annie and said – is this your new friend, Annie?

'Yes!' Annie said. 'I met her in the cafe where she works.

She's really interested in learning more, aren't you?' And then Dolores realized Annie didn't know her name so she said, 'Hello, I'm Dolores,' and the women all smiled.

She held her head high. She tried to remember, quickly, what the constitution was. She'd read the newspapers over the last week, she'd gotten the gist of what was happening.

The woman chairing the meeting had a rural accent. She was talking gently but firmly. She said they needed to show they were ordinary women, ordinary mothers and wives, with ordinary concerns.

'We shouldn't dignify their baby-killer talk with a response,' she said. 'Our campaign is not about that. We need to remember that, to keep to the messages we've agreed on, the issues that affect ordinary women, every day. The amendment won't help with any of that, and it's going to threaten all of the progress we've made so far – that's what we have to keep saying.'

The other women nodded.

'Abortion,' Annie said, suddenly, loudly. 'A woman's right to choose. I don't agree, Mary. We have to be able to say it, we shouldn't be afraid of it.'

Dolores felt that word 'abortion' reverberate around her body as if a bomb had gone off. The other women seemed to feel it too. Dolores had noticed, in her quick self-edification on the issue through the newspapers of the previous week, that it was only the other side, the holy side, that used that word. Again this confused her. Abortion – this thing they could not speak of – was already illegal, was going to remain illegal whether this amendment passed or not, as far as she understood it. She had assumed that the activists against the amendment, this small group of women would be, therefore, militant, given what they were up against. But here they were, as scared of the word as she was.

Mary looked at Annie, she looked tired and resolute.

'Annie,' she said. 'Please have some respect. We've been through all of this before, you know that. You have to understand that most people don't think like students. Most people don't talk like students.'

Annie blushed to the roots of her curls. She muttered something that Dolores could not hear. Another woman then spoke.

'You're right, Mary. We have to be able to hold our heads high. We are not pro-abortion, we are pro-woman.' She wore a brown scarf and a yellow brooch. She caught Dolores's eye and addressed her.

'Is this something you could do, Dolores? Could you stand next to us and talk about this issue, to women that you know, women in your family, women you are friends with?'

The faces in the room turned towards her. *This issue*, Dolores thought. *If you can't even say it, what hope is there for me?* She frowned at the woman. She sensed they all saw her as some kind of symbol. She realized she did not want to say what they wanted her to say.

'I don't know,' Dolores said. She spoke loudly, and honestly. 'I'm afraid I don't understand anything about this at all.'

There was a silence. This was not the right thing to have said. The woman who had asked the question looked at Mary as if to say, *I told you so.*

Mary looked back at the woman and then at Dolores.

'We're glad you've come,' she said. 'We need to be reminded.'

Dolores knew what she meant – we need to be reminded how people like you think, how thick-ignorant you all are. She felt humiliated, as if she'd been forced to take a test she had not prepared for.

They went to the pub afterwards – or around half of them did, the others went home to their children and husbands. Annie held her hand on the way over there, out of the campus, up Grafton Street, down one of the side streets. Dolores wondered why she was doing that – did she sense her upset? Or was this just what Annie usually did?

'I'm glad you're here with me,' Annie said. 'It's good to have someone younger with me.'

With a drink, everyone became a little looser. They talked of travelling to England, of husbands demented with drink, of bodies broken after eleven pregnancies, of unmarried mothers evicted from their homes, of wives abandoned, children neglected. But they also gossiped and laughed. They seemed to know each other well, to enjoy one another's company. They knew people who wrote for the newspapers and appeared on TV, and they spoke of them with an enjoyable irreverence.

'My father says women need to take more responsibility,' Annie said, after a while. She had been quiet, most of the evening, sitting on the edge of the group. 'He says change will only come when the women, the ordinary women themselves, push for it.'

Dolores tensed – already she understood that Annie's loudness, her way of speaking, were causing her trouble in this group. Again, she felt sorry for her. What a burden, to care so much.

'Sure what else are we doing here, Annie?' Mary said, before Annie could go on. She was softer now and there was affection in her voice. 'You go tell Dr Sinnot we're doing our best.' She paused and said then, 'And send our love to your mother.'

At closing time, Mary came up to them both. Annie was whispering to Dolores, telling her who had fallen out with whom, who was now in charge of the posters, how they decided what those posters might say. Dolores felt her grip on things slipping. Was this how important things got decided? She was more than a little drunk.

'Keep bringing her,' Mary said to Annie. She was on her way out the door, she wore a long, bright green anorak. 'We need girls like her.'

Dolores detected in that a slight to her new friend and she flinched at it. But at the exact same moment she felt a thrum of exaltation. Someone saw her and thought she was worth something. She noticed in Mary a capability, a clear-eyedness. She seemed like someone Dolores might know in her usual life.

That weekend, she tried to tell Liam about Annie and the meeting. He was in her room, he was kissing her all over. She felt his lips on her neck. She shut her eyes and he drew back and she felt him smile at her.

'Stop it,' she said. 'You'll kill me.' His lips were plump, she almost always wanted to bite them.

'That's my plan,' he said. He ran his fingers down her arm and his hands over her hands, which she was embarrassed about, they were red and raw from years of washing-up. He stood up then, and whistled and went and smoked a cigarette. He had good self-control. His older sister had had a baby taken from her, she now didn't talk to anyone. No one was supposed to know, everyone did know.

He came back to the couch and she lay with her head on his chest, his heart was beating a million miles an hour under his dark T-shirt, she smelled nicotine and motor oil and sweat and something deeply and darkly sweet. She knew he wouldn't stay much longer, she knew he had things to be doing. She wished he could stay the night. More than anything she wished that.

'This group,' she said. She tried to talk to him about it earlier, he had not listened. 'What do you think about all of it?'

'Women's lib?' he said. He was un-serious, teasing.

'It's not that,' Dolores said. She felt very cross, all of a sudden. 'It's not about that.'

She sat up on the couch.

'Yes, it is,' he said, laughing. He burrowed his face into the back of her neck, she reeled at his touch, she pulled away. 'You're angry now, sure,' he said. 'Women's libbers are always angry.'

She sat up properly and looked at him. She wondered if men felt the same as women about things, or if it was totally and utterly a different thing to be. He was so strong. He didn't ever seem to feel the cold. He could take anything apart and put it back together. She tried very hard not to adore every single thing about him.

'You try and change the world if you want, Dollo,' he said, looking at her directly, honestly. 'The rest of us are just trying to survive.'

'But do you think they really are – what they say they are?'

'What?'

'Baby-killers?' She felt very embarrassed saying that. But maybe they *were*. On the letters page, in the papers, that's what these women were called. By other women.

Liam shrugged his shoulders as if trying to escape the grasp of something.

'I don't know, Dollo,' he said. 'It seems more complicated than that.'

Dolores sighed. She didn't really know either. She wished she could stop thinking about it.

She would have stopped thinking about it except Annie kept insisting on being her friend. And Dolores didn't have very many other friends around then. The other girls on her course were locals who hurried home afterwards; her old friends from school were either at university – the few who had made it in – or at home waiting to get married, or training to be nurses, or gone to England. None of them were slumming it around Dublin like she was, living like some kind of – like some kind of *harlot*, Annie said and Dolores had giggled. She *was* some kind of harlot, what a surprise!

Annie had a lot of time on her hands, which surprised Dolores as she assumed students, especially those studying law, those who were going to be doing all of the important stuff that was to be done in a few years' time, she assumed they'd be busy. But Annie only had a few hours of lectures per day, the rest of the time she was supposed to be in the library.

'I know, I *know*,' she said to Dolores. 'I'm a terrible layabout.

But I just can't keep still for that long! It's too much to ask. I want to be out having adventures.'

Annie's version of having adventures was hanging around Dolores's bedsit, which was a short bus ride or long walk from the university. Annie got the bus, Dolores always walked. Two or three times a week, she'd come into the cafe early in the afternoon and Dolores would give her the key, and when she got home at half past five, Annie would be there, lying on the damp, check-printed couch, flicking through one of her massive law books and playing a tape on the new cassette player that she had bought. It didn't bother Annie that Dolores was often not home in the evenings – she'd go to the bedsit anyway and sometimes she'd still be there when Dolores got in from her course at half past nine, or sometimes there would just be a sense that she'd been there, a few crumbled notebook pages under the kitchen table, a mug of tea gone cold by the sink. These details gave Dolores a sense of warmth, of home. She never felt lonely, in those Dublin days, she remembers later.

It was because of evenings in the bedsit with Annie that Dolores finally fully grasped what the constitution was. She was very surprised. Just this little blue book that contained all of the main rules. How had she never known that before? She was fairly certain no one at school had ever mentioned it. How very reassuring to realize that the world was stable and ordered and could fit into a small book. It was funny to be discovering this solid bedrock of reality just at the same time as Annie was opening up the world to her and making everything seem multifaceted and complex. She was on a new sea, but she'd found a sturdy boat.

Annie criticized the constitution in the way people only ever criticize the things they love. She was always going on about it, reading bits aloud from it, getting Dolores to test her knowledge of it. She explained the wording of the new amendment that the dark, dastardly forces of the Church wanted to insert into it to make sure that abortion could never happen in the fair land of Ireland, and she did this in such a way that made it too hard for Dolores to ask her, *was she sure?* Like, did she think abortion *wasn't* killing babies, or did she think it *was* but that was okay because they weren't actually babies yet? Annie acted like Dolores already knew, and already agreed with her. It made it too hard and awkward to ask questions.

It was a good strategy, Dolores thought. It was exactly like the way her mother ensured she continued to attend Mass – by assuming she did, by making the mere idea that she did not seem essentially unthinkable.

5

She attended a few more meetings with Annie as a way to assuage this uncertainty. She felt that if she listened very carefully, the questions she carried in her heart, the questions she felt were too stupid, too fundamental, to ask out loud, would be answered. The first meeting had been, she later realized, a gathering of the most dedicated, those who decided upon and established strategy and talking points. The other meetings she attended consisted of bigger groups being addressed by one of those main leaders. At these meetings, she sat at the back, listening.

She always sat next to Annie, who nodded vigorously as some women spoke and sighed at others. Annie didn't like going to meetings without Dolores now, she had grown used to Dolores's anchoring presence at her side, and it was startling, to Dolores, to realize how much she meant to this much more educated, much more enlightened, girl. This sense existed alongside another, more painful one, which arose in reaction to Annie's scathing attitude towards her secretarial course. Annie sometimes tried to persuade Dolores to skip it so that she could attend meetings, she said that such work was one of the ways women were kept in their place. Dolores felt her face burn when Annie said that to her, she thought of her mother's pride in her attendance at that course, her mother's sense that being a secretary, in an office, working alongside professionals, in a busy city, was something so wonderful it was scarcely to be dreamt of. It was a shock, therefore, to learn that this dream, this barely obtainable goal which she was working so hard to try to achieve, was considered by the women's movement to be – incorrect, undesirable, demeaning, even. This feeling was one of the many obstacles in the way of her commitment, and meanwhile Annie did not even notice the turmoil her comments had created.

After a few months, Dolores still had not made up her mind fully, she still felt there was some essential dimension to this issue that she wasn't seeing. She felt, suddenly, very bored with her own indecision and she decided she would speak directly to Mary.

She sought her out after one of the public meetings – a good crowd of about thirty, a function room in a small hotel, the carpet black and yellow, the tea pale and grey. She told Annie that she wanted to speak to Mary alone and Annie looked surprised and then hurt. Dolores told her to wait for her at the Bordello – this was Annie's word for the bedsit and Dolores's deployment of it seemed to placate her and off she went.

She waited until almost everyone had gone and she approached Mary. She was gathering her pieces of paper and putting them in her bag, a wide, satchel-like handbag. Dolores glimpsed a Leaving Certificate honours maths textbook inside it and she wondered briefly at the awesome capabilities of this woman.

'Mary,' she said. 'I wanted to ask you something. I hope it's okay.' She faltered. 'I wanted to ask you. How do you know?'

Mary looked at her. She had feathery blonde hair and serious blue eyes.

'How do I know what, Dolores? It's nice to see you, by the way. I didn't know you were still coming.'

'I sit at the back,' Dolores said. 'Usually. Mary, how do you know it doesn't feel any pain?'

Mary sat back down in her chair. She leaned her elbows on the table and rested her chin on her hand. Dolores noticed that her arms were very white and thin.

'I don't,' Mary said. She sounded sad. 'I don't know if you can know. For sure.'

Dolores nodded. She also felt sad.

'So it is then?' she said. 'Baby-killing?'

'It's not a baby,' Mary said. 'It's not yet a baby.'

Dolores nodded again. 'What is it then?' She felt curiously close to tears.

'I don't know what it is, Dolores. I mean, I could give you the words for the different stages of development, but that's not what you're asking me. What I think is that it's not the same as a person, in the early days. It's not the same as a woman. And treating it as if it were, is dangerous, for women.'

Dolores nodded. She wanted to take these words away and use them herself. But she wasn't sure yet. 'I want to believe you and Annie and everyone here,' she said. 'I think

I understand what you're saying about women. I don't want to have a load of babies myself. And the idea of the priests being involved is ridiculous. But I can't help feeling that it's wrong. It's more of a feeling than anything.'

Mary looked straight at her. She wasn't defensive, she wasn't cross.

'It's not easy, Dolores,' she said. 'But do you really think you should be able to force a woman to have a baby if she doesn't want to? If that woman has become pregnant against her will? By a man she doesn't know or love? Or, and no one wants to say this, no one wants to even think about it, but if she's become pregnant by her own father or her own brother?'

Dolores shrugged. She felt Mary had moved away from the central question. She figured most people got pregnant the way she was trying to avoid getting pregnant – through love and pleasure, not through violence, not through pain. She saw that Mary knew she was thinking that.

'You're a very lucky young woman, Dolores,' Mary said. 'You have a good family, and you're clever, and you've been very well looked after.'

Dolores nodded. She wondered how she knew. It was a little insulting, to be appraised so summarily, but also comforting. There were people in the world who could see clearly, there were people who could see how everything fit together.

'Not everyone gets that,' Mary said. 'So I'm here doing this for the women who don't get that. Life and death are dirty and painful and very, very dangerous. Some people have money, some people can go to England and it's all grand. But not everyone can.'

Dolores shrugged her shoulders and wriggled her toes. She felt, suddenly, strong and young and free. She recalled how Liam had acted when they had discussed this, and how she had sensed him shrugging away from it — just like she wanted to now. It was really hard, when you had everything, like they did, to think about those who didn't. It was so inconvenient, it was so boring, to have to think about people who were not strong, or young, or free. She looked at Mary, at the thin, red skin on her fine-featured face. She wondered what had happened to her, to make her care so much. She didn't have to be doing this.

Mary got up, and started to put her jacket on, the same long, green one she'd been wearing all winter, it was not stylish, it didn't even look that warm. Dolores imagined she was too busy to go shopping, she had no time to think of her own comfort. She had three children, a job and a country to change.

'You don't have to be certain,' Mary said. 'You just have to care enough to ask questions. The biggest problem in this country is that people are so scared of asking questions. I don't know why we're all so afraid of each other.'

Mary laughed suddenly as if she had only just realized this. She looked at Dolores, as if they were both sharing in this joke, this realization, together, and Dolores laughed too, though she was uncertain, she felt there was so much she did not yet see. They walked out of the hotel together into the evening. It was, Dolores noticed, springtime, she could smell it on the air. She saw Mary notice it too, she saw her nose wrinkle in a small moment of pleasure.

★ ★ ★

By early summer, Annie's exams were done and she and Dolores planned on taking Dolores's first trip abroad, on the ferry, to London. Annie wanted to visit a friend of hers, Isabelle, a girl she knew from her law class. Isabelle was part of a feminist group in London, Annie explained – and they wanted to hear from them, Annie and Dolores, about what was going on in Ireland in relation to their activism and the amendment and all of that.

When Dolores told Liam about it, he was surprised. He asked her why Annie was spending so much time with her, why she didn't have friends of her own. Dolores shrugged these questions off but she knew the answers. Annie was a bit too much for most people. She didn't quite get how to modulate herself to fit in with a crowd; she often monologued about things she cared too much about, she was overly sensitive and sometimes cried, hugely, out of nowhere. Dolores did not mind any of these things – and she couldn't say why, exactly, only that she felt from Annie such a warmth of affection for her, Dolores, for who she was. Annie liked to hear stories of Dolores's brothers and sisters, she admired her for qualities – her calmness, her organized nature, her fortitude – that she hadn't even realized she possessed. Annie was very earnest and that was a hard thing to be, in those days, at that time.

Annie had begged Dolores to allow her to pay for the trip. She told Dolores that while she wasn't a socialist (because socialism had almost destroyed the Irish women's movement and, besides, she'd never met so many Marxists since she started at Trinity, which told you everything you needed to know about Marxism), she accepted that as someone born into good fortune, it was only right that she extend generosity when she could. But only on the condition that Dolores never, ever thanked her or dreamt of thanking her or of feeling grateful in any way.

'Money is a mess,' Annie said, 'it's all just a mess but it's not your fault, and it's not my fault, so please just let's go together and have a good time. You could call it rent for all the time I spend at your flat.'

Annie's presence did in fact cost Dolores as she turned the heating on when she arrived, and never offered to contribute – but the weather was getting better now and Dolores had forgotten to be annoyed about it. She said she'd go.

Liam wanted to go too but he didn't have the money. She saw that, in taking this trip, in going off with this odd rich girl, she grew in his estimation, she saw that he saw that she was a bit more than he thought. They hadn't seen each other a lot in the early months of the year; he had joined a band with some lads he met out in Dun Laoghaire, it was all he thought about. She'd been to see him play in a shed at the back of a pub, there were a load of punks there, Dublin girls with hair pointed like icebergs and boys with mascara. His band were a bit more Horslips-influenced than proper punk but the crowd were gracious about that, and she ended the night sitting on the floor of the ladies, talking to a girl from Crumlin who worked in Crazy Prices and dreamt of going to Africa to help the poor.

When she told Annie about it the next day in the bedsit, she got a bit funny and said, 'People never talk to me the way they talk to you, Dolores. It's either your gift or my failing, which do you think?'

Liam was there when she said that, they were in the Bordello and he said, 'Maybe it's because you make everything about yourself, Annie.' And Annie had gone pale and left, and Dolores had felt bad.

So Liam disapproved of Annie and was jealous of Dolores's trip. But he was also still very much encouraging of her – in fact, when she confessed that she was nervous about it, that the notion of meeting Annie's fancy friends intimidated her, he shook his head and said it was more likely that *they* would be intimidated by *her*.

'Sure look at ya,' he said, and he did just that. 'Just look at ya.'

There was a giddiness about that time and to look back on it is something Dolores later only lets herself do every now and again. Because it's so precious, it's like taking out a tattered photograph, she doesn't want to sully it with the sweat and the grime of the present. It was not unusual at that time to marry young but still she sometimes meets people who pity her for all that she missed, who pity her the fact that she's spent her life with one man. And that amuses her, this pity, not because she doesn't think they have a point – it is certainly true that she missed out on things, on so many things – but because of the assumption that the thing she is missing is intensity, is meaning.

She knows that memory plays tricks, but she also knows that when she stepped into that Dublin episode of her life, a whole set of experiences were brought into being, and often it seems to her as if the rest of her life was triggered by those days – a mechanism sprung and a life animated, a note struck, forever reverberating. It's impossible, for example, to think of the night at that pub, talking to that Crumlin girl, whatever happened to her, and not to sense the ghosts of her daughters, hovering there, somehow, daughters who, to her great pride, to her great joy, also had their share of nights like that, ghosts of the future, lighting up the past.

And so underneath the ordinary day-to-dayness of the life she ended up living (and it couldn't be more ordinary, it couldn't be more day-to-day), there is something else, there is a depth or a glimpse, or a something, and when she feels it or senses it, every now and then, it comes to her suffused with the dull hazy light that filtered through the frilled brown lampshade that hung in her meagre room in the Rathmines Bordello.

The meeting took place in a small room in a university on the Strand. Dolores didn't know that's what the road was called until her visits to her daughter many years later, she had thought the university itself was called the Strand and she blushed when she realized her error, feeling certain that she'd betrayed her muck-savage ignorance many unwitting times over the years. On the ferry on the way over, Annie told her that the women here were light years ahead of Irish women. She said they had no issues with sex. She said they would probably not really understand, but that wasn't the point. She said they helped Irish women get abortions in London.

'They're not afraid to talk about it,' she said. 'That's the main thing they won't understand about us. They don't understand that not only do we have no right to choose, they don't know that we can't even *talk* about having a right to choose.'

The women who had gathered to meet them were interesting to look at. One or two of them were beautiful, some of them had very long hair. A few were older, middle-aged or beyond, but they held themselves youthfully, their shoulders were square, their chins pushed forward.

The room was cold and dirty; the coffee in the polystyrene cups almost undrinkable. One of the English women had brought along a baby who woke halfway through the meeting, the woman calmly unbuttoned her blouse and let the child latch on, as casual as lighting up a cigarette.

Dolores tried to grasp what they were talking about. It seemed there was a march planned to go through Soho. There was also discussion around more practical actions to do with helping local families with housing applications. They spoke of Margaret Thatcher as if she were the Devil and this was something Dolores was familiar with but she sensed that here it was for different reasons. The mention of Thatcher prompted one of the women to say something about the hunger strikes and everyone looked at her and Annie, and Dolores did not know what to say. No one talked about the hunger strikes, even when they were happening; her father had looked stuffed up with words he couldn't say, her mother had been thin-lipped and weary. The feeling around the North was exactly the same as the feeling around stuff to do with women, with sex – it was forbidden, violent, sacred. There were only feelings, when it came to the North; there were no opinions, no ideas. Not in her home, anyway.

'Sectarianism divides women and gives the Pope licence to

run Ireland,' Annie said, smoothly, confidently. This comment seemed to deflate something in the atmosphere and the conversation moved on. *Sectarianism*, Dolores thought. What a word. She saw that Annie enjoyed using it, that she felt powerful using it. Dolores felt a curious hollow feeling – as if every real, painful thing could just be explained away in big fancy words by people like Annie. This feeling confused her and made it hard to concentrate. She felt very much like she didn't belong, she had a sudden vision of Annie examining her, and her family, and their life, underneath a microscope, taking notes and nodding as if there was nothing surprising to be learned from them at all.

It was then time for a tea break. Dolores stayed in her chair, she didn't want to move in case she said the wrong thing to someone and she didn't want to stick too close to Annie for fear of seeming pathetic. She watched as Annie spoke to Isabelle, her friend from university, the one who had invited them over. She was tall and angular and beautiful. She seemed, Dolores thought, vaguely surprised that they were there.

After the break, the chair of the meeting invited Annie to speak, telling the women that they were very pleased to welcome Annie and Dolores from Éire and they were going to report on what the women over there were up against, and what they were planning to do about it.

Annie began with a deft history of the country and its institutions. She explained that the Church had taken advantage of the chaos that followed independence to strengthen its hold on the people; she described how the visionaries of the early part of the century had included women as equals in their projections of how things should be, and how disappointed they would be at the state of things now. She spoke with a slight English inflection throughout. It was soothing, her version of events. Dolores had never heard it all explained like that before.

'And now my friend Dolores is going to give the rural, working-class woman's perspective,' Annie said.

All eyes in the room turned towards her and Dolores realized they were expecting her to talk – and if they were expecting her to talk, then she was going to have to say something, something *rural*, something *working class*. Her mouth went dry and her mind blank. Annie turned to her calmly.

'Tell them about your mother,' she said. Dolores experienced a brief, destabilizing moment of anger. Annie had never once mentioned to her that she was going to speak. But there was no time for that now.

'My mother,' Dolores said. She looked around. The faces turned towards her were kind and full of sympathy. She felt another flicker of outrage. What did she need sympathy for?

'My mother is a small business owner and the mother of seven children.' She heard her voice bounce off the walls of the room, and the clarity of that sound emboldened her. Her mother *was* a small business owner, she *was* the mother of seven children.

'I am the youngest. She had me when she was forty-one.' One of the women sighed loudly at this.

'So now my mother is sixty-one. And she still works every night of the week. Still serving pints to –' and here Dolores paused, thinking, *was this true, could this be true, yes, it was true* – 'still serving pints to the men from our village who come in to spend their money, leaving their wives at home alone with the children.' Dolores realized as she said this that it was all really quite true. This really was the state of affairs.

'But she doesn't mind,' Dolores said. 'She loves work. She doesn't think she needs to be rescued. She doesn't care about women's lib. Actually, she thinks women's lib is ridiculous.'

She felt brave, saying that last part. She felt a bit like she'd cursed at Mass. But it was the truth. And she wanted to present these women's libbers with the conundrum she was struggling with — which is that the women they sought to speak on behalf of often regarded them with distrust. She needed someone to solve that puzzle for her.

'What about you, Dolores?' asked one of the women. She had long blonde hair and bright, slightly hectic green eyes. 'What do you do?' Dolores experienced a moment of disappointment as she realized the women were not going to engage with her foundational quandary. But she also felt relieved. It was embarrassing to confront them with their own failures.

'I work in a cafe,' Dolores said. 'In Dublin,' she added, somewhat grandly, hoping that the women would realize what this meant, hoping they would see that she wasn't just doing whatever was expected of her, that she was reaching towards freedom, if that's what this was called, in her own way. She didn't mention the secretarial course. She had missed an evening to come here, she hoped she wouldn't get into trouble.

'Dolores is amazing,' Annie then said. 'She comes to all our meetings, even though she has to work all the time to keep food on the table and her rent paid. She didn't finish school or get to go to university, but she knows more about why we need women's liberation, and why we have to oppose the amendment, than anyone.'

The women in the room smiled at her as if they had figured her out and they now approved. It was a pity it was not all quite true – she *had* finished school, she didn't know 'more than anyone' about all of this. But there were truths and then there were truer truths, Dolores was learning. And the truer truths did not have to *be* literally true, they just had to *feel* literally true, they had to point towards a greater, nobler, collective truth. That's just the way it had to be, to get anything done.

After the meeting, most of the older women left. On the way out the door, one of them came up to her and squeezed Dolores's arm. Her accent was thick as butter.

'My mother was Irish,' the woman said. 'She ran away from that godforsaken place at sixteen, and never looked back.' Her eyes were black and round, and almost childlike, Dolores felt she'd seen eyes like that before. 'You are a fucken hero to be doing what you're doing.'

Dolores felt the jumble of confusion that was the hallmark of that trip – flattered to be suddenly awarded recognition for things about herself she had never considered worthy of notice, let alone praise, and then a bristling of irritation at the way everyone here seemed to think the place she came from so unspeakably dreadful, so dreary and forsaken. Didn't it bother Annie to have so many English accents – of all accents – talk about their country in that way? Liam called Annie a West Brit, and Dolores got angry at him for that, she felt it was ugly and unfair, but perhaps it was also kind of true.

The woman then handed her a piece of paper with a number written on it. She said it was the phone number for her flat in Elephant and Castle. She said to call it any time, to never be afraid and to stay strong. Dolores was moved by this, she felt this woman reaching out towards her in a sisterly way, in an adult way. She noticed the woman didn't look twice at Annie, that she didn't speak to her at all. Dolores then felt, as ever, vaguely fraudulent.

'She's a lesbian,' Annie whispered, in a salacious tone, Dolores didn't like it, as they watched the woman walk towards the door.

The house was the most beautiful place she'd ever been in her life. It was four or maybe five storeys high, the stairs were of stripped wood, there were paintings of all different sizes on the walls in the hallway, the door frames were wide, the windows huge. The ceilings soared above her, Dolores felt diminutive simply standing underneath them, the bare floorboards creaked under her feet and even this creaking seemed luxurious, as if the house were broadening to accommodate her presence, as if it were sleepily alive in some mysterious way. There were floor-to-ceiling bookshelves in the front room, stacks of old sturdy pots on shelves in the kitchen. The garden was long and brambly and it glowed in the light thrown on it from the big kitchen windows.

Isabelle had brought Annie and Dolores to the party at the house after the meeting. She led them through Soho towards a Tube station, and onto a train and then another train, and then down a long street lined with large white houses and then finally up some steps and through a blue front door.

Annie and Isabelle walked together the whole way, Isabelle continued to ignore Dolores, and Annie did too. Dolores did not mind, or much notice, there were so many things to see, she felt dazzled and blissful as the loud, bright impressions of the city rained down on her, washing away any lingering feeling of confusion. Lights, faces, smells, noises, sudden blasts of air, of music, of mad laughter, of traffic. She felt as if she herself had disappeared, that she was just a body, a clean, clear mind, absorbing, seeing, smelling. She felt her cheeks a little bit sore and realized she'd been grinning into the spring evening like a mad person. An old woman pulling a shopping trolley filled with newspapers and oranges grinned back at her.

There were boys at the party, they had soft, pale faces and floppy hair, they were all a little drunk and smiled as the girls moved around them. The girls were wispy and angular, and they wore flared jeans or long floral dresses. They called to each other in gentle, echoing voices, they sipped neat vodka out of delicate china cups. They smiled in a broad, general way at Dolores but they did not speak to her. She felt stiff and squat in her bright blue polyester blouse and tight jeans. She felt like a stuffed pig, she felt like she had an apple shoved in her mouth.

Dolores stood in the corner of the kitchen and looked across the room at Isabelle. This was her house, she realized this after noticing some family photographs on the wall on the way in. A sliver of envy cut through her body like a knife. She cleared her throat and shook her head. Isabelle looked over at her for a brief moment, and then her eyes slid away, as if Dolores were not part of this picture, as if there was no way she could really be here.

There was a small living room at the front of the house, painted a dark ivy green. A small, exclusive-seeming group of people were sitting in there, Dolores had glimpsed them on her way in. She decided she would go there now. She felt if she just stood rigidly in the corner of the kitchen then this feeling of bitterness would disfigure her and everyone would see. There was drink flowing, there was smoke hanging in the air like mist, there were people holding out hands to one another. She was not going to be miserable here.

In the room, a boy was picking out a song on a worn acoustic guitar and singing in a vague, gentle way. Dolores sat down on the sofa across from him. She realized she knew the words to the song he was singing, and she felt this knowledge a reward for her bravery in crossing the kitchen and breaching the threshold of this room. She began to sing along and the boy smiled. He then began to sing something more raucous and others – who had been chatting – joined in with them. Dolores's family was musical, her older siblings used to sing in the family pub on Saturday nights. Her own abilities were modest, no one paid them any attention at home, and it was always a surprise to be reminded that among average people she was musically quite competent, and to the tin-eared, she could even seem gifted. In this green room, her voice soared above everyone else's. After the song ended, the boy handed her his guitar.

She thought for a moment. A political song arose in her mind, it was sung often in the pub, her father shut his eyes when he sang it. But she knew it would be tactless to sing it here, and she was not usually a tactless or insensitive person.

But she felt that by coming into this room, by even coming to London in the first place, she had donned a different kind of costume, that she had become a different kind of person. She realized that people saw her differently, in this place, and she wanted to understand what the difference meant, she wanted to challenge them to acknowledge what it meant. Her cheeks burned with a shame she didn't understand when she thought of the women's meeting that afternoon; Isabelle had yet to say a single word to her. She was dimly aware in herself of a desire to punish.

She began singing. She felt her voice broadening, unnecessarily, on the vowels. She stopped pretending to play the guitar, and her voice filled the room. Everyone was watching her.

When she finished, there was a huge cheer. This surprised her. She noticed that Annie and Isabelle had come in from the kitchen and were standing by the door, watching her receive her applause. She handed the guitar back to the boy, her hands were trembling. He grinned at her; he had shining teeth and clear skin and dark glinting eyes. She was briefly unable to think. He held her gaze boldly and when he saw her blush he nodded as if settling a bet.

She looked back at Annie and Isabelle and she saw they were smirking at each other. She heard Annie say, in an exaggerated accent, *Down de glen wan Easter morn*, and she saw Isabelle laugh. She realized she had done exactly what they had expected her to do. She looked towards the boy again.

She woke early the next morning, feeling cold. She was lying on a couch in the small front room, the English boy with the glinting eyes was beside her, his body curled towards hers.

She recalled kissing him the night before. She recalled the surprising texture of his lips, and the way the bones of her face felt against his.

She got to her feet and looked around. The boy mumbled and turned over and she felt a detached affection for him. He was smooth and clean and new, like a gift she'd unexpectedly been given. He had been too drunk to talk much to her but he had been a not-terrible kisser. He was the only boy she had ever kissed other than Liam. She preferred to kiss Liam.

She walked across the carpeted room to the creaking hallway and into the kitchen. The sun thrust itself across the room in vigorous panels of light. She opened the back door and sat on the step. She looked out at the long green garden, its low old trees budding, its small brown birds singing. It felt like some kind of miracle, this rude preponderance of nature amid the hot concrete city.

Annie and Isabelle appeared in the kitchen then and she looked over her shoulder at them. She could smell the sun on her own skin. She hoped they would tease her about kissing the boy. She wondered if he was awake yet, she wondered if he was thinking about her.

Annie was walking around the kitchen in slow circles, searching for her shoes. Dolores spotted them underneath an armchair; she went and got them for her. Annie was like a child when she was hungover, she could not locate anything, Dolores's bedsit was full of her mislaid books and gloves and pens. Dolores smiled at this thought. It was nice, mostly, having Annie around.

'We have to get going,' Annie said, as Dolores handed her

the shoes. 'We have to get back to Camden and then to King's Cross to get the train.'

They had checked into a hostel in Camden before the meeting, it had been the plan to stay there. Dolores thought that she would be happy enough to abandon her things in London, to travel back home with just her ticket and her money. She felt free and light and unencumbered.

'I feel so sorry for you, Annie,' Isabelle said. She was leaning against the kitchen counter, wearing the same flared jeans and skimpy T-shirt as the night before. Her eyes were bright and clean behind her smudged mascara. 'Wouldn't it be so great if you could stay here?'

Annie's small face shone with delight.

'I have to study for the repeats,' she said. 'We're not all as smart as you, Izzy.'

Isabelle reached out and touched Annie's hair.

'You need to settle down now and work,' Isabelle said. 'Take a break from those meetings. They're not ready over there, Annie. It's a total waste of time.' She spoke in a tone of gentle admonishment, like a mother.

'If we're so backwards, then what are you doing studying there?' Dolores said. It was only as she spoke these words that she realized what a good question it was. What *was* Isabelle doing studying in Ireland if she thought it so beneath her? Dolores's question had come out of her mouth thick and coarse, because she was angry, she realized, she was suddenly very angry.

Annie and Isabelle looked at each other with an expression of vague surprise, as if a child had said something disconcertingly amusing. Dolores had the by-now tiresome feeling of missing something crucial.

'Annie has to come back over here when we're finished next year,' Isabelle said. 'She has to escape. You keep on reminding her of that, Dolores. Sure you could even come yourself, so you could.'

She did an ugly and exaggerated imitation of Dolores's accent as she spoke those last words. Dolores was startled – is that really how I sound? – and then immediately felt a disfiguring and humiliating sense of gratitude. Isabelle had paid her so little attention since they'd met the day before that she'd begun to wonder if she had somehow been rendered invisible in her company. But now she knew that Isabelle did see her, that Isabelle recognized her enough to be able to imitate her. In her throat she felt a thickness, making a reply impossible. She went back into the green room, but the boy had already left.

They slept most of the way on the train, it was almost empty, they had two seats each. They drank tea and Annie smoked cigarettes. Dolores couldn't afford to buy any, she didn't really want to smoke anyway. She watched the towns of England flash by. There were so many of them, it was unbelievable how many of them there were.

The crossing they had been due to get was cancelled due to stormy weather so they sat on the floor of the ferry port in Wales and pulled out a packet of cards and played Gin Rummy and then just Snap. Annie was competitive and fast, she slapped her hand down on the cards and pulled them towards herself with hungry glee. Her nails were short and bitten down, her hair big and wild. She was wearing a fisherman-style jumper and a nicely cut woollen coat. She seemed emboldened by their trip over, her flattery towards Dolores had faded away. She was sharper, grabbier, she didn't look her in the eye. Dolores had no money left to buy any food, Annie did not seem hungry, and Dolores could not bring herself to ask if she could borrow any more.

It was late by the time they boarded, after 2 a.m. People lay on the floor as well as the benches, the ferry was crowded due to the earlier cancellation. There were a number of young families with children in clusters of fours and sixes, they shared packets of crisps and bottles of lemonade. Toddlers slumped across their mothers in clammy abandon, older kids ran around wide-eyed and gleeful, fathers were resolute, mothers exhausted and cross.

Dolores and Annie sat together near the bar. Annie sleepily lay on her bag, and Dolores thumbed through magazines she'd bought with her last English money, thinking that Liam would enjoy them. A small, ferrety man approached them, as he got closer Dolores noticed his nose – purple, monstrous, in the fevered atmosphere of the night-time ferry, it almost seemed like a living thing.

'You two'd better watch out,' he said, in a mad, rasping voice. 'Someone is bound to get you some day. Bound to.'

He ranted at them for a few moments, he spoke of terrible things that could happen to girls like them. Dolores watched him, she felt sad and bored; there was nothing so familiar to her as the ravings of drunk old men. Annie drew her coat closer to her as if in fear, and this irritated Dolores. He was a tiny man, barely taller than herself, and what could he do to them here, surrounded by so many people? Sometimes she felt that Annie knew absolutely nothing about the world. She saw how clear and perfect Annie's face was, how lovely she was, and this annoyed her.

'Would you ever go away with yourself?' Dolores said at

last to the man. She spoke callously and tiredly, as if he were no more than a badly behaved child. His mouth twisted in surprise and he retreated. She saw in his flickering glance around the deck a mix of fury and bewilderment. She felt another twinge of sadness. Her mother had once told her that men like that, lost, angry men, with heads on them like bantam chickens, were usually the youngest of twelve or fourteen or more children, and had been forgotten or sent to industrial schools and therefore they spent the rest of their lives trying to annoy people into paying attention to them. 'Terrible oul bores, it's not their fault,' Brigid had said.

Dolores thought about this. It was puzzling that her mother was so very aware of the tribulations involved in having children and raising them and yet she had no interest whatsoever in any of the things Annie or the women's movement spoke of – in fact, she thought the mere idea of women's groups beneath contempt.

She should *learn* about it, Dolores thought, suddenly, as she watched the purple-nosed man approach a woman sitting with her young daughter, the little girl's scared face, the mother's hard impatience. Women like her mother had to learn or nothing would ever change. Suddenly she understood what Mary and others in the group meant by 'consciousness raising'. She had previously blushed at the thought of this phrase, but now she felt she finally understood.

Life was sacred yes, it really was, and it was wonderful and it was a gift. The city she'd left behind her reminded her of that, of the great blur of experience that was available, of the possibilities, of the adventure. But that was all very well for her! She was tough, she was smart. She could sing, she could deal with some English girl belittling her, she could take it on the chin, she could roll with it and let it make her stronger, let it become part of the great adventure of life. But a man like that — a poor, forgotten, abused, derided old fucker — he didn't have a chance. And while it was beyond her to say he shouldn't have been born, it was also beyond her to deny that life was miserable, just miserable, if there wasn't any love in it.

She suddenly got what Mary was on about that time. Mary understood that love was precious and, as such, limited. And Mary, and the other women, they weren't hiding from that, they were trying to explain that to the people of their country, the people of their buttoned-up, beleaguered little country. She saw, in a flash, why Mary and the rest of the women were speaking about it in the way that they were. They really cared about the broader picture, they were not just about that one terrible moment of ending a life in the womb, they saw the bigger, fuller context. They wanted things to be better, they really believed that things could be better.

She turned to Annie, and all of the irritation and hurt from the last two days fell away. She knew that Annie didn't really get it, not properly, but that didn't matter. It was thanks to Annie that *she* got it. She felt sorry for her, again. Poor Annie was never really going to get it, and it wasn't her fault. She was too rich. She was too fervent.

'Annie,' she said. Annie's head had lolled forward onto her chest, as if she were asleep. Dolores poked her in the side with her elbow.

'Annie,' she said again. She felt wide awake and excited, her heart was beating fast, she felt a warm, sunny joy inside her. She got it now, why Mary had laughed that time they had spoken. It was so silly, it was so *funny* for them to be tearing one another apart about all of this.

'I think I can talk to Mammy about this now,' Dolores said. 'I think I can make her understand, about the women's movement. About the referendum, even.'

Annie rolled her head up towards Dolores. She grimaced. Her lips were white.

'*Mammy,*' Annie said, and she shuddered as if she'd been sick. '*Mammy* is never going to understand, Dolores.' She rolled her head around on her slim white neck. 'That's your problem, though. Not mine.'

Dolores blinked. The contempt in Annie's voice was new, and shocking.

'If that's my problem, what's yours?' Dolores said. This she said calmly. She was curious whether Annie really did understand why she pushed people away, why the movement didn't want her, why Isabelle spoke to her as if she were a child.

Annie looked straight ahead, towards the bar. A heave of men in tweed coats, a tangle of girls in tartan skirts and knee-high white socks drinking lemonade and laughing.

'My problem is that I don't belong. I don't belong here and I don't belong there.'

This she said simply, as if she were speaking to herself in front of a mirror. Dolores did not say anything because she did not know how to disagree with what was true.

They arrived in Ireland as dawn was breaking. Dolores stood on the outside deck watching the coast appear. A man of about her own age let out a whoop, it sounded sarcastic, it made her smile.

They stepped out into the misty grey light, she felt salt on her cheeks, she noticed some crimson flowers nodding in a garden near the bay. She had ignored Annie after their discussion about her mother, but she turned to her now. Her lips were crusted with sleep.

Liam was waiting for them. He had borrowed his auntie's yellow Fiesta to bring them home, Dolores was surprised to see him, he'd mentioned that he might pick her up but they were almost half a day late. Her heart thumped in her chest at the sight of him, he grinned and she noticed that his arms were looking strong underneath his stripy T-shirt, it rippled in the breeze. He drove them to Rathgar first, the streets only starting to stir as they travelled north from Dun Laoghaire, still just about early enough to avoid the morning traffic. It was, improbably, a Monday morning. Dolores had got the day off, she was going to be so broke, she didn't know how she was going to get through the next week, she didn't care. Her stomach rumbled and she leaned her head against the window.

Liam asked them some questions, they answered vaguely, the talk faded. Annie hopped out of the car when they got to her house and Dolores watched as she sprang light-footed up the stone steps of her home, the windows glowing as if in anticipation of her arrival. Dolores pictured Betty, Annie's mother, welcoming her, making her breakfast and asking quiet, tactful questions. Betty was an artist, she had been somewhat prominent in the women's movement a decade or so before, but she couldn't take it, Annie had said. She's too soft. She's better off with her painting.

They made the short trip to Rathmines then. Dolores thought that her building must have started its life salubrious and proud like Annie's house, but it was now faded and shabby and carved up. The dusty smell of the red-and-black swirled carpet hit her in the gut as she unlocked the front door, but she did not mind it, in fact she felt welcomed by it. She had the sense of things waiting for her, of being back where she belonged. She led Liam to her room. She thought about the English boy for a brief moment and then forgot about him immediately and for ever.

6

A few weeks later, Dolores went home to visit her mother. She hadn't been home in six or seven weeks, not since before the trip to London, which she had not told her about. Brigid had never been out of the country, as far as Dolores knew.

She got an early bus because she wanted to see her mother before it was time to open the pub. It was now high summer, and the day was hot and blue. The village was quiet when she arrived and she felt like she was seeing it for the first time. She let herself into the kitchen and saw that her mother was out in the yard behind the house. She hurried out to help her, feeling the cold of the concrete steps underneath the thin soles of her shoes.

Her mother laughed when she saw her.

'It's yourself,' she said. She did not embrace her daughter but she took her bag – a new backpack, she'd gotten it in Dunnes, and she admired it. They went into the kitchen and Brigid made tea for them both. Her father was still in bed, he had worked late in the bar the night before, Brigid had also, but she couldn't sleep past eight, she liked the quiet of the place before anyone was around.

They talked for a while. Brigid informed her how May's children were doing, Dolores missed them, she was pleased to hear about them. They had a new childminder, one of the women from the village, and it was all working out more or less all right. May lived in a new bungalow up in the hills, built by her father-in-law's family. James and Declan, the brothers nearest in age to Dolores, were the only ones still living at home, on the dole but not too miserable about it, Brigid said. They were keeping as busy as they could, they helped in the pub but there was not enough money to pay them properly. They talked of England, they talked of possible jobs in the county council, they talked of music, money and girls.

Her elder siblings Dolores saw less often and knew less well. Rita, the oldest, twelve years her senior, was long married and living in the west; Walter, the dreamer, the wanderer, was in Manchester, alone. Brigid worried about him constantly, he wrote rarely. Dolores didn't like to mention him, she saw it pulled on her mother's heart to hear him spoken of. Martha was the soundest, the strongest, she had somehow managed to get to teacher training college, she had a solid permanent job, on her way to being school principal, Brigid said proudly, she had excellent Irish, she always had everything worked out. She was also married but had no children yet, her husband was in the army.

Dolores wanted to see James and Declan, to boast lightly of the gigs she'd been to in Dublin with Liam, to mention casually her trip to London, but they were not awake yet.

They rarely stirred before noon, Brigid said they'd be around later, she'd told them she was coming home. Dolores had missed the loudness of home, the feeling of being peripheral but still essential, the sense of being carried along by everyone else's routine. She kicked her shoes off under the table, feeling happy and at peace.

When she grew a bit older and reflected back on these particular years, Dolores realized that this time in her family's history was one of uncertainty, of contained fearfulness. The seventies had been all right, the pub had done well, but then in the bad times of the early eighties, when her parents had all of these children but nowhere for them to go – she didn't quite know it at the time but it weighed on them, it weighed on her mother in particular. Brigid worried about the boys most of all – the girls would get themselves married, would get themselves babies, the girls were always steadier, more able to look after themselves. But the boys – especially Walter, but also James and Declan, so young and with so little to hang on to – the boys troubled Brigid.

After the tea, Dolores helped her mother roll a beer barrel onto a trolley and then into the darkened quiet of the pub. She polished the bar and the tables, most of the other tasks had been completed the night before in the manic, determined energy that took over at the end of the night when everyone just wanted to get to bed. She opened the windows and the front door to let in some air, Brigid watched her.

After everything was ready, there were still a few moments before opening time at midday so Dolores persuaded her mother to sit outside for a cup of tea and a cigarette. She told her that she'd been to London a few weeks ago.

'Well, that's some jaunt for you,' Brigid said mildly. 'Was it Liam you went with?'

This question she tried to put lightly but it was weighted anyway, weighted with all that such a jaunt with Liam would represent.

'No,' Dolores said, with conviction. She felt emboldened by the way she could honestly and righteously deny the very idea of London with Liam, Sunday mornings in Rathmines with Liam notwithstanding.

'I went with a women's group, actually.'

As she said that, Dolores realized she'd almost never said the word 'woman' before she met Annie. In her world, they were *girls* and then they were *ladies*. The word 'woman' sounded posh, almost. Kind of obscene, actually.

'A prayer group, was it?' Brigid said, and she laughed. 'You should have told me you were into that oul claptrap. We could go to Knock together and pray for me knees.' Brigid was a pious woman – somewhat – but she was wary of people who took it too far. She went to Knock, but mainly for the craic, she avoided the Legion of Mary, she hardly ever went to Confession.

'No, Mammy,' Dolores said firmly. 'It was a women's group. You know the referendum they're having. To prevent women from getting, you know, reproductive rights.'

She was surprised to hear those words come out of her mouth. They were not the words that most of the women at the meetings used. Those women preferred to talk about the amendment itself, how it was unnecessary, how it had bad legal implications. But Dolores did not have the equipment to speak of those things. She felt she had to go to the heart of the issue, with her mother, she could not talk to her mother of broader contexts, of legalistic challenges.

Brigid was sitting in a slice of shadow, she did not trust the sun, Dolores could not see her face. She watched as her mother got up and went back into the pub without saying a word.

Dolores was not brave enough to follow her, so she stayed outside, sitting in the yard. She thought about how different she felt, after just a few months living away from home. As a child, she'd wanted more than anything to be a 'big girl', like her older sisters, to be as tall and strong and all-knowing as they were. She remembers clamouring at them, wanting to be picked up, wanting to be part of whatever they were doing. They rarely did pick her up and for that she couldn't blame them. Her eldest sister had been a teenager when she was a small child. Rita had a cool, collected demeanour, she was very like Brigid, she'd done her duties in the home conscientiously but carefully, she'd moved to the opposite side of the country as soon as she could, she'd started her own family young in order to escape the demands of her siblings. Dolores understood all of that, she'd pretty much always understood all of that.

But still it had hurt, still it had been a huge hurt, to always feel left behind, to always feel slower and smaller than everyone else. And it would have hurt so much more if her mother hadn't seen it, hadn't picked her up, held her, cherished her not despite her slowness, her smallness, but because of it. And it was throughout her entire life maybe the biggest question Dolores had – how had Brigid done it? How had she managed to stay not only sane, but good-humoured, not only hard-working, but competent, not only calm but – quite often – joyful? And not only loving – anyone could be loving, deep down – but affectionate? Comforting? When Dolores found herself with two (only *two*) small children, feeling like she might drown, feeling like she might choke on her own isolation and loneliness and frustration – it was this same question that came back to haunt her – how was it possible to be such a lesser woman than her mother was? And how did she ever think she had the right to tell her what was what about anything?

Dolores had not been scheduled to work in the pub that day but sunny days brought out the drinkers, and so she slunk back inside halfway through the afternoon to help. She worked steadily and quietly alongside her mother and Rosalie, a fifty-something matron who helped out behind the bar whenever required. She watched the side of her mother's face, it was still and normal.

At six o'clock, she bought a bag of chips from the chipper across the road, then sat out in the yard eating. When she finished she returned to work and then Brigid took a break, boiling potatoes and turnips and frying sausages for herself and Patsy, Dolores's father. He was not working that night, he had a bad back, he sat in the kitchen with the curtains closed watching television. Dolores went to speak to him, he responded with the mild affection he reserved for her. He always seemed vaguely surprised to encounter her, she often had the sense that he forgot, sometimes, that they'd had a last daughter. It didn't bother her much, because she sensed from him that to recollect she did exist was a pleasant surprise, like realizing there was one biscuit left in the packet, or a smoke in the box. He was ten years older than Brigid, he was carrying too much weight, they all worried about him.

At closing time, Dolores poured herself a pint and sat at the bar, tired after the night's work, waiting for her mother to join her. They always had one drink before starting the clean-up, the only drink they'd have all night. It was much more pleasant to mop out the gents with a drink inside you, Brigid said.

'They were lovely women,' Dolores said, the minute Brigid sat down. 'I told them about you.' She felt she'd started this whole thing so she may as well finish. She couldn't bear to return to Dublin with all of this still unsaid between them.

Brigid was sitting in front of her usual, a glass of whiskey.

'Sure if they had their way, you wouldn't even be here,' she said. She spoke with a great, casual clarity. Dolores felt her heart hammer in her chest.

'But Mammy,' she said, her own voice low now too. 'Not every woman wants to have seven babies. *I* don't want to have seven babies.'

'Well, you know what not to do then. You're not a fool, Dolores.'

Dolores wondered why it was so impossible to talk about sex with her mother. The sheer physical impossibility of broaching it made it easier to believe she had been conceived by the Holy Spirit than by her parents.

'But Mammy, look at all this. Look at how hard you have to work. While Daddy – well. You did it all. You had nothing for yourself.'

She wanted to mention the fact that her father had been

sitting on his backside in the kitchen all evening while they worked but she did not have the courage to go that far. Her mother would not hear a word said against him. Annie would say that was the patriarchy, working through her mother. Annie talked about the patriarchy like it was some kind of ghost, some kind of spirit that inhabited men and made them monsters and inhabited women and made them act against their own interests.

There was a newspaper on the bar and on the front of it there was something about the North. Brigid reached for it and looked at it.

'You know what's happening up there, don't you? People killing each other. People who believe in the same God shooting each other, blowing each other up. That's what happens when ideas become more important than people. And that's what's happening in the North and that's what's happening with these – *women* that you're talking about.'

Dolores felt this a weak argument, but she didn't know what to say in response to it. She remembered the word Annie had used in relation to the North when they were in London. But she couldn't figure out how to get at it.

'They want to be like men, so they do,' Brigid said. 'They want to kill things that are innocent for the sake of their ideas. And for women like me, they don't have the time of day. They think we're thick, they think we're nothing. They don't even know we exist.'

Dolores tried in that moment to pretend that was not true, she tried not to blush as Brigid described Annie without ever having met her.

'But Mammy,' Dolores said, and even as she spoke she knew

how thin her words would sound. 'How can you treat a two-day-old *zygote* –' and Dolores knew as she said that word that the battle was lost. Because to speak to a woman of seven births and who-knew-how-many pregnancies of *zygotes* was not something Dolores felt able to do. Maybe this was the kind of thing they taught in university, how to talk to people who had lived as Brigid had lived, who had survived, who had endured, when you yourself had merely read a few dusty books. Maybe you needed to go to university to be able to do that.

She finished anyway, she felt like she was swallowing a foul-tasting medicine – 'How can you treat a *zygote* –' she didn't even know if she was pronouncing it correctly – 'like a full-grown person?' She couldn't say *woman*, she didn't have it in her.

Brigid shook her head at her and laughed. Her laugh was powerful and callous and it lent Dolores the tiniest bit of outrage she needed to finish her speech.

'It's women in power that would stop killing like that in the North,' she said, but she only said it in a whisper. 'But how can we ever have power if we're never finished having babies?'

Dolores rested her head on her hand. She felt frustrated with herself.

'So you have one kind of killing to prevent another?' Brigid said, and Dolores felt momentarily surprised that her mother was deigning to actually engage with her line of debate. 'And wouldn't they be only delighted, the men, able to do whatever they want, to whoever they want, and no fear of a baby? Do you not think the best thing that ever happened to me and your father was all of you? That you give us something to get up for, to work for, to be proud of? We don't care about ourselves, we care about you and your brothers and sisters. That's the way it's supposed to be.'

Brigid was not one for sentiment, in general. Her affections were always leavened by humour, she never wanted to be the kind of mother who tormented her children with demands for tribute. So this speech was agonizing to remember, in later years. It was the closest Dolores could ever remember her mother had come to saying she loved her.

'Mam,' she said, gently. Her mother was looking straight ahead, at the bottles of spirits behind the bar. They were all perfectly lined up, gold and glinting in the tobacco light of the pub. 'It's you that I want this for,' she said. 'For women like you.'

Brigid stood up. Her eyes were blazing behind her thick glasses. She was a tall, strong woman.

'You want this for you, Dolores. Go after it if you want, but don't tell me it's for anyone but yourself.'

Dolores woke early the next morning and felt wide awake straight away despite having slept little and poorly. The narrow room was mainly empty of her things now, and that pleased her. It was good, she thought, to have so few belongings, it made it easier to come and go. She felt the small thrill that kept burgeoning underneath her skin those days, a feeling of possibility, a feeling of freedom. She had shared this room with two of her older sisters once, years ago, the three of them – herself, Martha and May – across two beds. But now it was empty, though Declan or James could have claimed it if they had wanted to. They probably thought she'd be back before long and they could not be bothered moving their few things across the hall.

She heard the front door open and shut – her mother, leaving for Mass. She felt a little thump in her stomach, she had not called up the stairs to ask her to go with her. She never made the boys go but she liked a daughter to accompany her, if one happened to be around. She looked out the window and saw Brigid walk up the hill, her stride confident and almost masculine. She wore trousers, unlike most other women her age, they were navy and well-tailored underneath her grey coat.

The day was warm and still. Dolores looked at the houses huddled against one another on the far side of the street, their walls thick, their windows small and mean. She felt full of energy, of a blaze that needed to be spent.

She walked loudly and vehemently down the stairs. She had not seen her brothers the night before and she wanted to see them, she wanted them to see her. So much had happened since they'd last been together, they didn't even know that she'd been to England. They should know that, she thought.

In the kitchen, she made toast and tea and eventually, Declan came in. A large white toe poked out from one of his socks and the sleeves of his shirt were too short for his arms. He always had his shoulders up near his ears when he walked, and his stride contained within it a pent-up energy, as if he might at any moment burst into dance. All the girls at school had been crazy about him. It had been a thing of status, to have been his younger sister.

'What-*a* bout-*a* cup-*a* tea?' he said. It was his and Dolores's habit to talk to each other like that sometimes, they could not remember why, possibly in imitation of an old man who used to come into the pub. Declan walked jaggedly across the kitchen and picked up a potato from the vegetable rack near the sink and threw it at her.

'Catch a fairy,' he shouted at her.

This was another of their games, to throw something unexpectedly at the other while calling it something else. Declan said it was good to scramble the brain, he said it kept you sharp.

Dolores did not attempt to catch the potato. She felt irritated by Declan's messing. She wanted to talk to him properly. She wanted to tell him all about the things she was learning, to tell him about Annie. She felt suddenly that it was her duty to show him that there was another world out there, and that he could be part of it too, if he would just get his act together. Declan had not done well at school but not because he wasn't clever.

'Too good to catch a spud,' Declan sang softly to himself as he got a mug and reached out to feel the belly of the teapot. Dolores sat down at the table, wrapping her hands around her own mug.

'I went to England, Declan,' she said proudly. 'Did you hear?'

'She went to Eng-ga-land,' Declan said, still in his enraging singing voice.

Dolores said nothing. Declan sat down opposite her and poured himself some tea.

'How'd ya get the money?' he asked, with a sudden, exaggerated eagerness. 'How in the name of all that's holy did ya get the money to go to England, Dolores Reidy? Did ya rob a bank? Did ya find a rich husband?'

Though this was still annoying, the fact that he'd used her name made Dolores smile. She wanted, always, to be recognized by her older siblings, and most especially by him.

'A friend,' she said. 'A very rich *friend*.' She leaned back in her chair.

'The only kind of friend!' Declan said.

'Really, Dec,' Dolores said. 'We walked through Soho. We went to a party! With – students!'

'Soho!' Declan said. 'Students!' He clutched his chest and lay down across the chair beside him.

'Oh, shut up,' Dolores said. 'It was very interesting. I went as part of the Women's Movement.' She said this grandly but with plausible self-mockery built in. She hoped that Declan might understand what she was doing. He was not like the other young men of this area – he had no interest in Gaelic football, he liked Thin Lizzy and soccer and English music magazines.

Declan stared at her, as if fascinated. He then turned abruptly and picked up the racing newspaper from the day before, and began reading it. Dolores knew now that he was bored and that he'd ignore her for the rest of the day. She knew he'd go back to bed and only get up when it was dinnertime and she had gone back to Dublin. Her heart thumped in dismay and she felt, for a terrible second, as if she might cry.

She grabbed a tea towel and tied it over her hair.

'Sure they think we're nothing but a shower of eejits over there,' she said, in a voice she found suddenly inside her. 'Poor Holy Marys who do whatever the Pope tells us to do.'

Declan looked up from his paper.

'And sure aren't they right?' she went on. 'So it is and to be sure.'

Declan curled his lip upwards like an old man. He stood up and put his thumbs inside a pair of imaginary braces and stretched them outwards.

'Well, ya know, it's like I do be saying, Dolores. You can never say too many Hail Marys.'

Dolores grinned. She saw her mother's housecoat hanging from a nail by the cooker and she grabbed it and wrapped it around herself. She then stood up on her chair.

'Pray for us, Declan,' she said, in a croaking voice, it was at once both loud and feeble. 'Pray for us poor little Brigids and Bernadettes, who are never finished having babbies. Pray that we never end up like those Brits, with their sins and their *sex* and their terrible carry-on.'

Declan laughed properly then. In his laugh she detected a note of surprise. She felt proud. He thought her so predictable, he thought her so well-behaved, he thought her so *young*. She wondered what he thought about the referendum. He probably didn't think anything about it. He didn't have to think anything about it.

Declan sat down and returned to his newspaper.

'The poor little babbies,' she said, in a loud voice. 'Who will protect the poor little innocent babbies?'

She heard a noise on the stairs and she stopped shouting. James would not approve of this, he was of a much softer nature than Declan, he would not countenance any mockery of their mother. He came in and saw her standing on the chair.

'Good morning, Mammy,' he said.

'Good morning, Jamesie,' Dolores said, in a voice halfway

between her own and the one she had been putting on. She looked down at him. He needed to learn about this stuff too, she thought. He would probably actually listen to her. James read philosophy, sometimes. Dolores smiled at him. James would be the one, he'd help her make them see.

'Good morning, children.'

Dolores turned around. Her mother was standing at the back door of the kitchen. It had been open all morning. It was always open, on warm days, the kitchen had only the tiniest of windows and the room quickly became stuffy. The back door led into the delivery yard, her mother's domain. She always came back into the house that way, Dolores remembered. All too late, she remembered that.

Brigid was leaning against the door frame and she had a still, clear look on her face. Her gaze did not seem fixed on anything in the room, it seemed to be looking somewhere far beyond that. She reminded Dolores suddenly of a movie star from an old film, she couldn't remember which film, which star, but she recalled a kind of resoluteness, a toughness, a blankness. Brigid's face was so clear, so pale, she was not frowning, or smiling, or speaking. She remained in that suspended moment, for what felt like for ever.

Dolores was frozen to her spot on the chair. Her mother walked into the kitchen and began to take off her coat, shattering the stillness, causing life to begin again. The boys scrambled to help her, to take her bag, to hang up her things. Dolores tried to tell herself that she hadn't heard anything and that if she had heard, she hadn't understood, and that if she had understood, she took it good-naturedly.

'Mammy,' she said.

Brigid turned around and looked up at her.

'Yes, Dolores?' she said.

'How was – Mass?' Dolores said. She saw that James's face was red. Declan was calm and smooth, he took rashers from the fridge, he started whistling as he warmed oil on a pan.

A look finally passed over her mother's face, and it was one of anger but a kind that was contained, a kind that said, *I will not cede to you, I will not redeem this for you.*

Brigid did not answer the question.

Dolores felt she had erased something – she had wiped away something that had always been there. She got off the chair. She noticed then that she was still wearing her mother's housecoat, she still had the tea towel over her head.

7

At Brigid's funeral, Declan and James had to hold their little sister upright. She stood between them and she felt like they were a unit, the smallest ones in the clan, and she felt grateful that they did not hate her. Her sisters had organized everything, they did not have time to speak to or comfort the younger siblings. Dolores felt certain that they knew what she'd done. Walter came home and was dead drunk the entire time, sodden and robotic in grief and an expensive-looking navy suit, he even wore it to bed, Dolores knew because he slept on the couch in the sitting room.

She saw that the family had split into separate constellations: Rita, Martha, May – all married, all sorted, all polished and competent; then Walter, off by himself, speaking about poetry and dog-track racing and things no one else cared about, sometimes lapsing into an English accent to the consternation of everyone, was it an affectation or was this who he was now, either way it wasn't great; and then Declan, James and her – the children, the babies, in jeans and badly ironed shirts, standing together trying to pretend they weren't afraid, trying to pretend that it wasn't unfair to have lost their mother before they were fully grown, trying to pretend – to themselves, to everyone – that they *were* fully grown.

When she got the news, she felt like God himself had come down to earth to slap her across the face. She had a terrible feeling of having been paying attention to the wrong thing. She felt dizzy, concussed almost. She had not spoken to her mother in the two months before she died. She kept meaning to ring her, she kept putting it off.

She couldn't hear properly, she couldn't walk straight. *What?* she kept saying to people who spoke to her at the funeral, at the reception after the funeral. *What did you say?* She didn't yet feel sad, it was as if her guilt was a dam, preventing access to the rush of grief and heartache that she saw the rest of her family were immersed in. She longed for this sadness to come for her too – she longed to be swept up in it, to be taken away by it – but she was not entitled to that mercy. Her eyes were sore and dry.

She couldn't face her father. He didn't seem to care or even know about the falling out, but she couldn't face him anyway. He sat in front of the telly and wept silent tears, her older sisters came and looked after him. She had no role to play. The day after the funeral, she sat with May's children in the yard outside the pub and traced shapes in the dirt with them, and then May came out and gave out to her for messing up their clothes.

James told her that she had to stop thinking of Brigid as some kind of fixed-in-time entity, that the Brigid who was upset with her in the days before her death was not any more real than the Brigid who had loved her so well over all the years before. And that was the first time Dolores heard someone else put into words the fact that she *had* upset her mother, that the last time her mother had seen her, she had been mocking her, she had been disrespecting her. She had been keeping that reality at bay, because she didn't know for sure. But now she did.

This feeling knocked her off her feet and so she went to bed for a week – a bed in Liam's auntie's house in Dun Laoghaire, of all places. She had lost her job (Mrs McGrath was not sympathetic) and she had nowhere to go. She had stopped paying her rent on the bedsit, she had stopped attending Miss Lacey's, even after finding a letter from her in the shared hallway at the Rathmines Bordello, a gentle enquiring letter, saying she hadn't paid her fee, she had missed the most recent shorthand test – but that she was welcome back whenever she liked.

Brigid was not one for martyr-like rebukes, no matter how hurt she was, she never would have died just to stick the knife in. It was a stroke, she had not been ill. Dolores saw it erupt on the surface of her mother's brain like an explosion on the surface of the sun – an explosion that led to the extinguishing of the entire universe, just a thing that happened, no rhyme, no reason. She kept seeing it like that in her mind, it soothed her somewhat to see it like that.

The referendum happened in the thick of all of that. Dolores did not vote. Not out of principle, not for any reason other than that it seemed irrelevant, laughable. She was vaguely surprised at how fully Annie and the women's movement lost but she did not feel anything about it. The whole thing felt like a pile of papers that she'd forgotten she'd read. She didn't know if Annie knew her mother had died, she didn't tell her, Liam didn't tell her. After she'd returned to Dublin following the fight with her mother, she'd seen Annie only a few times, she'd been busy studying for her repeats, she didn't have time to mess about in Dolores's bedsit any more. So Dolores spent those summer evenings swimming in the sea with Liam, building her resistance to the cold, feeling her body get strong under the waves. He teased her about the men's-only bathing place nearby, asked her why she wasn't picketing it, she ignored him, she lay back in the water and watched the tender purple sky of the never-ending summer dusk.

Over the years, she occasionally felt a sudden piercing of sadness when she remembered Annie, when she remembered how much fun they'd had, they'd sometimes had. But when her name emerged in the papers or her voice came on the radio as it sometimes did – Annie became an academic, in women's studies, in gender studies, Dolores was glad she managed to find a place for herself in the world – but when she encountered her, when she heard her, Dolores mainly turned over the page, she mainly switched her off.

They went to England, for a while. It was Liam's idea. She had no money, no job, and he was barely making anything at the garage either. He said, *c'mon, let's just go*. It was early the following year, early 1984, they'd been staying with his auntie, she was growing impatient with them. She was starting to weigh how much porridge they ate in the mornings, Liam said he didn't know if it was meanness or senility, either way it seemed time to get going.

They got the ferry to Wales and hitch-hiked to Bristol. It was March. They both felt the desire to be in the countryside so when they heard of jobs going in a pub in a village near Weston-super-Mare, they jumped at it. When they got there, they found it offered accommodation too, a small room above the bar, and Dolores felt giddy with good fortune.

In the village, through the job, they met a lot of different types of people. There was a woman in her fifties who told long, disorganized stories drawn from Cornish myth. She told Dolores she had grown up in a children's home, had never known love, and didn't trust any man, though she flirted gently with Liam. She lived in a caravan behind the pub, she told fortunes to tourists in the summer, in the winter she slept in the front sitting room of the guest house to which the pub was attached. There were three Welsh-speaking young men who wanted Wales to become independent, they slept in a cluster of tents near the village green from March to October, they survived by working as handymen and pub bouncers. There was an eighteen-year-old girl who could draw famous cathedrals in magnificent detail from memory, she confided in Dolores that she wanted to become a vicar, like her father, and drive around a country parish providing spiritual succour to old ladies, although she didn't believe literally in the Bible.

Many of the wanderers they met eventually revealed themselves to be from wealthy backgrounds which intrigued Dolores and Liam; they couldn't quite figure out why they had chosen to slum it like this. They generally quite liked them, they knew a lot about the world and were usually very generous.

THE AMENDMENTS

There were wild-eyed Marxists, there were gentle Marxists, there were confused Marxists and there were women's libbers – although they used the word 'feminist' more so here. There were discussions about nuclear weapons, nuclear power, nuclear waste, breastfeeding, Greenham Common, folk music, abortion, the IRA, witchcraft and football. Their first year there, Christy Moore played Glastonbury and people were getting into the Pogues. Dolores was surprised by this, feeling her culture reflected back at her, its rough hearty texture made sharper, more counterculture, more commercial, it was confusing, it was exciting.

No one in the village near Weston-super-Mare cared where they were from or how they spoke. Everyone she met was seeking a quiet, temporary refuge from the storm of their usual lives. When she woke up, particularly in the spring and summer, and felt the house underneath her begin to stir, she felt like she'd stepped into some kind of separate kingdom, like in a story, one that existed alongside the ordinary regular world, but one only some people were permitted access to, one in which no one could stay for ever.

She felt that the people she moved among here in this charmed place, during this charmed time, had the same basic concepts of life as she had, as people back home had, but that here they had access to different ways of talking about those concepts. She felt that ways of talking about things seemed to count for more than the things themselves. She sensed that this business of language was connected to status, but her thinking about it ended there, she couldn't move beyond this conclusion, she didn't feel troubled to try and reach beyond this conclusion. She felt happy to exist at the intersection of all sorts of new, vaguely felt ideas. She had three jumpers, two pairs of jeans and four T-shirts, she wore them on rotation and washed them by hand in an outdoor sink in the summer and in the winter she barely washed them at all. In the cold months, she wore a dark brown duffel coat, sometimes she even wore it to bed, if Liam were working late and she was going to sleep alone. She sometimes scandalized herself when she remembered they weren't married, but no one here thought to care. She sometimes called him her husband and she felt it was a very fine thing, to be a young, strong, freckled wife pulling pints behind a bar.

They lived upstairs, their room tucked into the eaves, the house was hundreds and hundreds of years old. In the mornings, Dolores would come down and sit in the field behind the dark sitting room and watch the frogs jumping in the longer grass at the back of the meadow, beyond the Welsh boys' tents. She was on the pill now, but she felt it a strange thing to do, to outsource the rhythm of her body to pharmacology, she missed the feeling of noticing her cycle, she hated the dribble of blood she now experienced, puny and miserly compared to the full rush of before. She also hated that she felt like sex less often, what was the point? She talked to Beatrice, the caravan lady, about this, and Beatrice said that everything came with a price. She wondered at the miracle of being able to talk to a woman of Beatrice's age about these things.

It was after their second summer that she realized she was pregnant. She'd come off the pill, they'd been using condoms, she was not that surprised. She told Beatrice, who stroked her arm and told her it was time to go home.

'You have the luxury of being from a real place,' Beatrice said. 'You need to give that to your child. The least any mother can do is pass on the best of what she's had herself.'

Liam also said it was time to go back. Since they'd found out about the baby, she noticed that he stood up a little taller, he walked a little straighter, he drank a little less. He said he wanted their child to be Irish, he said things were just about as bad in Britain as they were back home, so they might as well return. She could tell he sometimes felt destabilized here. She did not – or no, she did, actually, she felt as if she were living in a totally different reality – but she knew she could come to like it, she knew she could stay and never look back, never go back. She felt the certainty of this within her and it shocked her. It was too strange a feeling from which to anchor an argument, and so she simply agreed with Liam's plan.

They got married one cold clear morning in October in the Catholic church one village over. She had their baptismal certs sent over via the parish office, but she didn't tell anyone else at home. Lainey, the cathedral-drawing girl, was her bridesmaid, Mr and Mrs Jones, the pub owners, their employers, signed as witnesses. Mr Jones's small eyes smarted briefly with tears, Mrs Jones got very drunk, Liam and Dolores were very touched. Beatrice told them they had lost a child, a six-year-old, many years before and never had another. Beatrice didn't come to the ceremony because she thought her presence was bad luck – as a spinster, as she put it – but at the party afterwards, she told everyone's fortune.

Dolores felt like she was bursting at the seams of her body, she was exhausted in a new and strange way, sleep was incandescent, food tasted deliriously good. She had no idea where they were going to live or how they were going to make money.

When she came home, married and pregnant, her sisters were hugely hurt that she had not invited them to her wedding, had not told them about the wedding, and a rift set in that took many years to mend. While she was in England, Declan had gone to America and when she found this out, it was like being shot in the stomach – why had no one told her? *Sure how could we tell you, we didn't know where you were!*

James was still at home, working in the pub, Patsy was crumbling and confused, ever more stuck to his chair in the kitchen. It was a miserable, horrible time, she felt she'd stepped into a black pit of guilt, of grief and guilt. The constellation that was her family was wheeling through space, and Dolores could not find her place within it – so she and Liam and their unborn baby broke away and formed their own unit, their own pattern.

8

She never told Nell she was conceived in England. She had barely mentioned that episode in her life to her daughter at all. When she came back, she walked straight into a wall of grey, of grief, of stress, of no-money, of family drama, of estrangement. Liam found them a damp, smelly bungalow on the edge of a town she did not know. She could not drive then and she sat alone with the baby, all day long, feeling like some terrible trick had been played on her.

She thinks of that time now, thirty-two years later. She's thinking that her daughter fled this country too, but she was brave enough to stay away. She feels a perverse and sour envy for a second and this surprises her. She then calls her. After a short moment of conversation, she says what she's called her to say.

'Martina Power is very unwell. She's in hospital, in the County, and she's asking for you.'

'What?' Nell says. 'Who?'

'She's talking about you. She's asking for you specifically.'

It's funny, Dolores thinks, how grown-up children pretend they remember nothing of their silly, childish ways, their antics, their obsessions. That's why they can't bear to be around their mothers, she reckons. They don't want to be reminded of who they once were.

'The County,' Nell says. 'You mean she's gone mad?'

'Yes,' Dolores says. 'I suppose she has.'

Nell says nothing for a moment.

'What does she want with me, Ma? I haven't seen her in years.'

Dolores sighs. She reflects that only Nell herself really knows the answer to that question.

'You meant a lot to each other,' she says, carefully.

She senses Nell on the other side of the phone, she pictures her eyes darting about the room and then she pictures her closing them and sighing as she makes up her mind.

'I can't, Ma,' she says. 'Not with Adi. Not with work.'

'She left that group,' Dolores says, suddenly. 'Did you know she'd left?'

Nell doesn't say anything. Dolores realizes she's been storing up that fact, to use it as a trump card, to shock Nell into some kind of reaction.

There is a long, controlled pause on the other end. Dolores finds herself rolling her eyes. Sometimes all the unsaids and unsayables just become tiresome.

'I can't,' Nell says then, firmly, without any trace of curiosity or surprise in her voice. 'I just can't.'

'All right,' Dolores says. She feels weary but also relieved. It's a terrible thing, how selfish children make you. She knows that another woman's child is suffering but she doesn't want to put her own at risk. That's the way things always are.

She feels guilty about that. So she drives out to Martina's mother's farmhouse, and she talks to Martina's mother. Dolores is the type of woman who knows people, the fact of her not being from this town originally means that a lot of people confide in her. Her parents are both dead, and her siblings are not local, and in this still clannish, still family-orientated culture, this lack of a visible network, of deeply embedded blood connections, means that Dolores carries with her an aloofness, a separateness, that some people, many people in fact, find attractive. And so she had been told about Martina, and so she knew how to establish contact. Lucy, Martina's sister, was the link in the chain. Dolores knows her through a friend at her book club.

The old woman is baffled by her daughter's madness. Dolores holds her hand across the table and lets her cry. It's February and the light in the farmhouse is gloomy, the sky outside white as milk. Dolores can tell that Mrs Power has not cried much, she can tell she's not the type to cry much. She feels from her an exhausted helplessness. She feels from her a sense of *when will there be peace?*

9

London, 2018

Nell has been planning on telling them about Martina. She wasn't going to leave her out, it wouldn't have been possible to tell even the most abridged version without including her. But the phone call from her mother makes her uneasy, it makes her angry. She feels she is being forced into thinking about Martina as a real person, not as a memory, not just as the slightly odd *spiritual mentor* (she imagines this is the phrase she'd use in the therapy session, she imagines Madeleine nodding as she uses that phrase) she'd looked up to during her more impressionable years. And she doesn't want to do that. She wants to keep Martina where she belongs – in the past.

She is shocked to hear that Martina left the movement. She is even more shocked to hear she's gone mad.

For the next few days, after the phone call, she carries around a new, more alive dread. She works from lunchtime to close with an hour off at 5 p.m. She drinks on her evening break, and then after closing she stays and drinks with the younger floor staff, a habit she had grown out of, a habit she'd had to grow out of. She gets home to Adrienne at around 1 a.m., slipping quietly into bed beside her, and she doesn't get up until after she's left for work. Adrienne doesn't say anything, Nell thinks she doesn't notice, she thinks there is nothing to notice.

On the morning of the next therapy session, Adrienne taps her fingers gently on Nell's collarbone to wake her. In the kitchen, Nell makes coffee. It's a bright day, it's late February, it feels like the dark mantle of winter is finally starting to crack. It's time to start feeling better about the world; she usually feels better, in the spring, in the summer.

'Where's your notebook?' Adrienne says. Something in her tone irritates Nell. It is so pathetic, this notebook, this revisiting. It's self-indulgent, it's stupid. She sometimes thinks the world is ending, because of vapidity, because of people writing about themselves in notebooks, on the internet. Nell mainly loathes the internet.

'I'm not going today,' Nell says. 'I don't feel up to it.'

Adrienne walks across the kitchen and pulls the notebook out from under a stack of papers and magazines on the coffee table. She opens it up and without looking at any of the writing, she lays it out flat on the kitchen table. It's a spiral-bound one, it sits open easily, waiting and innocuous.

'Sit here and write some more words,' Adrienne says. 'I'll meet you at Madeleine's at lunchtime.'

Nell sits in the bleak silence that Adrienne always leaves in her wake. She remembers what she is doing all of this for. She tries for a moment to think about Martina. But she can't. So she thinks about someone else instead.

★ ★ ★

To be in the movement was to enjoy many opportunities to travel. Rebecca had been all over the world – to Spain, many times; to Germany, where there was a big group; to the US; and even once to Brazil, where the movement was extremely active and successful. Nell was very envious of all of this. She had been abroad just once, to Wales, a trip she and her sister had bullied their parents into taking just so they could say that they had been out of the country, though Nell quickly learned that to someone who had been to Brazil, Wales did not exactly count as *abroad*.

In the summer after her Junior Certificate exams, Nell was fifteen and she was finally allowed to go on her first trip out of the country, to Spain, with the hermanas. It was the year 2001, it was the future, her father said, and he was delighted about it. He was raking in the cash working on building sites, he was making up to a grand a week, sometimes more. He liked to have barbecues in the garden at the weekend, he bought Dolores a car of her own, he walked around town with his head held high. When Nell was younger, they didn't have a landline in their house because phone calls cost too much, and now her dad had a mobile phone clipped jauntily onto his belt. He even told Nell that she could get one too, if she wanted, though Dolores disapproved, she thought it would be too distracting.

Her father had given her the money for the hermanas trip without a second thought, he peeled off the fifty-pound notes from a stash he took from a little cash box in his office – a tiny box room at the back of the house – with relish and he told her to have a ball, he told her not to pray too hard but if she did pray, to make sure she prayed for him. Liam went to Mass every Sunday, he said it gave him space to think but he also seemed proud that his wife didn't go, or didn't always go. She's too wild, he liked to say, and Nell was slightly destabilized by this description of her mother.

When she was a child, Nell liked to crawl onto Dolores's lap and to lie across it, her head dangling under her mother's legs, her heart knocking against her knees. She liked to feel her mother's sturdy, capable hands play with her hair and stroke her back. But as she entered adolescence, she sensed Dolores seeing her far too clearly, understanding her much too easily, and she also sensed Dolores backing away from this understanding, and Nell did not want to be backed away from, not because she didn't want privacy, but because she didn't want anyone seeing or acknowledging there was anything in her that *needed* to be backed away from.

For example, Nell knew that Dolores was uneasy about the movement. She didn't know why, exactly. Most people thought it a bit weird – 'It's not a cult, it's *literally* part of the Church, the Church that everyone in this country pretends to be part of,' Rebecca said, but Nell also suspected that Rebecca might secretly enjoy the idea that people might think she was in a cult. In any case, she certainly had the kind of popularity that made it possible for her to do whatever weird thing she liked – join a cult, or just be really extra holy – and no one made fun of her for it.

Dolores didn't seem to care whether or not the movement was part of the Church, nor did she think it a cult. But she deployed a certain caution around it. Any time Nell came back from a meeting in a good mood or the few times she tried to share with Dolores something interesting Martina had said, Nell sensed in her mother a feeling of *steady now, don't get too involved, be careful*. And this drove Nell crazy. Why *not* get involved? Why *not* get excited? What was it that Dolores was so afraid of? At the time, a couple of lines from the TV programme *Father Ted* were much in circulation, *Down with this sort of thing, careful now*, and they struck Nell as capturing a particular attitude common to the grown-ups in her country. They didn't ever want to name the things that were to be avoided, but you were expected to know to avoid them all the same. It made her feel rebellious. It made her feel like becoming really fucking holy, just to show them.

Dolores did not, of course, forbid her going on the trip abroad with the hermanas, to do so would have involved having to explain what her reservations with the movement were, and Nell knew that she wasn't going to do that. And when it came to it, her mother actually seemed quite keen for her to have a good time, she helped her pack her things, she made sure she brought enough sun-screen. Mrs Clery drove the four girls to the airport, they had to leave at 5 a.m., the August morning was misty and pale. When they got off the plane at the small airport somewhere in the middle of the big square country that had birthed this strange organization, the heat felt bracing, electrifying. And Nell then realized she had no idea what they were going to be doing now that they were there.

The theme of the gathering was *that all may be one*. Nell thought that this had to do with forgetting yourself, with getting yourself out of the way in order to see what was in front of you more clearly. She figured that unity – another core value of La Obra – could only be achieved if individuals accepted the limitations of their own understanding. She looked at the girls arriving in this hot Spanish city from all over the world and wondered if they saw it in that way too. She wasn't sure if she was getting it, but she saw, she sensed, that there was something very different in the air here. The sky soared above them, it was very blue and everything felt bright and clear.

On the first morning, after a short Mass, the girls gathered with their core hermana group from home for a check-in before the day began. Martina shared a reading from the Gospel with them, and there was space for any of them who were feeling a bit troubled by anything to speak about it. Fiona had recently started a relationship with a boy, and that morning, she spoke shyly about it. Nell was jealous of this relationship, she didn't like to hear about it. She saw that Martina also disapproved, but she didn't say so. She just let Fiona speak.

The boy, Brian, was a typical boy of their area. He played hurling, he went to the boys' school, his mother was a teacher, his father a farmer. Fiona had recently turned sixteen and had grown her hair a bit and stood up a little taller and she had just discovered her skinniness as an asset. Nell had not yet kissed a boy and had no desire to. Brian therefore represented a bridge to a new world that Fiona was standing on the edge of, leaving Nell behind. She didn't want to be reminded of that and she felt primly satisfied when Martina reminded Fiona how young she was, and how God wanted her to stay open to many things, and how she shouldn't tie herself down to one set of attachments.

At this, Ursula smirked. She was surely thinking, as Nell was, that *set of attachments* was quite the euphemism. Nell caught her eye and she smiled too. Fiona blushed and Rebecca rolled her eyes. Rebecca – seventeen to their fifteen and just-turned-sixteen – had never had a boyfriend but so many boys were interested in her that it didn't seem to count against her. Rebecca did not approve of talking about romance in the meetings, she thought it a waste of time. She said, often, that God needed them to be tough. To *go against the current* was Rebecca's favourite of the movement's slogans. It meant you didn't just do what everyone else did. It meant you did things because you thought they were right.

After the hermana meeting, there were activities – normal ones, not holy ones – basketball, art, music, debating. This was when the girls got to meet the other hermanas in attendance, of whom in total there were about two hundred. Nell and Rebecca opted for basketball on the first day, Nell watched Rebecca glide around the court as if she owned it. Ursula had come with them, though she didn't like sport and after a few moments she lay her body down on the hot tarmac on the side of the court. Nell could tell this irritated Rebecca; while the two were close friends, Rebecca disliked when Ursula became too playful, she did not like, Nell thought, when Ursula behaved in ways she could not predict or control.

Following lunch – Nell's highlight – the hermanas all gathered as a group in the convention centre of the hotel to hear lectures delivered by some of the senior people from La Obra on matters to do with spirituality and theology. Specially chosen hermanas got up to address the meetings about particularly challenging situations they had faced and overcome with reference to the ideals of the movement. The senior people spoke in their home languages – mostly Spanish, though there was Portuguese, German and Italian too – and translations were provided by hogareña volunteers and delivered to the girls through 1980s-style headsets. The girls sat in their chairs with the headsets plugged in, and they listened intently and they sometimes fell asleep. Some of the talks were interesting, some less so. The hermana testimonies were very earnest and Nell wished she could see how those saintly girls comported themselves in their ordinary day-to-day lives, among ordinary day-to-day people.

They ate outside, on their second evening, it was a delight to Nell how warm it was so late in the evening. She was feeling a little shy, many of the girls here knew each other already. Opposite her sat an American girl called Pilar. She had been one of the 'chosen' hermanas who had shared an experience at the gathering in the hall earlier; it had to do with her sister who had Down Syndrome. She had spoken clearly and fearlessly and with a great, humorous, unbridled affection for her sister, and for her sisters in the movement. Nell observed her across the table with interest, noting how confidently she seemed to move, how at ease she was within herself. A large group of girls – twenty or so – were in attendance from the US, and it was not hard to pick them out, their clothes plain but of gleaming quality, their voices clear and certain, their movements slow but sure.

Pilar smiled at her encouragingly, as if she could tell Nell was thinking about her and wished to speak to her. Nell was just about to ask a question when Rebecca, seated beside

Pilar, cut across and said, 'Pilar must be the first black person you've ever spoken to, is she, Nell?'

Nell's mouth dropped open, and she blushed and she hated herself for that blush. If it were not for the blush she could have pretended not to hear.

'*En serio?*' Pilar said.

The girls spoke little bits of Spanish to each other throughout the day, mainly for laughs, and Nell felt therefore that Pilar was making fun of her. She took a bite of her rice; she was determined that she was not going to say anything. It was not her fault she hadn't travelled, it was not her fault she didn't know anything.

'It's not her fault,' Rebecca said – and Nell felt further infuriated that Rebecca had read her mind. 'She's never been abroad before, have you, Nell?'

'You don't have any black people in Ireland?' Pilar said.

'We do,' Rebecca said. 'But Nell wouldn't know any. I know some through the movement. They mostly live in Dublin.'

Pilar smiled at Nell in a warm way, like a teacher. 'Well, I've never talked to an Irish person before, so we're even,' she said.

'You've talked to *me*, Pilar,' Rebecca said. It was important to Rebecca that everyone in their hermana group, especially Nell, should know that she had met all of these girls from before, that this was her territory.

'Right,' said Pilar, in her straightforward, American way. 'But I always think you're English. From like, Manchester or some place?' She darted a look at Nell.

'That's the other Rebecca,' Rebecca said, coldly.

As well as being English, the other Rebecca was bucktoothed and insipid. Nell looked across the inky blue of the evening and tried not to grin.

Pilar played guitar and described herself as Afro-Latina. She attended a private Catholic school outside Atlanta and was hoping to get into Emory, whatever that was. Pilar assumed Nell understood all of her cultural references, and Nell liked this about her, it flattered her and also made the world feel cosy and knowable. Pilar was doing a lot of volunteer work — which she loved, it was very humbling — but she was troubled by the degree to which such good works enhanced her scholastic career.

'I worry that I'm not doing it for the right reasons,' she said to Nell. 'Sometimes I feel like I should find a project that would make me look *bad*, something that would even get me into trouble. Just so I know I'm doing it for *Him*, not just to get into the right college.'

'What about you?' she then asked, and Nell didn't know what to say. It was very hard to explain to Pilar what it was like to live in a world where everyone was exactly like you and so no one ever had to describe themselves.

'It's different,' she said. 'Where I'm from.'

It was the third day of the trip and the girls were sitting in the courtyard of the convention centre. It was late afternoon, the ground in the courtyard was hot and tiny little stones stuck to the backs of Nell's knees when she stretched out. She revelled in the feeling of the sun on her pale limbs, she felt like her body was gobbling the heat down, hungry as a dog. The day had passed its peak now but there was no hint of a breeze.

'You're all real prayerful there, I guess?' Pilar said. They had eaten lunch together that afternoon and then sat together in the lecture hall. Nell had struggled not to fall asleep, the talk had been very boring, but Pilar's polite wakefulness had kept her alert.

'Eh, not really,' Nell said. *Real prayerful, I guess.* She felt that was a very beguiling way to speak, it echoed around her mind, it made her lips tug into a smile. It was also so hilariously inaccurate that she didn't know where to begin explaining.

'I imagine it's real peaceful,' Pilar said. 'Not too many people. Proper seasons.'

'It's boring, mainly,' Nell said. 'The weather is terrible.'

Pilar smiled harder at her. She had that hogareña habit of intensifying her Jesus-inspired optimism whenever anyone complained.

'What do you do for fun?'

'Drink alcohol,' Nell said. She couldn't help it. She couldn't cope with the wholesomeness of these foreign hermana girls.

'You don't!' Pilar said – whether she was actually shocked or just humouring her, Nell couldn't tell. She was flattered that Pilar was paying so much attention to her, but also a little wary, a little suspicious.

'Like, what kind?'

'Beer. It's disgusting. Or vodka. I like to mix it with Coke,' Nell said, hearing the boastfulness in her voice, and feeling idiotic for it. It was stupid to be proud of drinking alcohol, she knew that, and yet everyone she knew who did, *was* proud of it.

'Kids at my school drink sometimes,' Pilar said. 'But not me.'

'I play sport too,' Nell said, remembering this suddenly.

'That's awesome,' Pilar said.

'And I train my sister's team,' Nell said, hoping Pilar wouldn't ask what sport. Camogie seemed so brute and embarrassing. Everything about herself seemed brute and embarrassing next to Pilar.

'So awesome,' Pilar said. 'I have a sister too.' Nell nodded, acknowledging the speech Pilar had given the previous day. Pilar bowed her head, as if in acceptance of a token of deference.

'She is so precious to me,' Pilar said. 'Can you imagine a world where she wasn't allowed to live? Because of who she is?'

Nell knew she was supposed to shake her head in horror at the idea of abortion here; she did not. But she did not want to delve into a discussion of the movement's principles, she did not want to think about things like that. She tried hard to create a space in her mind between what she knew the movement's stance on issues around sex must be, and what she herself thought of such issues.

'I call her Precious, actually,' Pilar went on. 'But Maria is a good name for her too. Like, pure. You know, like in the movement, we're supposed to be like little children? That's what Maria will always be like.'

Nell thought about this. The way Pilar spoke about the world, the way many of the hermanas and hogareñas spoke about the world, made things seem very simple. Perhaps things really could be this simple.

The girls of the movement touched each other a lot. They hugged and walked around with linked arms or clasped hands. They giggled and sometimes made jokes about sex when the hogareñas weren't around. Some of them had boyfriends, some of them were doing stuff with those boyfriends, some of those doing stuff with those boyfriends felt conflicted about it, some of them didn't. Fiona talked a lot about Brian on this trip and Nell was surprised and moved and a little hurt to discover what a lot of emotional turmoil this burgeoning romance and its attendant sexual demands was causing her friend. She'd never said anything about it at home. But that was the beauty of these trips – it was a place of freedom, Martina said, a place where we can see ourselves anew.

Nell liked Martina's calmness. She liked how she seemed to stand apart from things. She liked that she disapproved of coarseness, meanness, stupidity, but in such a way that didn't make you feel like she thought she was better than anyone who was coarse, who was mean, who was stupid. Nell was trying to figure out what the best way to be in the world was, and she was interested in Martina. She didn't seem like what people said religious people were like. She seemed happy. She seemed *free*. She dressed simply, wore little make-up, didn't have a boyfriend or a husband or children, didn't drink, didn't smoke, played sport and sometimes spent time with her mother on the family farm. She had a slight, youthful figure; she put Nell in mind of a mythical fairy creature, a Peter Pan sort, it seemed impossible that she would ever get old. Nell sometimes tried to get her to talk about herself in more detail, she always gently resisted. This was another remarkable thing about her. Everyone else was always dying to talk about themselves.

On this trip, Martina seemed happier than ever, in the sun she seemed to bloom and shine. Everyone here at the gathering knew her, everyone respected her. She spoke excellent Spanish, and when she spoke it, her body moved in a different way, she held her face in a different way, she seemed more direct, more certain. Martina saw Nell watching her speak, and a slight pinkness came to her cheeks, as if Nell had caught her showing off. It made Nell feel happy, to see her in this way.

The city in which the gathering was taking place was small, medieval, inland and hot. In the evenings after dinner, the girls would walk around the city, arms linked in groups of twos and threes, winding their way through the groups of Spanish families out strolling together. Nell enjoyed the sight of portly old women sitting on kitchen chairs outside their houses, gossiping with their neighbours. Pilar spoke beautiful Spanish and she sometimes chatted to the locals, old ladies were surprised and delighted by her, young men looked at her with interest.

Americana, someone called after her one day, and Pilar turned around. It was an elderly lady she had spoken with the evening before. Nell had overheard the conversation but little understood it – other than the fact that it involved God (what else) and faith and young people. The movement was always talking about *young people* which was not what young people were generally called, in Nell's world – they were girls, young lads, teenagers, juvenile delinquents. *Young people* felt much more respectful, she thought and yet she also found it a little pious, a little proper.

The lady approached them, holding out a miraculous medal to Pilar. Her bosoms strained against her fading house dress, her hands were smooth and spotted, her eyes watery and grey. She looked at Pilar like she was a queen or the president or something like that. Nell had in fact begun to call Pilar *Mary Robinson* after the very good, high-achieving girl who had been President of Ireland during the previous decade, first ever woman in that role, serious, brainy, well-coiffed, much loved by everyone's mother. Pilar, when informed who that was, thought this extremely funny. Pilar was not used to people making fun of her, and at first she seemed surprised, and then she seemed thrilled by it. Nell didn't know anything then about the kind of pressure a high-achieving young woman from an ambitious family like hers would be under in the US. She just sensed, correctly, that Pilar needed to let her hair down a little.

Pilar smiled mildly and accepted the medal from the old lady. Maybe this kind of thing happened to her all the time, Nell thought. Pilar was the 'white' of her hermana group; that is what they called the holiest girl, the lead girl of each unit because white contained all the colours of the universe within itself. Nell was 'green', which she resented. It was to do with nature, and she wasn't that bothered about nature, people just thought she was because she liked sport. Rebecca was the 'white' of their group, which showed that even God sometimes made mistakes.

'I think Spain is my spiritual home,' Pilar said, kissing the medal before putting it in a zipped compartment at the front of her backpack. 'Maybe when I'm a hogareña they'll send me here.'

'You want to be a hogareña?' Nell said. They were now walking back up the hill towards the hotel. It was getting dark – a deep, vibrant, pulsing dark.

'Of course,' Pilar replied. 'Don't you? A married one, at the very least.'

'I want to be a doctor,' Nell said.

'So?'

'So – that's what I'm planning.'

Nell didn't feel pressured to say much more. She was not totally committed to all this stuff yet. Her attendance here was provisional, she could not yet feel whatever it was that Pilar and, increasingly, Fiona seemed to feel. She was ashamed of this, but somewhere she was proud of it too. She wanted to hold on to it, this uncertainty, this scepticism. It felt like a little goblin inside her. Sometimes she wanted to throttle it but other times she wanted to protect it. She couldn't imagine who she'd be if it went away.

'I'm going to be an economist,' Pilar said. 'I want to study different systems of government to figure out how best to serve the poor.'

'Oh, right,' Nell said. 'Cool.'

They walked along in silence for a moment. Nell wondered where an economist might work and what exactly they might do there. The evening darkened in little pools around them, they had fallen behind the other girls, their voices came to them in sparks and wisps on the air.

Pilar grabbed her hand, and Nell looked around, thinking someone was following them. The previous night, a drunken man had leered and shouted obscenities at the group of girls – one of the naughtier Spanish hermanas translated for them later. It was pure filth, what he said, the girl cackled as she told them, she had small thin fingers that she used to roll cigarettes around the back of the hotel, she spoke eagerly, and sometimes angrily, about *Jesús* but she was also really into Nirvana. Nell was a bit scared of her but at the same time relieved to see you could retain something of an edge and still belong to La Obra. The girls had found the whole thing with the creepy guy hilarious but Martina had been angry and shouted that she would call the *Polizia!* and the man had slunk back into the shadows with a sullen scowl. Martina and a couple of other hogareñas accompanied the girls on these strolls but always at a distance, she didn't want to insert herself among their intrigues. On this evening, she had been drawn into conversation with Rebecca and Nell noticed that the older girl was trying hard to ignore the fact that Nell and Pilar were spending time together.

'I know what you're thinking,' Pilar said, still holding Nell's hand.

'*El bastardo?*' Nell said. That's how they referred to the pervert when Martina wasn't around, it was extremely amusing to them.

'You think I'm just another rich girl who wants to save the world because I feel guilty,' Pilar said. She spoke quickly, in an urgent, confessional tone, she kept her eyes on the road ahead of them. 'But I try not to indulge my guilt. Samantha says that's a waste of time, none of us can help the circumstances we're born into. She says all that matters is that we use our gifts to serve.'

Samantha was the American girls' hogareña. She seemed a bit dim-witted in her starry-eyed enthusiasms to Nell but Pilar spoke of her with the utmost respect.

'That's true,' Nell said. 'No one can help what they're born into.'

'I know it must be hard for you,' Pilar said. 'I so respect what you're doing.'

'Oh,' said Nell. She had again that weird feeling of Pilar seeing things in her that she herself didn't know about. It was flattering, confusing and – somewhere in the hinterlands – a little irritating. 'Thanks.'

She didn't understand until later that Pilar thought she was *poor*. She was lying in bed, thinking about the conversation, picturing the way Pilar had looked at her, the way she seemed so concerned about what Nell thought of her, as if she feared – yes, *feared* – Nell's judgement.

She started laughing to herself, when she realized. She would try and correct her the next day. Liam Larkin's family were a lot of things at that moment in time, but *poor* was not one of them.

She fell into a delicious sleep – something to do with the clarity of the air, the silkiness of the darkness – and she dreamt about her. She dreamt chiefly about the softness of the palms of her hands. She had a very subtle way of blushing. She dreamt of that too.

At breakfast the next morning, Pilar put her tray down next to Nell's in the dining hall, she did so with a startling vigour, her small white cereal bowl wobbled and almost fell over. They were staying in a chain hotel, the hermanas and their accompanying hogareñas comprised about half of the guests. The breakfasts were delicious – slices of fruit and cheese, pastries, hot chocolate. It all seemed very elegant to Nell, she especially liked the watermelon, the way the red crunch dissolved on her tongue.

'I was up at dawn for a jog,' Pilar said. 'It's so beautiful here, I can't deal with it. Do you want to come with me tomorrow morning? You like running, right?'

She said all of this very fast. Nell felt the pull of reasonings and motivations that were not being made explicit.

'Okay,' Nell said, assuming the dry ironical tone that Pilar seemed to locate in and withdraw from her. 'But I'm very fast, I have to warn you. You might end up feeling really bad about yourself.'

Pilar laughed and laughed as if Nell had said something extremely funny.

For the rest of the week, they met early in the morning to run through the city streets and up to a small wooded area near a church. Pilar was stronger and faster than Nell but Nell's lightness meant she managed the hills better, and the city was mostly hills.

Nell was sharing a room with Fiona and Rebecca. They both liked to sleep until just before breakfast, so they didn't ruin things by insisting on coming along too. Rebecca was displeased at the friendship developing between Nell and Pilar; to retaliate, she spent more time than usual with Martina, cultivating an air of maturity. Nell had a huge amount of trouble not rolling her eyes at Rebecca's never-ending talk at their meetings this week about how she was going to manage at UCD next year when there were going to be so many people there who *challenged her spirituality*. Fiona spoke more of Brian; Nell felt her chest harden at this and this hardness seemed to form a barrier between her and Fiona, one that made it seem ever more natural to spend her free time with Pilar. Fiona, sensing but not understanding this, reacted by assuming a coldness that was balanced – somewhat manically – by an intensified playfulness that reached towards Ursula, who, sensing she was being utilized, in turn reacted by spending more time lying prostrate on the hot basketball court, and, as the days went on, skipping the hogareña lectures and smoking cigarettes with the Spanish Nirvana fan near the staff entrance to the hotel.

On their last day, Nell and Pilar decided to walk around the city instead of going for a jog. This meant they wouldn't have to take a shower afterwards and that they would have more time therefore to enjoy the morning in the city before the sessions began. It was Pilar's idea.

'We can grab a coffee and some breakfast too, if we can find someplace,' she said.

Nell loved the way she used language – to just casually grab a coffee, it never would have occurred to her, she never really drank coffee but suddenly it sounded like the most delicious and elegant thing in the world. She felt as if she didn't understand the opportunities that were out there, opportunities for coffee, opportunities for breakfast, opportunities for fixing the economy so that there might be no more poverty. But Pilar understood, and she could show her.

The morning was clear, the air cool on their skin but the sun white in the sky. The city was built from some kind of prickly yellow stone, Nell liked to run her fingers over it, it was extremely old and hot. They found a small cafe in one of the squares, and sat outside. Nell knew they were breaking the rules but since Pilar was known to be one of the most spiritual girls at the gathering, she didn't worry about it too much.

'I'm going to miss you, Nell Larkin,' Pilar said. She had taken to calling her by her full name. She said it was an awesome name. Nell told her that her real name was Ellen but that her sister had called her Nelen as a baby and then it became Nell and that it stuck. Pilar said that was also awesome.

'Well,' Nell said, 'once you figure out how to lift me out of poverty, I'll have enough money to come and see you in Atlanta.'

'You are never going to let me forget that,' Pilar said.

'Never,' Nell said. She touched Pilar's arm. 'I'll always be your *campesina*.' She had learned that word at the tiny agricultural museum in the city which had clumsily translated English blurbs alongside the Spanish – or Castilian Spanish, as Pilar urged her to refer to it. *Yo soy una campesina* she had said to Pilar, they had giggled over it endlessly, helplessly.

Pilar put her hand on Nell's and then brought it to her lips and kissed it.

'*Para siempre*,' she said.

They strolled back to the hotel holding hands, which was normal, very normal for them all. The day – their last – was to begin with a meeting with their respective hermana groups. Nell found the room and took her seat before the other girls arrived from breakfast.

She knew she was in trouble when Fiona didn't meet her eyes as she walked in. Rebecca followed, her face like thunder, and then Martina came in, looking tired and sad. Ursula seemed a little upset – she did not care for conflict, she was used to being in trouble at school and it unnerved her when it happened to someone else.

'Nell, can I speak with you?' Martina asked in a careful voice.

Outside in the corridor, Martina lectured her, firstly about the safety issue. She should not have left the hotel without telling anyone, it was dangerous and it put her, Martina, in a very difficult position. If something had happened, what would she have told her parents?

'But it's not only that,' Martina said and Nell braced herself. She knew that something had happened to her, something that perhaps should not have, and she knew that Martina could see that.

'The special unity that you have built with Pilar is beautiful,' she said. 'But it has become a source of pain to your hermanas. They feel –' and Martina paused, and Nell could sense her trying to find a better, less pathetic term than *left out*.

'They feel hurt, Nell. Remember, this trip is about you all as a group. You are all growing together and while it is wonderful to meet new people who share our spirituality, we must never forget that the people in our unit are the ones who are there for us when we face the challenges of day-to-day life. And it is those challenges that are hardest to overcome. I think your hermanas feel as if you have forgotten them, Nell.'

Nell felt her face get hot. Rebecca, who had tried to humiliate her in front of Pilar, who was just jealous that she was not the favourite for once, was trying to use Martina to get her to feel bad, to get her into trouble. Where was Jesus in all that?

'Don't you think that's a problem for the girls' egos?' Nell said. 'That they can't just be happy that I have created Jesus in the midst with Pilar?'

Nell could not usually say the phrase *Jesus in the midst* without blushing, and she knew that Martina knew this. Still, she held her head high.

Martina put her hand on Nell's arm.

'Nell. I know you understand.'

Nell's ears blazed and she felt like she might cry. The thought of this made her even angrier. She would not give them the satisfaction.

'I can't go in there now,' she said, fiercely.

'You can,' Martina said, calmly, almost indifferently. But then she softened a little.

'But, look. I'll give you some time.'

'Thanks,' Nell mumbled, her voice low and sulky.

'Just don't go anywhere,' Martina said. 'I really was worried. Stay in the grounds.'

Nell walked out of the hotel and around the back to the courtyard. Pilar was there too, sitting on a bench. She looked up and they both burst out laughing.

Nell sat down beside her. She still felt charged up by everything that had happened. She was not used to getting into trouble with teachers or authority figures, she didn't like it, she didn't like how much she didn't like it.

'I didn't even know we were doing anything wrong,' she said. 'I mean, come *on*. We're not children.'

Pilar didn't say anything.

'It's so ridiculous,' Nell said.

She got up and picked a pretty pink flower off a nearby shrub. Its leaves were dark green and spiky. Everything was sharper here, everything had definite outlines. She thought of home, where everything was soft and mushy and grey. She felt a wave of not wanting to leave, a helpless sense of how unfair it was that she had to do what she was told, go where she was brought. Her joining this movement had come of her wanting to understand things, of her wanting to be free, but here she was, just wrapped up in yet more authority, yet more control.

'They can't control us like this. I'm *fifteen*.'

Pilar started laughing. She was wearing a blue summer dress, the same colour as the sky.

'You really didn't think we were going to get into trouble?'

'No,' Nell said, sullenly. 'Did you?'

'Of course!' Pilar said.

'Well then, why did you suggest it?' Nell said. 'I could have done without the hassle.' She affected a grumbly tone to hide the fact that her heart was starting to beat faster and that her cheeks were becoming warm.

Pilar was still sitting on the bench. Nell was standing opposite her, in the middle of the courtyard. The American girl's eyes were in her lap. She looked so demure. She looked as if she had something to say. She also looked – in her blue dress, against the deep green and pink of the bushes behind her, her feet soft and manicured in a pair of worn-out brown sandals – she also looked so beautiful that Nell thought her heart might burst.

She looked up and met Nell's gaze and Nell regretted saying anything about hassle. She regretted ever saying anything that was not beautiful or graceful. The week had not yet finished and she already knew the only thing she would remember from it was these mornings with Pilar.

'I wanted to be with you,' Pilar said. 'That's why.'

Nell returned to the meeting, it was almost over, it was about John the Baptist. Afterwards, there was a farewell Mass and then it was time to fetch the bags from the rooms, check out, and leave. Amid the headiness of the goodbyes, the promises to stay in touch, the declarations of everlasting fidelity scribbled in big fat letters in La Obra-branded homework journals, girls crying like they were being wrenched from a Siamese twin, Nell and Pilar alone were calm.

As she said her goodbyes to the other foreign hermanas she had got to know over the week, Nell felt imbued with a sense of purpose, of control, of brisk appropriateness. She felt like a mother, holding her vast knowledge of the world quietly to herself while her children swarmed around her. She sensed Pilar feeling the same thing, she was aware of where Pilar was at all moments, the American girl was not crying either, she moved carefully around the mass of throbbing adolescence, checking bags, comforting any particularly hysterical hermanas and squeezing the arms of the hogareñas she wouldn't see for a while. And she was aware, Nell knew, of the way the hogareñas were looking at her, she was aware that she was one of their great hopes, and she bore all of it, their expectations, their dreams, and the roar of her own young heart, with such grace, such calm. Nell tried with all her might to keep her eyes off her.

The Irish and British girls were heading off to the airport together, before the Americans. Nell slung her bag into the belly of the bus and went over to say goodbye to Pilar. They looked at each other and shared a moment of amusement, as if they were grown up now, more grown than anyone else. It was not possible for them to articulate anything about what had happened between them, but it was possible – just about – to acknowledge that something *had*. Like everything else about those days, the most important things were unsayable and transcendent and deeply, giddily, profoundly funny. Nell remembers for ever the pink flowers in the bushes and the glare of the light on the white flank of the bus and her skin bristling thirstily as it soaked up the rays of that miraculous and benevolent sun.

In Kennington, Nell smiles. She stretches out her body fully. She had been hunched over the table, she had been writing unselfconsciously. She is amazed to feel a feeling of grace come over her, a feeling that is also, troublingly, reminiscent of other feelings of that time. Most of all, she thinks how ordinary it was, how very usual to go on a trip abroad and fall in love with someone from another world. What a beautiful relief to finally fully realize that.

10

Ireland, 2001

Back home after the trip, the dreariness was very depressing. Nell thought about Spain and Pilar and her blue dress every day. She was impatient with her mother and her father, critical of everything from the food they ate to the way they ate it. She saw her people, her culture as apologetic and cowed, a place where no one ever said what they meant and no one ever meant what they said. We are just like our weather – grey, dithery, and just nothing, Nell thought. She felt like her boundaries were all loose, and when she thought of Pilar, she saw her in strong colours, strong lines, vividness, decisiveness.

She figured it was also time for her to sort out her own spirituality. She could not very well express exasperation with her culture for being wishy-washy if she herself could still not fully commit to being a hermana. She started going to Mass more regularly, and tried hard to concentrate on what was being said there. She started reading the Bible, much to her mother's alarm, they didn't even own a Bible – what Catholic owns a Bible? her father said, gently, jokingly, and Nell gritted her teeth. Fucking typical, signed up to a faith they don't even understand. It filled her with fury, her father's amusement, her mother's quietness. How could they bear to be like this, how could they bear to live like this?

Thank God she didn't have to, thank God she was out of here. She felt an enormous sense of guilty relief – how was she so lucky to have been born when she was born, when she could have been her mother, making sandwiches and driving up to the school every day, and nothing else, that was it, her whole life leading up to that. Since Spain, Dolores had been more watchful than before, asking questions about what she had done there, what friends she had made. This was irritating too – what business did her mother have in understanding her when the things that Nell wanted to understand belonged to a realm her mother could not possibly imagine?

She wrote a letter to Pilar. She told her about being at home. She tried to write about trying to get closer to God, but on the page, the words felt stilted, Nell felt as if she was trying to adopt Pilar's own idiom rather than just using her own. It was frustrating because when they'd been together, their way of communicating had been so natural, so easy. She tried several versions of the letter and the one she ended up with was shorter and terser than she intended, but she posted it anyway. She got one back a few weeks later, and it was full of chat about school, about grades, church, her sister – and it was very careful too, it read a little bit as if it had been written as a homework assignment. It felt to Nell like a punishment for the failures of her own letter. It gave her a pain in her chest, she carried it around – the letter, the pain – for days afterwards.

★ ★ ★

There was an extra year between the junior and senior exam cycles at secondary school in Ireland, a recently introduced, optional extra year that Nell was only half-inclined to do. Why delay the freedom of leaving school? But all of her friends were doing it and she knew that she was more likely to do well in her Leaving Certificate examinations if she were a year older when taking them, and she knew that for medicine she needed to achieve almost unachievably high grades. She talked to Liam about it, and he said, 'Girl, if I were you, I'd prefer an extra year of fun now rather than an extra year of pain and strife if you have to repeat. Doing the Leaving once is enough for anyone.'

He also said that you were one hundred per cent less ridiculous at eighteen than at seventeen and that the fact that she was thinking strategically about it at her mere fifteen – going on sixteen in January – meant that she was one hundred per cent less ridiculous than ninety-nine per cent of people her age anyway. 'Play to those strengths, girl,' he said, 'and you'll go far.'

People talked a lot about 'Transition Year' being a time of personal development, of opportunity, of growth, it was all very open and exciting and ill-defined. They did a module on yoga, they were encouraged towards independent learning, there was a lot of group work, there was hardly ever homework.

The other thing that was important that year was to be seen to make progress in terms of one's romantic life. This was an issue for Nell. To not have been kissed at this stage in her career marked her out as *a frigid* among her peers. The word was said with hatred and contempt and derision. Nell wanted not to care about the things everyone else cared about, she wanted to be her own person. But to be considered desirable by boys was one of the main things that would shape one's life – Nell could see that. And that made her angry. It made her really angry. It made her angry because she could see how stupid it was; it made her angry because she wanted it – male approval, male desire, *admit it* – too. She returned to school that September feeling as if the things she used to count on were all changing in ways she did not at all approve of and this disapproval extended to include her own feelings.

After the Spain trip, the Clerys' house was unavailable to the hermanas for a while. They were redecorating, Rebecca reported, and Nell felt a throb of envy. How much better could that house get? Their meetings were therefore held in a classroom in the girls' primary school in town. Martina had a friend who worked there, this friend allowed Martina to host her weird little prayer thing there. 'Go right ahead,' Nell imagined this friend saying, and then changing the subject – for a supposedly religious country (*real prayerful*), most people could not cope with any kind of religious talk at all.

At their September meeting, Fiona announced she was breaking up with Brian. 'He doesn't understand,' she said. 'He doesn't understand how important to me it is to wait.' Fiona was sixteen already by then, which was, Nell the grown-up thinks, below the age of consent, but she doesn't have any sense of Martina reporting any of this to Fiona's parents. She doesn't recall thinking about that at all in the session. Rather she was burning with hurt. Why hadn't Fiona told her about this?

Nell confronted her on their way home after the meeting.

'Why didn't you tell me about you and Brian? You never tell me anything. You think I can't understand anything because I don't have a boyfriend?'

They were walking towards the chipper's, it was their habit to get a bag of chips after the meeting. Nell could smell the vinegar as they approached.

'You know why, Nell.'

'I don't, actually.'

'It's because you hate boys,' Fiona said, stopping and turning towards her on the narrow footpath, forcing Nell to lean against the outside wall of someone's house. 'You act like they have leprosy. You act so superior to them, and it's not fair. They can't help being who they are.'

Nell was speechless. She realized that Fiona was right. She did hate boys. She did resent the way the world revolved around them. But she didn't know that anyone had noticed.

'Brian always says that he feels like you're just waiting for him to leave whenever we hang around together.'

'Of course I'm waiting for him to leave,' Nell said. 'I have nothing to talk to him about. I'm not going to do the things you do with him – so he's not interested in talking to me either.'

Fiona shook her head sadly. 'You have no idea what it's been like for me. And you don't care. Why can't you try to see – to see the best in him? In all boys? That's what we're supposed to do, Nell.'

Fiona and Nell hardly ever referred to the ideals of the movement outside meetings. It was tacitly understood between them that to do so would be not only to invite the scorn of their other friends at school, but to break something of a spell, to be putting something delicate at risk. That Fiona was almost doing so here – she was essentially saying that Nell should try to *love* Brian, because they were, as Christians, as hermanas, compelled to try to love everyone.

This was unprecedented, this was shocking. Nell did not know what to say. They reached the chipper but Fiona kept walking. Nell stopped and watched her.

She turned to walk back towards town, feeling hopelessly alone and without any idea of what to do with herself. Saturdays were a funny thing those days – sometimes she went to friends' houses on Saturday nights where beers and vodka were drunk; once or twice she'd managed to sneak into one of the nightclubs in town, Fiona came too, they were with other girls from school, they had an excellent time. But she knew of no one going out or doing anything that evening and she sensed that Fiona did, and she also sensed that she wasn't invited.

She was back by the school before she realized, and in the car park there was Martina, getting into her car. She saw her and waved. 'Did you forget something, Nell?' she said. 'I didn't find anything in the classroom, but go in and check if you like.'

'I didn't forget anything,' Nell said.

'Well, good,' Martina said. 'Do you want a lift home?'

Nell got into the car – a big old rickety one, a strange car for a woman without children, she thought.

'What are you doing this evening?' Nell asked and Martina smiled.

'Lots of work to catch up on for a conference in a few weeks,' she said. 'Boring stuff.'

Nell could tell Martina didn't think this was boring stuff at all.

'Do you want to go for a drive?' Martina said. 'It's a funny time of day, isn't it? When I lived in Spain, everyone slept through the afternoon. You'd wake up around four, feeling nice and calm.'

'When did you live in Spain?' Nell asked.

'Oh, a while ago,' Martina said.

They drove in silence. Martina told her to text her mother telling her where she was, Nell told her she didn't have a phone but her mother wasn't expecting her until later, that she usually hung around with Fiona after the meetings.

'Fiona is angry with me,' Nell said. 'She thinks I'm mean to boys. She thinks I'm judgemental and *superior* towards them.'

Martina laughed.

'And are you?'

'Yes,' Nell said. 'I mean, you said it yourself. We're too young to get caught up in all that nonsense.' She looked out the window as the dull green and grey of the countryside slid past.

'I just feel really annoyed when I see girls making a fool of themselves over boys,' Nell said. 'It makes me so furious. That's why men get to run the world, because girls do everything for them and make such a fuss over them. It drives me crazy.' Nell's face got hot as she spoke. She felt a choking, gulping feeling inside her. She felt as if there had to be a better way to articulate all of this, she hated herself for not being able to find it.

'It can be silly, all right,' Martina said, mildly.

'Is that why you became a hogareña?' Nell asked. 'To escape from all of that?'

'There's no escaping men,' Martina said. 'We share the earth with them, I'm afraid.'

'Not in the Church anyway,' Nell said. 'They run everything there too.' She was surprised at her bravery. She had decided not to think too much about the way the Catholic Church was run by men. She had found a little enclave within it, a very female enclave, that gave her a sense of peace, a sense of possibility, and she was engaging with it in a limited way, for a while. She did not feel she had to answer for all of the obvious ridiculousness of the broader institution.

But Martina was a different story. She had given her life to God via this one, holy, catholic and apostolic Church. So she should answer for it, Nell thought, but she probably wouldn't. No one, even Martina, was fully honest about their own hypocrisies.

'Women will one day run the Church,' Martina said, calmly. 'I feel sure of that.'

Nell was surprised, Martina had never struck her as a rule-breaker. 'Isn't that sacrilege?' she said.

'Yes,' Martina said. 'Don't tell anyone.'

Nell felt a little annoyed at the humour in Martina's voice, she felt like the woman was cajoling her back into a good mood. But she couldn't help her interest in this revelation.

'Well, why don't you do something to make that happen?' Nell said. 'I never hear anyone in the movement talking about that kind of change.'

Martina didn't say anything, she was gliding through a roundabout, Nell wondered if she'd heard her.

'You might actually get more people involved, if you talked

about things like that,' she said. 'Instead of weirdos like me and the girls.'

'You're not weirdos,' Martina said, matter-of-factly, as if she had known many weirdos in her time, which Nell did not doubt she had. But she was right, Nell thought. They were not. Still, there were only four of them.

They had left the town now and were on a main road, leading to the next town over. There was little traffic. The day had been cloudy earlier, there had been rain, but suddenly the sky was clear and blue.

'Anyway, Nell,' Martina said. 'That's a good question you asked – why I don't do anything to make this change happen. And I think there are two answers to it.' She kept her eyes on the road. Nell had the sense that she had defended her position on this before.

'One is less important but let's get it out of the way. The movement wants to stay part of the broader Church and so it can't be seen to adopt fringe ideas or progressive ideologies. It would alienate us from Rome, but also from the global Church, which is much more conservative than us Westerners like to admit.'

'Politics,' Nell said, with a world-weary sigh.

Martina smiled. 'Exactly.'

Martina suggested they go for a walk in a forest park she knew nearby. But first she made Nell call her mother from her own phone to tell her where she was. Nell let it be understood by Dolores that the other girls were there too, she didn't know why. Dolores said fine, don't be late, she asked if she was going out later. Nell said, 'No,' defensively, and Dolores sighed.

'You said there was another reason,' Nell said. They walked down a path into the woods, pale sunlight slid through the trees, the ground was wet from the rain of earlier and the mud at the edge of the path was thick and fresh. In the hills in the distance, Nell could see a crop of trees with a burn of blazing pink on their sun-facing side. The beauty of it hit her in the heart. It made her feel, suddenly, miserable. She felt separate to all of this, as if she had been made in a factory when everything and everyone around her had simply grown.

'I did,' Martina said.

'Well, what is it?' Nell said.

'You're not going to like it,' Martina said. 'I'm just bracing myself for your reaction.'

Nell was surprised by this, she had not thought Martina knew her well enough to tease her, to tease her so gently. She felt flattered and suddenly – appreciated. She knew she could be difficult, she knew she could be prickly. She was used to it causing her trouble, she was not used to it drawing affection.

She looked at the side of Martina's face and noticed she had a dimple in her cheek, she had a pink-and-white complexion, she had the tiniest crinkles around her eyes.

'I've accepted what my place in the world is,' Martina said. 'And it's a quiet place.' She stopped walking as she said this – they had reached the top of a small hill, there was a clearing in the trees, they could see across the fields, and again Nell felt that terrible piercing sadness, it made her throat feel dry, it made her unbearably thirsty.

'It's not my role to agitate or to push for change. I know, deep down, that if I were to do so, it would be for shallow, egotistical reasons, rather than because I felt I really could make a difference.'

Nell felt disappointed. She felt that it was a bullshit reason. She also felt irritated that Martina had predicted her reaction so accurately. They walked on for a while and Nell tried to compose her thoughts and arguments.

'What about it being the right thing to do?' she said. 'Wouldn't having women in power in the Church prevent . . .' And she faltered then, she didn't want to bring sex abuse into it, she felt, somehow, that it was cheating to mention that. But then she rallied. It was unthinkable, those things. Which meant they had to be said. 'And what about the abuse, Martina? That's all men, doing that. You know that.'

'I don't think I would help bring about the change, Nell,' Martina said. 'I think that, given my particular gifts and strengths, and my failings and weaknesses, any impact I could have would be a negative one.'

'If everyone thought like that, then nothing would ever change,' Nell said.

'I don't agree,' Martina said, again mildly. 'I think it's best to take one's own feelings, one's own private agenda, out of it. And to think, what will truly matter, in the long run? If I were to campaign for women priests, given my limitations – I'm not a public speaker, I'm not an organizer – then all that would happen is that the unity of La Obra would be weakened. I would make no impact on the broader Church at all, but I would weaken my own part of it. And I think the movement does good work. It's humble work, it's not big work. But it's good work.'

Nell thought about this. It was an attitude that ran counter to everything they learned about history in school – the people who mattered noticed an injustice and then they changed it. Everyone else just did whatever the done thing was. This humility, this placid way of just accepting things – that was the way ordinary people behaved, the sheep people, the forgotten, ordinary people. But Martina was not ordinary.

'What do you get out of all of this?' Nell asked. The path wound back down towards the car, she could hear the roar of passing traffic in the distance. She wanted to get to the bottom of things before the conversation was over.

'Peace, mainly,' Martina said. 'I feel that I know what I'm supposed to be doing.'

Nell didn't say anything. What she was thinking was – that's because you've accepted being told what to do, that's because you have let an institution tell you how to live your life. But it was troubling to her, how happy Martina did seem, happier than almost anyone she knew. Maybe this was the only way to survive; maybe most people were too feeble, too weak to survive without instruction. Maybe she was too.

Back in school the following week, Nell felt bored and sad without the anchoring presence of Fiona, who was not speaking to her. She had other friends, but Fiona was the one who made the days fun. Nell was also uninterested in much of what they were supposed to be doing. She did not like group work, she missed the intensity of having to study for exams. They were learning to play bridge in the science room, it was cold, there was a vague stink of sulphur in the air. Nell sat grumpily at the back, thinking, *Bridge? Really?*

She ran into Rebecca on her way home one day that week.

They spoke amicably for a while. She sensed that Rebecca knew that something was up between her and Fiona, but she wouldn't give her the satisfaction of filling her in. When Rebecca invited her over to her house, saying she was studying too hard, she needed to take a break, Nell suspected her real motive was to get Nell to tell her about the drama.

She went along anyway. She'd never been inside Rebecca's house before. Also, maybe Fiona would call over – she lived across the road – and maybe they'd make up and everything would be right between them again.

They sat in Rebecca's front room watching *Friends*. Rebecca had many of the episodes taped. Her mother brought them cups of tea and biscuits.

'Thanks, Ma,' Rebecca said, her tone large and expansive. Her mother, a slight woman in a floral skirt, blinked and looked curiously at Nell for a moment before retreating to the kitchen. Rebecca was the youngest of three girls, Nell wondered if all of them were like Rebecca, she hoped not for the sake of their mother.

An episode came on featuring Ross's ex-wife who had left him for a woman. Nell very much liked the actress playing Ross's ex's new partner, she wondered if she'd been in anything else, she thought she had seen her in something else, she could not remember what. She said this to Rebecca – and Rebecca smirked. 'Of course *you* like her,' she said. 'Have you heard from Pilar, by the way?'

What a little bitch, grown Nell thinks, almost admiringly. How did she know? How did she know before Nell herself knew? Or before Nell was permitting the knowledge that she held in her body to be known by her mind? Later, Rebecca went through an about-face; she studied politics in university, and then broke with the movement at some point in her twenties. She then, later still, frequently appeared in the media in Ireland as part of the pro-choice campaign trying to repeal the Eighth Amendment, she once even appeared on a special on BBC *Woman's Hour* to talk about it. At that time, the issues of backward Ireland and its backward abortion laws were much reported on in the British media and Nell could not bear it, she could not bear it at all. So when Rebecca, of all people, popped up on the radio talking about it in the way she talked about everything – superciliously, piously – Nell felt as if some monstrous jack-in-the-box had leapt out at her, in order to torment her, in order to remind her that there was nowhere she could hide.

But that's a few months ago now. This new Nell, this therapy Nell is able to think about Rebecca in-and-of the context of Rebecca. How clever and cunning she was. How much pain she must be carrying under all that clever and cunning. How she must love telling people what to do, what to think, how to live. How she must alienate everyone in her life by so doing. Nell goes online and she sees how much she tweets, and in what tone. She feels it all makes sense now. She enjoys understanding her, she enjoys feeling superior to her through this understanding. She enjoys feeling like she forgives her.

II

The Transition Year programme presented new opportunities to mix with the boys' school. Nell told herself that it was little wonder she didn't understand the appeal of boys when she barely knew any – she had only a sister, attended an all-girls school, and because of the number of times she had moved house as a child, she did not have any male friends from her childhood either. *So*, she thought when they were told that they would be doing a play with the Transition Year boys from the CBS and the eighty girls packed into the hall giggled and shrieked and whooped, *so*, she thought, *maybe this will be the time*.

She didn't want to be in the play as she knew she couldn't act, and she didn't want to do behind the scenes because she wasn't very good at building things, and while she did want to get to know boys, she thought the building work would perhaps be too many boys all at once. She had no interest in costume or make-up – indeed, she privately thought being too interested in such things was frivolous and inane.

Which left directing.

The Transition Year play had started to become a tradition between the schools – Transition Year itself only existing for a few years now – and so far, the play had always been directed by a boy, with assistance from the drama teacher at the boys' school. This was nothing to do with sexism, Nell was informed when she asked about it, it was just that the drama teacher at the boys' school was *very experienced in the theatre*. When Nell told Dolores this, her mother grew a little red in the face and said carefully, not too excitedly, 'Would you like to have a go at directing?' And Nell, to her surprise, said that yes, kind of, she maybe would. And then she said, 'Oh, maybe not, I've never directed anything before,' and her mother said, 'Nell, you're not yet sixteen, of course you've never directed anything before.'

So Nell went back to the teacher at her school and told her she'd like to try directing and the teacher, looking surprised and then pleased, and then a little defensive said, 'Well, good for you, Nell, good for you. And you know what, you're dead right.'

That's what everyone said – *you're dead right*. The local arts scene was almost entirely male – the bands who played in the pubs were male, the musical directors were all male, the amateur dramatics were always directed by a man, the local classical music school was run by a man and the visual arts scene, such as it was, seemed only distantly aware that female artists existed. Nell had not quite realized this until friends of her mother and mothers of her friends stopped her in the street and said, 'Fair play to you, Nell, and you know what, *you're dead right.*'

Fiona – who had come back to her, who was apologetic,

who had sworn off boys completely, it seemed – could not stop laughing about this. She and Nell decided that one day they would write a play about making this play, called *You're Dead Right*, but Nell was starting to feel somewhat uneasy. What if there was a good reason for women not getting involved in things like this? What if she made an almighty fool of herself?

Martina was the only person who seemed to share this trepidation, though she didn't say anything about it, which was the way of things with the hogareñas. They did not explicitly or even tacitly forbid one's participation in things that were not connected to the movement, but they demonstrated a gentle indifference to it, which was of course all the more effective than outright disapproval would have been. When Nell talked about the play at the hermanas meetings, she felt Martina watching her in the way a mother might watch her child play with her dollies. Nell felt foolish. The play was going to be terrible, inevitably, and her participation was, deep down, just a way to meet boys, which was, even deeper down, a way to smother her panic over her feelings towards girls – and she both knew and didn't know all of these things, all of the time. Sometimes she thought how peaceful it would be to surrender, like Martina did, to let go of any desire for anything, to rest in deep, peaceful acceptance. And when she prayed, on her own, which she sometimes did, she sometimes felt that peace, that acceptance, and then she got up and left her room and buried it deep, alongside all the other buried things.

They were doing *A Midsummer Night's Dream*, though the play was to be performed just before Christmas. It was a very silly play, Nell thought when she read it, but the language in it was fun, and not too difficult, and it had good parts for both boys and girls. The Transition Years didn't usually do Shakespeare but there was a sense that the girls had to be held to a higher standard than the boys; that while the boys might get away with something charming and scrappy and original – last year's had been a Tarantino-inspired take on the 1916 Rising, very confusing, Nell recalled – a play directed by a girl, and led, therefore, by the girls' school, needed to be more proper and enjoy the stamp of some already existing authority.

There were some nice boys in Transition Year at the CBS that year. Nell knew some of them a little and she found as the weeks went on that they were not in fact all that terrible after all. She saw very quickly in most of them the scaredness she felt in herself, of herself, most of the time. She felt a tenderness towards them that she nurtured and tried to enflame towards something she could conceivably call attraction. It was hard work. Some of the boys quickly became quite nakedly vulnerable on the stage under her calm and watchful eye, and this vulnerability was surprising, disturbing and interesting – if not at all sexy.

A boy called Daniel played Demetrius. He had sandy hair and brown eyes that were a bit too big and a doleful way about him. The other boys liked him because he understood how to make fun of himself. He called himself Eeyore, after the ponderous character in *Winnie-the-Pooh*. And he was mad about Nell.

Everyone knew. She felt his eyes on her and she felt the eyes of everyone else on him, with his eyes on her. It made her very cross, at first. How embarrassing. How dare they. How dare *he*.

But then they walked home together. He was obsessed with *The Simpsons*, and she was surprised and charmed to find his favourite character was Marge. He said he liked how unpredictable she was, that you never knew what she was going to say or do. He said the entire thing would collapse without her, he had a whole theory about it. He said he wanted to study animation or video game design when school finished, he showed her some large, hard-backed notebooks he kept with character sketches and ideas for stories. She flicked through them and realized that it was possible, for some people, to just enjoy life, to just play with ideas, to not feel like they had to solve everything, and she felt a deep, painful pluck at her heart.

She looked up at him as she was feeling that, and she saw that he noticed that something had stirred in her. He blushed – assuming, she assumed, that she was moved, that she was awed by his work. She smiled at him then, feeling touched and surprised that he cared what she thought about his work.

She decided that he would be the one. She felt very tenderly towards him and he often said things that surprised her. Their first kiss was messy and he apologized and said it was only his second ever. They were in the lane behind the girls' primary school, it was a damp, late October day. She looked at him with dizzy relief. She was no longer *a frigid*. They enjoyed corresponding levels of attractiveness and popularity.

Her body did not tell her when he left the room, the way it did when she'd been around Pilar. This thought crossed her mind one day and she tried to squash it. His hands were always warm and soft, he called her late in the evening, she felt his penis harden in his grey trousers when he leaned against her when they kissed, she tried not to notice how the very idea of it made her shudder. He and his friends liked to pretend to hump each other from behind – she had no idea why they did that, it was puzzling and very irritating but everyone seemed to find it funny. There had been several American teen films in the cinema over the preceding few years, the boys tried to behave like the boys in those films, there was much open discussion of masturbation. Nell disliked this immensely, Daniel could tell that she did, and he sometimes frowned at his friends, but he did not have the kind of personality that could influence the tenor of a wider group of people.

It was a great relief, to Nell, to be in charge of the play. It gave her an excuse to stand apart from the wider group, it meant she could hide her shyness behind the pages of the script. She was surprised at how heavy and cumbersome a body could feel on the stage – she'd never done any acting before and when she stepped into the role of one of her actors for a moment, she was shocked at the sudden weight of her limbs, at the sudden, frightening feeling of visibility that moved through her. She was sympathetic therefore to the actors and they liked her, and the rehearsals went well. The boys' school drama teacher had given her some tips before rehearsals began and then stepped away.

They performed the play just before Christmas, in deepest midwinter, and they made a virtue out of this seeming infelicity in the timing, they put on the poster: '*A dream of summer in midwinter . . . a dream of a world turned upside down . . . a midsummer night's dream.*' Dolores laughed at this. 'Well played,' she said. She was looking forward to seeing it. She very much approved of Nell doing the play, she said that it was a wonderful opportunity. Dolores liked Nell to have fun, she liked her to do creative things and Nell felt glad that she could, for once, allow her mother to think everything was fine with her.

The week of performances felt like another kind of dream. They had been given access to the local theatre, which was not a given, last year's group hadn't had the honour. Before the performances, Nell moved in and out of the rooms backstage, making sure everyone was ready, trying not to feel like too much of a teacher, but she did feel separate, she did feel like this performance mattered, and mattered hugely, whereas for many of her fellow students, it was just an excuse to have fun, it was just an excuse to flirt and mess about. She had forgotten about the emotional subterfuge that had led her to participate in the play in the first place, by the time it opened she lived and breathed and dreamt it. She wanted it to be perfect, she felt very determined that it would be perfect.

There were teachers present backstage too, supervising everything, and she sensed them being impressed by her, and she sensed some of the performers, some of the other kids, whispering about her, rolling their eyes at her. This stung, a little bit, but Daniel saw that it did and he squeezed her hand and whispered to her, *these are the forgeries of jealousy*. She loved him, fiercely, completely, briefly, in that moment. She kissed him suddenly and vividly and he blinked and looked at her, mesmerized, in a moment that would remain frozen in time for her for ever.

It was a triumph, Dolores said to her afterwards. A total triumph. Liam said he'd never laughed so much at Shakespeare, but to be fair it was only the second Shakespeare play he'd seen since school. Nell had sat in the front seat, watching, and as it unfolded, she felt a profound sense of letting go. She had done her part, she had made the girls and boys on the stage feel like they could pull off this play, and they did. It was truly a thrill to not be seen and yet to still know how much influence she'd had over the thing that everyone was watching, that everyone was afterwards discussing, celebrating.

The show ran for four nights, and on the final night there was a party, and at that party she and Daniel kissed in front of everyone. She felt that she was showing the ones who had bitched about her being so bossy, who had bitched about her being a teacher's pet, who had probably bitched about her being *frigid* that she was in fact totally wild and cool. She walked to school the next day with a new swagger. She had directed the best play the schools had ever seen, and she had a boyfriend. At the last hermanas meeting before Christmas she now had a secret to keep, a very acceptable, very ordinary secret.

There were several more parties over the Christmas holidays and into the early months of the following year. At these parties, they celebrated the New Year, and then, a few weeks later, her sixteenth birthday. She and Daniel met at these parties and kissed in corners and then in bedrooms at them too. She felt exhilarated by all of the different roles she was playing – wild party girl, celebrated director, hermana. She was drinking properly for the first time too, and this again was a relief; it was a duty to drink. Her parents trusted her, they didn't mind her drinking a little, they picked her up after the parties. They believed in being realistic as to the antics of teenagers, they would rather know where she was, and when they could get her, they said.

Nell knew also that her mother was relieved. Dolores could see that Nell had shaken off the sadness that had been brewing inside her, that had been growing since Spain, since before Spain, probably. Dolores felt, Nell sensed, that a little teenage drinking was a price worth paying for that.

His penis had made itself known to her on a couple of occasions and once, in his house, in his room, one Saturday afternoon, she had touched it for him, and he had ejaculated almost immediately due to the fact that they had been kissing each other for a long time beforehand. He looked bewildered after that happened and her first instinct was to apologize to him.

The first time they had sex, it had been the same sort of situation. It seemed that the fact of the previous ejaculation meant that he thought this was par for the course now. He kissed her a lot and she grew desirous of him. They were in a bedroom at the house of a friend, during a party. He had not touched her before, and this time he did. It made her gasp and she came almost immediately; it was the first time in fact she had felt it like that. He was rubbing himself against her excitedly – triumphantly, in fact. He was wearing a condom – she had told him to – and he had slid it out of his wallet and held it for a moment as if it were a holy thing. He was a little older than her, but not much.

It was a struggle, to get it in. He was flustered and then he lost his confidence. He withdrew without having needed the condom and she hugged him. She recalled that in films, women always apologized to men when this happened. She reckoned she was still a virgin, that could not possibly have counted for anything. She was interested in how taking one step and then another, and then another, led her over a threshold.

They were now boyfriend and girlfriend. Those words reverberated around her in their wrongness. She felt tenderly for him but she did not feel for him the way she should. But the social approval she received from her relationship masked this very well. She was doing the things she was doing with him because she thought that was how she was going to prove to herself and to the world that she was normal. She was going to do these things – these things that everyone talked about, all the time, in films, in songs, in giggling groups in school – and that was how she would finally feel real and normal.

She didn't think, at the time, that she was doing anything particularly wrong in the sense of her role as a hermana. She knew that everyone in the movement in theory went along with all of the rules around sex but she sensed, from Martina, and from some of the other hermanas too, that these rules were made, if not to be broken, at least to be danced around. She felt like the whole fuss over sex was a distraction.

For her, the movement was a way to escape the inanity, the narcissism, the cheapness, the selfishness, of everyday life. She felt, sometimes, that through it, she was reaching towards something bigger, something more enduring. Talking to Martina, listening to Martina, made all of the tacky, meagre problems of everyday life seem just that. She didn't want to give that up just because she had a boyfriend now. She said that to herself in the mirror: *I have a boyfriend now.* As she said that, she felt she couldn't quite see her reflection, it was like she was looking through herself.

She barely ever thought about him when they were not together. And when they were together, at other people's houses, at other people's parties, she drank so much and so fast that she did not really ever have to speak to him. He felt hurt by this and would often text her and call her phone – she'd gotten one for Christmas, she hated it because it seemed to tie her to him, no one texted her as much as he did – and she often wouldn't answer. But then when it was time to go to a party, she would remain close to him. He made her feel safe at these parties, he liked her so much.

The second time they had sex, she had been extremely drunk. It was the drunkest she had ever been. She had been extremely drunk and suddenly very intimidated. The group of kids they were with at the party started singing IRA songs and that always made her furious and a little scared. She didn't know anything about the IRA – well, she did, of course, but only the history books kind, and she knew from the spittle and the mad-eyed urgency of these kids that such knowledge was something that would get in the way of this kind of singing. And she felt deep within her that there was something wrong with her – that for her, knowledge was something that seemed to get in the way of living, of singing, of being, of just going along with things. And she hated, hated, *hated* herself for that.

So she led him into a spare bedroom in order to escape the singing and the confusion of her own feelings. He didn't really want to go with her – he didn't, to be fair, like those songs either, but he'd been having a good time – but she so rarely initiated time alone together that after a moment's hesitation, he followed. She was sleepy with the drink and she thinks now that he may have mistaken this sleepiness for desire of him. She was so sleepy that when she lay down on the bed her limbs felt almost entirely immobile. She said something to him, something like, 'I'm glad you are here with me,' and in the moment of saying it she felt its falseness. She was glad that he was there with her but not for the reasons he thought she meant. To her he felt like nothing so much as a dog – a comforting shaggy dog that she could lean against for comfort and protection.

In the play, he had struggled to learn his lines, he had stumbled over the words. She had been impatient with him, but she had swallowed this feeling, and she gave him space and time to figure his part out and for that he was grateful. On the night of the performances, he brought something of that scared vulnerability to the role and for some reason it shone through and he was good, he was actually really good. And he had been a little bewildered by his competence in the role, it made little sense to him. He was, like her, deep down, quite shy and in need of approval. In later years, when she met some actor types through Adrienne, she thought that if he had gone to one of those posh English schools with full-time drama teachers and award-winning arts programmes, maybe he would have gotten on TV, maybe he would have become an actor. He was soft and dark-eyed and handsome and would have played the husband of broken but determined women in BBC crime dramas. It hurts her to think of that.

In the bedroom, the air was fresh. They had been smoking downstairs but the newly washed laundry in the room made it smell cool and inviting. She remembers the colour blue – was it the light, maybe moonlight was filtering through the curtains, or was it perhaps just the colour of the sheets? The pillow was cool on her cheek.

Daniel was kissing her, and he whispered something to her, she thought it was about a condom. She was distantly interested in what was going to happen next. She felt no corresponding rise in desire in her body, she was too sleepy for that, but she did run her fingers through his hair because she felt very affectionate towards him, his lust seemed to render him very vulnerable. He must then have put the condom on his penis and he must then have slipped down her jeans – or maybe she did, she really can't remember, but it seems unlikely to her that she would have, but it also seems unlikely to her that he would have, because he was gentle, he had always been gentle. She does remember feeling that a point of no return had been reached but also feeling curious about what kind of girl she might be now, in this act and after this act. She was sending a version of herself into the world to perform a role, she felt a surge of pride at the kind of power and control this involved.

Again he came in about two seconds flat and even though it was technically the second time, it seemed like the first because he was properly inside of her and did manage to thrust and she thought, *oh, so this is what it is, is this it, really?* And then it was over.

In later years, in more proper relationships, she understood that she got particularly wet when having sex but she didn't know that then, and doesn't even know now – would she have gotten wet if she didn't feel any conscious desire? *Did* she feel any conscious desire? Wasn't it therefore her fault? Or not her fault, but her body's fault? And how was he to tell the difference between her and her body?

It was so shameful, either way. So shameful to have a disgusting, wet body, so shameful to not want to have sex, so shameful to want to have sex – there was shame, or at least embarrassment, underneath his desire too – this is what made him seem so vulnerable to her. His vulnerability in that moment was unbearable to think about.

After all of that happened, and she was dealing with the plus sign on the test, the solidity of the plastic felt like a slap, a rebuke, a punishment. Not for being a slut – funnily enough, she never really felt that – but for being a girl who didn't know who the hell she was. If she could just have played along with other people's certainties and stayed in the living room singing up the *ooh ah up the ra*, or stayed home on Saturday nights playing board games with her hermanas, or if she could have done what her mother would have wanted which was go to the doctor and get a prescription, or – and this was not a thought she had at the time because there was no iteration yet of this existence, as far as she could see – but if she could have accepted the feelings she had for Pilar were real, if she could have just made up her mind about what kind of girl she was, then all of this would have been avoided.

The only way to survive was to give yourself a solid outline, like Martina did, like Pilar did, like Dolores did, like Fiona was starting to do. That is what she was being punished for, she felt, when she saw the test, for not knowing who she was, for being an absolute nothing, a total fake, someone who performed rather than someone who *was*. And the shame of that was the worst shame of all.

12

Ireland, 1971–2018

The farm was going to Patrick but he didn't want it. That was the humble tragedy of the family. Patrick was the kind of son every mother dreamt of having – polite, handsome, athletic, studious. But those blessings were also a curse, and it meant he was destined for better things than life on the dairy farm twenty miles from town and four from the village.

Next came Niall who was born with a learning disability. It manifested itself slowly and then undeniably. He could not manage a farm, he could not even live independently.

And then Martina. A woman, but what of it. And Martina was so capable. So attuned to life in the country, maybe too attuned; not many friends, a little dreamy, too connected to Niall, which was a blessing of course but one that was easily taken advantage of and misunderstood. But she had a powerful sense of duty and so Martina was the obvious choice. But then, Martina . . .

Finally, there was Lucy. The baby, the drama queen, the little princess. Lucy was wild, and she hated the farm, she wanted excitement, she wanted out. She wanted the life she got, which was a moderately misspent youth followed by a secure adulthood funded by her solid slab of a husband who had a decent job at the dairy plant and her own career as a midwife inside in St Luke's. Lucy was fun, Lucy was tough, Lucy was fake tan and French manicures and twice-yearly trips to the Costas. Lucy was Michaela's favourite, her anchor, her most reliable source of grandchildren – four from her, just one from Patrick, none from Martina or Niall, of course.

Michaela was so named in an uncharacteristic moment of poetic weakness by her own mother who was to be permitted these indulgences after ten children in almost as many years. Martina liked the way with just the addition of that tiny letter *a*, Michaela transformed the most bog-standard male name into another sex and clothed it in drama and elegance.

Michaela was a presence in the community, she had airs and graces according to some, she was a bit of a witch, according to others, she was a woman of the earth, the soil, the trees, the fields. Widowed at forty, with four children and fifty cattle, with Niall a bit touched and Patrick having a faraway look in his eye – sorcery was the very least she needed to survive. But Michaela was determined to do more than just survive. Her family, her people, had tentacles that stretched throughout the county and back for centuries; she was born a Brennan, she married a Power. She was born into a house with no running water or electricity, she was well able for the dark and quiet, and she did well, hiring a cousin to help her with the milking and keeping up with the modernization that was then transforming the way the land was being worked.

Martina – whose own name echoed her mother's, but

lacking the drama, she always thought, appropriately enough – felt very small in her mother's presence. Michaela was a tall woman, elegant, with a sloping nose and an unhurried way of talking. She wore a shawl and dangly earrings. She liked listening to Gay Byrne and Marian Finucane, she thoroughly approved of Edna O'Brien. Sometimes, she read fortunes for neighbouring schoolgirls, giggles echoing through the house. Every Christmas, she'd host a 25s tournament, one of Martina's earliest memories was of Michaela's irritation the year the priest won. *Sure what does he need with a turkey and the parish covering his every expense.*

Martina inherited her mother's dislike of the priest and her distrust of sanctimony. They went to Mass, of course, but there was an attitude from Michaela, one of style and of ever so slight defiance in the tilt of her chin. Martina dreamt her way through the services, mouthing the prayers, chewing the Communion wafer, untroubled, happy. That was something Martina held closest to herself, in later years – her phenomenally happy childhood. She adored her mother, she admired her elder brother Patrick, and she doted on gorgeous, golden-haired Lucy. And then there was Niall, who needed her, whom she understood, whose soul flickered oddly in his round brown eyes. He never lost the uncanny stare that small children have; it unnerved people, they turned away from him. The strongest, smartest, bravest people were the ones quickest to turn away, Martina noted, she saw that they feared the disorder someone like Niall represented, to them he didn't add up, he didn't contribute, he wasn't going places. That was probably it, really, the foundation of her entire philosophy. The way the strong turn away from the weak, the vulnerable.

The strong can't ever just *be*, Martina reckoned, they had to *do*. They had to dominate.

Martina always felt that she had been given so much. She felt that her gift was this deep, quiet, solid joy from which she could draw in order to build unity and love in the world. The loss of her father – he died when she was three – did bring a kind of poignancy to her memories of that time, her childhood, but there was no grief, she couldn't remember him, he was merely an imagined soft hand on her head, a fading image in photographs on the dresser in the sitting room. But she knew he had been a good man, she could see it in Patrick who everyone said very much resembled him.

Patrick was a fervent scholar of the Irish language, a nationalist, a patriot. He found his way to a job at the Department of Education and it was his tragedy that he had not been born two generations earlier and thus able to demonstrate his love for his country by dying for it. Martina could sense from him a sadness with the unfolding of the modern world; he hoped for noble things, he ascribed to higher ideals, he liked gentleness, politeness and for things to be in their right place. He liked classical music, he talked about art; loud, coarse things seemed to physically hurt him, and they were living through loud, coarse times. He was not persuaded by the Church, however, and Martina did try, for a time, to get him into the movement, feeling certain, or at least hopeful, that its combination of deep-rooted spirituality and forward-thinking internationalism might suit him, but it never stuck. Later it was clear that he was just gay, and the obviousness of it all when he finally told them, approaching his fifties with a marriage behind him and a daughter almost-estranged – well, it took a long time for Michaela to forgive herself.

'We didn't know,' she said to Martina. 'We just didn't! Sure how was I to know?'

And then, when Martina couldn't find the right words, she never could find the right words, when it came to her family, Michaela said, *I was his mother. I should have known.*

That it all happened around 2015, the time of the same-sex marriage referendum, made it more painful than it should have been. They couldn't turn on the TV without discussions of it all, Michaela bewildered and enraged by the sudden preponderance of rainbow flags.

'Those fuckers,' she said one day as Martina drove them home from town. 'Where were they, with their flags, thirty years ago? On their knees saying Novenas is where.'

Martina didn't say anything. In the movement, discussion of homosexuality was not forbidden, or even uncommon. But it was always conducted in a tone of sadness, of wistful regret. She would have liked Patrick to think she had left because of that. Because she could no longer countenance her connection with an ideology that viewed the very existence of her brother with deep regret.

But that wasn't the reason.

The reason she left was the same as the reason she joined. Both decisions – if one were to call them that – felt preordained. There was little choice involved. The difference was that first time round she thought it was God leading her, that she had become still enough to hear his voice, and that voice was leading her to the movement. It had been a change that felt as natural as the spring arriving in March – inevitable, joyful, peaceful.

But then – the force that drove her away – that was something much darker, much emptier. It came from an absence. It came from a falling away of something. It came from a brutal, infantile fear. She recalled reading that a baby feels terror in the night because it does not know itself, that the mother's act of mirroring the child's distress is how the child knows it exists and it is therefore comforted – because to know one exists is an immense relief, even if in the moment of so knowing, one is screaming, one is weeping.

She did not return to Michaela screaming or weeping. She did not wish to see her pain reflected back to her by that woman she admired so much, that woman who understood her so little. She wanted absolutely nothing, she saw herself as a small bird living in the eaves of the old house, that's what she would be. She had no money but she felt no shame, she was incapable of feeling shame, or maybe if she had allowed herself to feel shame, then all of the shame and regret would come at once, knocking her out of the eaves and onto the hard floor of the farmhouse, her body dashed, her brain spilling out of her head.

She would not do that to her mother. She needed to come home, she had nowhere else to go.

As a child, Martina had difficulty concentrating. That didn't seem so important in the early days, at the tiny two-teacher school she got to by walking the quiet country roads in the company of her siblings every morning. The teachers – a Mrs

Stacey and a Mrs Dowling, a mother and daughter – got to know the children so well over the course of their years together that education seemed a pleasant by-product of their existence, something that just seemed to happen alongside learning songs, how to identify trees and lots of stuff about Cú Chulainn.

Everything changed when she moved to the secondary school in the village. It was also a country school, but the only secondary within a twenty-mile or so radius and was as such attended by children from all of the surrounding townlands, very few of them known to her, many of them terrifying. It was a mixed-sex school and as the bullying got particularly bad towards the end of Second Year, she thought longingly of the girls' school in the big town, but there was no way of getting there, the bus didn't come their way and it wouldn't have been fair to expect her mother to make a thirty-mile round trip every day in their rickety old car, just for her.

Especially as she wasn't all that good at school, anyway. She had trouble keeping words and symbols straight in her mind, and her nature didn't really lend itself to urgency – other weaker students pulled themselves up the grades through diligent repetition, but she just didn't really see the point. There were too many other things to think about and to take care of, and there was part of her too that hated the idea that mastery of the things they were taught in school was the way you established your worth here on this earth. She found that way of thinking puzzling and preposterous. So the teachers thought her lazy, but she was also quiet and gentle and had what her geography teacher described to her mother as *a lovely temperament*, so it was not the teachers who troubled her in those worst of days.

She didn't fit in with the brainy girls – she was too dreamy and lacked the competitiveness that enlivened the dynamic of those friendships. She didn't fit in with wild, cool girls either because she was neither wild nor cool. She was okay with the outcasts and misfits – but they were, by definition, unreliable and could never be counted on to stand up for her when things got bad.

And then there were the boys. There was one, a troubled, violent and often foul-smelling one called Johnny, who by unhappy accident found at this school an audience eager for his performed vulgarities, a group of boys who found in him a safe or at least safer, more deniable way to explore the violence they for some reason felt they must channel. Martina felt sorry for Johnny; his clothes were threadbare, he could barely read, his fingernails were bitten down to stubs and wild rumours circulated as to the fate of his mother. No one knew where she was, he was being raised by his grandmother at the bottom of some lane, his father was gone to England.

Johnny was six foot one at fourteen years old and his trick was to show off his erection at the back of the classroom. It would poke upwards towards the desk making a grotesque outline in his grey trousers. The other boys encouraged him in it, the girls made sure to sit as far away as possible. Martina – dozy Martina, they sometimes called her – was always the last to cop on to anything and the day she first saw it, and then saw that Johnny's audience were waiting for her to see it – that was the day she learned who she was. Because in Johnny's altered state, his sweating, his dilated pupils – and in the muffled, terrible laughter of the other boys – she felt her soul leave her body and align with the tormented party, and there was never any doubt in her mind but that the tormented party was Johnny.

Even after he raped her, she still felt that. She knew, without having to be told, the kind of life he lived. Michaela was a storyteller, which really meant a gossip, and Martina had heard all sorts of tales throughout her life of terrible neglect and suffering and darkness. The sexual element to many of these stories bubbled underneath them, she never knew when she learned about all of that, she thought there was never a moment when she didn't know.

He pulled out of her before he came. That was a great mercy. She told her mother and she put it like that, clear and simple, he didn't let it happen inside, is what she said. She told her straight away because she didn't know what else to do. Michaela stood up from the table and grabbed her around the head and hugged her close to her body and told her, over and over again, *I am sorry, I am sorry, I am sorry.* Martina remembers the feeling of her mother's thin wool cardigan on her lips, the tightness of her grasp. She smelled like flour and butter.

Johnny was removed. And three years later, he shot himself with a shotgun in his grandmother's farmhouse on a mid-term break from whatever juvenile institution he had been sent to fester in.

Martina could not stop crying when her mother told her. Michaela thought it was because she was relieved, that she was safe, but Martina had always felt safe. Even in the moment of the rape, she knew it was going to end, she knew she was going to run home, as long as he didn't kill her, and she really didn't think he would. It had happened in the woods behind the school, on a route she often took home, it had been the most glorious spring day, the countryside just waking up, the bluebells new and damp, the sun pouring through the trees, everything green and fresh and frenzied. He got her by asking her if she could help him with some homework, and she turned to get something from her bag and he walked up to her slowly, and suddenly he was too close. He pushed her over and fell on top of her. It was like having a tree fall on you, it was as if he had himself been felled by some outside force.

But she knew her mother was there. When she realized what was going to happen, she looked up at the birds in the trees and she thought of Michaela, and she knew she would always be there for her, and all she had to do now was to keep that thought in her head and hold on to it until it was over. She recalls clinging on to the grass beneath her, when she got home her palms were green. When he pulled his penis out of her, she winced with pain but took the opportunity to roll to the side, to pull up her knickers and pull down her skirt, and run, she'd always been fast, leaving her books behind her, not knowing if he was following but sensing that he was not, sensing that she had left him alone in a state of darkness, a state of rotten abandon, a state so dreadful that she could not even then begin to hate him for it.

The ones she really hated, the ones she had to draw on God's mercy to find forgiveness for, were the ones who had egged him on, the ones she suspected until her dying day of having told him to go after her, of having pushed him towards a savagery he would never have reached on his own. Those other boys, the ones she had to sit alongside for the rest of her years at school, several of whom went on to careers of prominence in the community, a guard here, a primary school principal there, they were the ones she hated, the ones she feared. She didn't tell anyone about these boys because to do so would have been – it would have been to drag the whole world down on top of her. She should have told the teachers, shouldn't she, when they started all the nonsense with the erections in the back of the class, and if it came out now, maybe the teachers would think that it was a little bit her fault after all, that the stirrings of something she felt in relation to all of that, buried underneath the disgust, or maybe bound up with the disgust – she didn't ever want to think about that. And so those boys, those nice boys from nice farms and nice homes, they got off scot-free, while Johnny died in disgrace, his mother never heard from, his father in England.

It was difficult to make sense of it. Martina turned towards the Church but it was a cold, lonely place. She didn't like the priest, he oozed the kind of respectability she knew could never withstand true torment, a respectability that lacked imagination, that lacked humility. Michaela worried about her constantly – there were often nightmares and Martina would crawl into bed beside her mother, frightened at what the world had revealed itself to be. Fourteen and fifteen and then sixteen years old, barely seven stone and sleeping beside her mother inside in the bed in the back bedroom underneath a red satin quilt and a pile of scratchy yellow blankets.

★ ★ ★

She came across the movement when there was a news item on the TV about an event in Rome that was bringing together young people from across the world to celebrate Jesus. The coverage depicted happy, good-looking people singing and holding hands. But it wasn't really that which appealed to her – it was something one of them said to the camera when interviewed about why they were bothering with the Church when so many people their age were turning away from it. The question was asked of a young, curly-haired man with a European accent, Martina couldn't tell if it was French or Spanish or what. His answer was really in the broad grin of his young face. 'Because of the joy,' he said.

It was such an odd thing to say. Joy was not something Martina ever heard much about, especially in the context of the Church. But it was something she often felt, and almost felt ashamed of herself for feeling. Until what happened had happened, and then her joy was swallowed by sadness and fear – not that she might be attacked again but by what the world was capable of doing to a person, that circumstances could conspire to create such a person, such a life and such a death as was Johnny. She knew that the Church understood such things – darkness, sin – but here for the first time she realized that within it, it held the solution to this darkness too, the solution being this joy that the beautiful young man had spoken of.

Joy, she knew, came from love, and she had been born in and of love and therefore she had a responsibility to make this joy something real in the world. If Johnny had known real joy – not the sniggering, contemptuous regard their classmates had given him, and him so hungry for it, so hungry for anything that looked even remotely like respect – if Johnny had known what she had known, what she saw her mother give Niall, give Patrick, give Lucy, then maybe he wouldn't have hurt her like he did. Maybe he wouldn't have hurt himself.

So she went to the priest and asked him if he knew anything about the groups that had attended the gathering for young people in Rome and if so, could he find out how she might find them. A few weeks passed and finally, an address and a phone number. And a name, a mysterious name: *La Obra de los Hogareños*. This priest seemed to know Spanish and his accent morphed when he spoke those words in a way that startled her, that thrilled her.

And after that – it was all so easy. It was exciting, it was interesting, it was hard work – volunteering, organizing, studying – but she was so eager to do it, so full of energy she didn't know what she might have done otherwise. When she saw regular people go about their lives, their jobs, and they all seemed so tired all the time, she felt so sad for them. She had a normal job too, she was an administrative assistant in several different small organizations through the years, and around that she had to fit all of her La Obra work, but she was never tired.

She initially joined the hermanas and then the group for young adult women, and then she went off and followed el camino – which was what you did if you thought you might have the makings of a fully-fledged hogareña. She studied theology at a Catholic university near Madrid, her language skills good enough to take some of the courses in Spanish. It was intense, immersive, challenging – she had never been very academic, but she had an instinct for the Word, it all made such sense to her – so that even though the language in her essays was simple, it was also elegant, in the way the truth is always elegant.

And it also solved the problem of love of the more prosaic kind. Martina never had any interest in romance, it seemed silly to her. When she learned more in her preparation to be a hogareña, she understood her anathema to it as one rooted in revulsion of the ego. Romantic love as it existed in their culture was about finding one person who thought you wonderful, who thought you special, and then shutting out the rest of the world on that basis. It was selfish, exclusive and, ultimately, if all the films and books about the stultifying awfulness of marriage were to be believed, utterly unfulfilling. Martina couldn't understand why more people didn't see it like that – sometimes, listening to pop music on the radio, observing the covers of women's magazines, turning on the TV – it felt to her that everyone around her was in the grip of some kind of fevered, insipid propaganda, as fantastical and deluded and controlling as anything dreamt up by any authoritarian regime. And, like all dissidents, she often wished she could just go along with it, she often wished she was not burdened by the clarity of her understanding. But the movement relieved her of that wish. The movement showed her it was okay to see the world in the way that she did.

She softened her stance on romantic love somewhat through her experiences in the movement, where she encountered many couples who found a way to have a marriage that was built on less flimsy premises, who seemed devoted to something beyond just themselves and the material acquisition of their families. Still, it was not for her. She never had any doubt about that.

There was another path for her and how lucky, how incredible that she had found it. She shuddered to think what she would have done if she had not – few of the convents were taking on novices any more, and even if they were, she recoiled from that fusty, old-fashioned, respectable Catholicism. It was old, it was dying, it had nothing for her. She knew she was supposed to be embarrassed, that her old school friends – not that she had been particularly close to any of them – thought she was in some kind of cult. She knew that Lucy, who partied her way through school and college, found the earnestness of the other members of the movement excruciating. But she didn't care. She felt totally and utterly free.

Theresa, her first mentor, from a vaguely aristocratic British family – one of those classy English Catholics untainted by Irish blood – was amused by what she called Martina's *unquiet soul*. Theresa recognized that Martina was fleeing something, that she distrusted Confession, that she could be impatient with older, more conservative members of the movement. Martina confided in Theresa that she struggled with the lack of women in the ministry, that she secretly recoiled at the ostentation and wealth of the Vatican, that she found many, if not most, priests tedious and careful and totally devoid of the charisma necessary to share the message of Christ in an increasingly godless world.

La Obra had been founded by a woman and devoted itself

to the Virgin. The Vatican promised the founder that the group would always be led by a woman. Theresa told Martina that was the reason God had led Martina to La Obra, that he understood that the gifts she had to give needed the nurturing of other women, of other, holy, women.

But she also cautioned her. We have to find our way towards our role, we can't push for too much, because then it becomes about us instead of about Him. We have to think in centuries, not in the mere years of our own little lives, Theresa said.

Theresa knew about Johnny too. Martina didn't want to tell, but she figured it was an act of egotism to keep it a secret – it had been the thing that had propelled her here, it would have been untruthful not to disclose that.

She had asked to speak to Theresa in private – this was when she was still on el camino, and her progress was made through her meetings with other young women, and most of them told the group everything about their lives. She didn't want to talk about that part of her journey because she worried that they might think she was holding it as some kind of trump card, its salaciousness (sex, death) meaning that her hermanas whose experiences had not been so bombastic might feel less tormented by God and therefore less worthy. And she didn't want to do that, she didn't want to mark herself out as special in any way.

She was also wary of the alliance between rape and martyrdom in the history of the Church. She did not think the violation, as she learned to call it, marked her out as special, as more worthy than her hermanas, and she didn't want them to think that either – and it was possible they would think that, being, as they were, so very pious and excitable and young.

She also wanted to clarify things around her virginity. She still thought of herself as a virgin but, of course, she wasn't, quite. (Or was she? He had ejaculated on the ground beside her.) And she was by no means asking permission to continue on her journey towards full hogareña status – they assumed virginity, they required celibacy – in fact, the mere idea that this act could disqualify her in some way aroused in her the irritation she often felt at the silly contortions the Church tied itself up in with regard to sex. But she just wanted to be really clear on it. She wanted to be clear and truthful about everything.

So she was maybe a little defensive when she told Theresa, who listened with a stern expression and then told her that she was a true messenger of Christ and that she was blessed to know her. They were in a room off a conference room in a conference centre somewhere in La Mancha and Theresa hugged her and Martina was so surprised that she forgot to ask anything about the technicalities around her virginity. Theresa did not, to Martina's relief, seem to think that the violation meant anything other than what it was, and her impression of Martina's holiness was to do with Martina's concern for her violator, which, Theresa said, was an act of profound love, and one that she herself could not imagine being able to perform. And after that they never spoke of it again.

13

Martina never spoke to anyone about it again, not even to Nell, who came to her having been through the same thing – or so Martina wanted to think, wanted to believe. Nell came to her at a point at which Martina was beginning to feel restless, at a point at which she was beginning to feel complacent. She felt that all of her struggles had been overcome, all of her questions had been answered. She was only thirty-one, in that summer of 2002, and she was too young, she knew, to feel so – arrived.

That feeling had crept up on her. She returned to Ireland in 1999, having been away for just over a decade. She first completed her studies in Spain, her camino, and then the next four years she spent in Peru and Ecuador – a blessed, beautiful time, she didn't want to leave. She would have happily stayed there for ever, living first in a small house, a shack, really, in a barrio in Lima, followed by a short stint in Quito, where she observed the hedonistic backpacker trail through South America, and heard the first Irish accents emerge from it. She avoided them carefully, she felt further away from her fun-seeking compatriots than she did the impoverished children she helped in the schools as a volunteer assistant, her Spanish so good by then that the locals made fun of her for her Madrid-influenced accent. Many of them thought she was actually Spanish and as her tan deepened she felt no need to correct them.

But then she was summoned home by the movement who were alarmed to find that things were diminishing at a rapid pace in Ireland, that several families who had once formed the core of the organization there were starting to fade away. The hogar she was sent to – there were only four in the entire country – was located only thirty miles from her home, from the farm, which was presented to her as something to celebrate. She did not feel celebratory about it, and she knew that they knew she did not feel celebratory about it, the senior hogareñas understanding better than anyone the complicated relationship most of their adherents had with their respective notions of home. But she had signed up to go where they needed her and so back she went, and got a job quite easily as a receptionist in the office of a prosperous local solicitor in a town only twenty miles away from the town where the Clerys lived; the Clerys who seemed to have spearheaded the growth of a little outcrop of holiness among a group of young teenage girls there.

And it was then clear to her why God had sent her back. She felt an immediate connection to those girls coming of age in this moment of enormous change – a change they could not even recognize, being, as they were, as they had to be, so much of their moment that they were blind to it. And even though she was only a decade and a bit older than the oldest of them, she felt she could see in three dimensions things which they could only see outlined in flat, terrifying colour.

At first it was Rebecca she felt especially concerned with, her religiosity oddly placed alongside a strange, angry sharpness, which Martina quickly understood was born out of a difficult situation at home – her mother was flaky and fragile, her father glib and often elsewhere. Rebecca adored her aunt and uncle, the committed hogareña family with the perfect children and gorgeous house, and it was through them, Martina saw, that Rebecca sought to find a place to dig in and build herself from. But as the years passed, Martina was saddened to find a lack of empathy in Rebecca – and an oddly unquestioning attitude towards the movement. Again, at first Martina was heartened to observe such devotion in these increasingly godless times, but as time went on she began to suspect that Rebecca was merely using the movement as a way to build a protective shell around herself, and, more worryingly, as a place in which she could exercise control over girls less certain than she was. Martina alone among the hermanas unit knew how thoroughly Rebecca had been bullied in primary school (her aunt had told her), and it was disappointing to see how this past humiliation seemed to motivate the girl not to greater tenderness towards those younger and less sharp-witted than her, but towards a bullying of her own. Martina felt guilty about how long it took for her to recognize this, blinded as she herself was by Rebecca's surface-level piety.

Most of the girls felt some kind of embarrassment around the holy stuff, and it was understandable, it was not in their culture to be earnest about things. Martina felt a little impatient about this, she so wanted them to get over it, to feel the joy that was available to them if they could just stop caring what their peers thought. Back in Ireland after so long away, she felt more alien than ever and it was often hard not to feel a little hopeless in a place of such compliance, such conformity, such head-down acceptance.

And then God revealed Nell to her and again her hopes soared. At first, she had thought it highly unlikely that Nell would stay the course; she seemed completely mortified by anything remotely spiritual, and sceptical and questioning about everything. Martina knew she only joined in the first place because of her friendship with Fiona – a solid, if unexciting recruit – and she was very surprised to see Nell turn up, month after month, and even start to listen properly and think about the gently theological subject matter the movement prepared for its youngest members.

She was still surprised – and touched and delighted – by how Nell seemed to think that she, Martina, held real answers for her as she moved through ages fourteen and fifteen and she stayed behind after the meetings to interrogate the older woman about what the hell God thought he was doing by putting her through this dreadful adolescence business. Martina was even more surprised to find that she could in fact provide answers to this girl, that she could help her. Martina was pretty sure that if she had been at school with Nell, the girl would have scorned or at the very least overlooked her, and it was yet more evidence of the enlarging power of Jesus's love that they should be able to connect in this way.

She envied Nell her intensity. Martina felt that she lacked passion, that she was too complacent, that her life would always be small. She didn't want to be a leader, she didn't want to be known by the world. But she did sometimes worry that God was disappointed in her for accepting her modest lot so readily.

Nell did not accept her lot, acceptance of anything was not in her nature. She seemed furious about all sorts of things, but underneath that was a deep well of love, of tenderness, of something really singular. Martina could sense it, and she knew Nell could sense it in herself, and she prayed hard that Nell might find a way to channel it, that she might find a way to live peacefully while not wasting this resource that she had. She thought it might be hard; she had no idea how hard it would turn out to be.

Martina knew that Nell's mother was unhappy about her attending the movement. She could tell in the way her eyes slid over her face when she came to collect her daughter from a meeting, from the set of her mouth as she waited in the car. Martina wished she could talk to Dolores but she also felt a little afraid of her; someone told her that she had been an activist, a women's rights activist back in the eighties, and Martina felt uncomfortable around any discussion of those matters. When Nell interrogated her as to her ability to accept what she clearly saw as the subordination of women in a man's world, Martina felt more than capable of explaining her position. But she worried that if so challenged by someone like Dolores, someone who seemed to carry with herself a deep knowledge of how things really were – she worried that she would crumble, that she would get defensive, that she would fail.

When Martina was twenty-one and back and forth to Spain, discovering the new life that was to be hers, thrilled about this new life that was to be hers – she recalled she used to sleep poorly, so excited was she for the next day to begin – a news story exploded onto the front pages at home, one that she could not avoid. A fourteen-year-old girl travelled to England from Ireland for an abortion. Her parents were with her, the girl was pregnant as the result of rape. The parents contacted the Gardaí, to enquire, sensibly, innocently, if they should obtain DNA evidence from the foetus in order to prove who its father was, in order to prove what its father had done. The police contacted the Attorney General who instructed that the parents should return from England with their child, that what they were attempting to do was unlawful due to the Eighth Amendment to the Constitution which stated or implied or seemed to imply a duty of care on the part of the state to protect the life of the child inside the child who had been raped.

The parents and the girl returned, the case was turned to the Supreme Court which ruled that because the girl was suicidal, the threat to her life was real, and that therefore she was entitled to an abortion. The girl returned to England and she miscarried the baby before the procedure could take place.

Martina was horrified by this story but she could not think about it in any coherent way so she did her best to shut it out of her mind. Her feeling on abortion was that it was wrong, totally wrong. But she had real trouble reconciling that feeling with the photographs of flat-capped farmers holding signs proclaiming things about Holy Mary that appeared to represent her 'side' of the argument. She felt mortified by them, she felt enraged by them, they had no compassion, all they cared about was respectability, she knew exactly what kind of men they were. But she couldn't, wouldn't think about abortion without being filled with horror. The situation with the girl at the centre of all of this was unbearable but she felt sure that the death of the tiny child at the heart of it was not going to make it better in any way. In later years, when it became the idiom of the age for people to use their personal experiences to prop up their political positions, she wondered why she had never thought to do that herself, even in the sanctity of her own mind — she never thought, *oh, I was raped too*, therefore I think that this girl should just have her baby and be done with it, that's what I would have done (and that is what she would have done, she never feels in any doubt about that, though she was also only fourteen too, and an incredibly babyish fourteen at that).

She felt compassion for the girl and she prayed for her and when she read that the baby had been lost anyway she wondered if that was God's way of rescuing the girl from whatever pain she might have felt if she had gone through with the termination. But then she felt that was her, putting her own spin, her own interpretation on things, and it was not her place to do that and, besides, where had God been throughout the long process of torment that preceded the pregnancy and the loss of the baby? These were not questions she could answer, so she was glad to escape to Spain where abortion was contested but more legal than in Ireland and hence not as present an issue on the front pages of the newspapers and hence not something she felt she had to think about. And so she didn't.

And she didn't have to think about it again until another referendum was held on the issue in 2002 — only a few years home and it rears its head again, but the issue duly faded when it was decided that no one could decide. She was not a political person, she barely kept up with the news. She felt guilty about this sometimes – and Nell's questioning did in fact force her to consider her quietude, her meekness – but when she watched how politicians and activists and journalists and public people operated, she felt nothing but revulsion. She had no desire to proselytize, that was the problem; while she knew that a life rooted in God was the only life possible for her, the enormity and profundity of that knowledge rendered the squalid politicking of argument and debate a nonsense, a complete waste of time. She knew that from time to time exceptional people appeared on the scene, people who possessed the ability to both walk with God and engage in the fray of political life – she also knew that she was not one of them. Her humility protected her, but perhaps it did so too well. That is what she was starting to feel when Nell came to her, shell-shocked, wide-eyed and pregnant, late in the summer of 2002, asking what she should do.

It was the play that changed things, Martina could see that. She observed in Nell around that time a strengthening, a discovery of power within herself – but Martina had thought this awakening a more intellectual kind, one that might lead Nell towards more literary or philosophical pursuits. She knew the girl wanted to be a doctor and she admired her determination in that regard, but she could never quite picture it, she secretly hoped that Nell would study theology or philosophy and help to form the body of writings around which the movement built and sustained itself.

Nell came to see her at work. It was a grey late summer

day, warm, damp. They sat in the meeting room on the middle floor of the creaky Georgian building in which the offices were located – it was quiet that day, most people were on holiday. Nell took her time getting to the point; she sat quietly, saying nothing for a few long moments. Martina poured a glass of water for her, the quiet between them was so intense that years later she could recall the sound the water made as it landed in the glass.

'Martina, I'm going to have a baby,' is what she said, is what Martina *thinks* she said. And years later, she told herself that this meant Nell never intended to end the pregnancy. If she had, she would have said, *Martina, I'm pregnant* which had a different meaning, a more open one. She was twenty weeks by then, too late – not technically, as the law in the UK permitted it up to twenty-four weeks but this was not something Martina thought about at the time. The option itself was not available in her way of thinking, nor in Nell's, she assumed.

Martina cannot remember later what the first thing she said was. She thinks she said nothing, she was so shocked and – *admit it, admit it* – appalled and – yes – disgusted. What business did this child have being pregnant, what business did this child have even knowing about sex? Martina felt overwhelmed with revulsion before the first coherent thought came to her. And she does remember asking the question, in the next breath, almost no gap between thinking and saying –

Was it taken from you?

Such a strange way to put it, but it came out like that – born of her prudishness, born of her fear. Nell looked at her then, her eyes wide and green and scared. She nodded. It was a tight, curt nod.

The details then came. The drink, so much drink. Nell told Martina how much she had drunk, and Martina asked her how her body felt. Nell described it as *heavy*. And then *impossible to move*. Martina felt calm coming over her as those words were said, she reached out and held Nell's hands, as if to draw more of those details out. She knew what she was doing. Even in the moment of it, she knew she was pushing the girl in a certain direction, but she wanted, she so wanted to believe that's how it had been. It felt essential to believe that's how it had been. It crushed her spirit, it made her sick to her soul to realize – later – that she wanted, she *yearned* to believe some violence had been done to Nell. It sickened her – later – to think she could sit easier with that truth than another; she realized – later – what sordid truth of herself as a person had been revealed.

Martina felt sorry for men and she didn't like them very much. She lived with women, in a modest, quiet, feminine house, and her closest friendships had always been with women. And because of this, it was comfortable for her to think of the boy, Nell's boy, as selfish, a lust-driven opportunist, a sloppy, disgusting, ignorant pig. She never quite thought of him as a rapist – but she would have, if that word had been circulating more at the time, she would have been more than happy to think of him as such. She did of course know that Johnny was a rapist, in the classic style, but her forgiveness for him was total – any anger she had was towards those other boys, those mainstream, ordinary, respectable boys, who had egged him on.

Therefore she understood this boy – Nell's boy – as one of those mainstream boys, callous, unthinking and – most troubling of all – utterly incomprehensible. She simply could not understand what it would take to drive someone to impose their lust on someone else. It was beyond her imagination. She could imagine killing – if she had to, to defend herself, or to defend someone weaker, she knew she could do that, or at least she could contemplate it, her mind could go there. And she could imagine, almost, why Johnny had done what he had done. Everyone knows what it's like to seek approval from those more powerful; we have all, at one point, behaved cravenly in the face of authority.

But to already have power, to already be accepted, and to still want that? It was the pleasure thing, she supposed. Men must experience sex as such awesome pleasure that the other person becomes nothing but a vehicle through which to obtain it. It was abhorrent. She couldn't think about it. Had they no shame?

And she thought also in that moment of another thing she tried her very hardest never to think about, which was the sexual crimes visited upon children by men of the Church. It was spoken about in hogareña meetings sometimes, they spoke of it like it was the Devil made incarnate and come to destroy God's creation, his Church. And she thought, she did, she thought, *bullshit*. It's not the Devil. It's men. It's just plain old men. It is in their nature to do these things. And then she quickly, hurriedly, pushed this thought aside.

But in that moment, that moment with Nell, she allowed herself to feel all of that anger, all of that rage, all of that disgust. Why would He make them like that? What was a person to do in a world with people like this? What was a woman, a girl, a child, to do?

★ ★ ★

'How did it happen, Nell?' Martina asked. She asked this after she'd already asked, *was it taken from you?* and Nell had nodded, and then had spoken of her drunkenness. Martina didn't want to ask this question again, but she forced herself to.

'I didn't want it,' Nell said. She spoke quietly and clearly. Her tone did not contain within it the tiniest note of self-pity, or any hint of persuasion.

Martina felt her body flood with relief. Her shoulders, which had been tense and held at her ears, slumped and she sat back in her chair.

'It was a violation,' Martina said. She felt her eyes move towards the window as she said that. She spoke mildly, as if asserting an incontrovertible fact. 'He violated your trust. He violated your body.'

Nell sobbed loudly, suddenly, and Martina was startled. Nell buried her face in her hands and her shoulders shook. Martina watched her and felt it was right that she should sob. She stayed quiet for a long moment. She sensed Nell wanting her comfort but she withheld it. Nell had behaved badly, she had been drinking and socializing with people who did not share the ideals of the movement, with people who would never share the ideals of the movement. Martina thought of those people and they were indistinguishable in her mind with everything that she hated most about her own country, about her own people.

'But he's not important,' Martina said eventually. She allowed a note of softness into her voice, she was aware of her power, and she exulted a little in it, she who so rarely felt anything like that. 'What's important now is your baby. You have to forgive him so you can love your baby.'

Martina heard her voice crack. She felt a sudden swell of emotion at the thought of the baby, and then she felt weary. Another baby, another life, another child, more struggle, more suffering, more pain.

'God will give you the strength you need, Nell,' she said, again finding a place of control, of authority. 'God loves babies and mothers. He will look after you.' She watched the girl's face and she noticed how her eyes had flickered towards the window, as if she weren't listening any more, as if she had already moved on to somewhere else. And Martina felt the familiar loneliness.

14

London, 2018

Adrienne didn't know anything about Pilar until the sessions with Madeleine. She is very interested in her. Nell tells her that they had written to each other on and off for a while after the Spain trip, then emailed, and then, when social media came, the emails gradually stopped and that while they are still friends on Facebook, they haven't actually communicated directly in years. Nell knows that Pilar is married to a man, that she is a lawyer, he is also a lawyer, they have three children, they are members of their local Catholic church. She supports pro-life groups on Facebook but she didn't seem to go for Trump, or if she did, she did so quietly.

Nell once received a Christmas card from Pilar, in the early days of her marriage, just after the birth of her first baby, one of those personalized family ones that Americans like to send, so cheesy, such brilliant smiles. Nell had been living in London for just a few months then, feeling like she was nothing more than a flicker of reality, feeling like she could very easily disappear. When she saw the card on her trip home to her parents' house for Christmas – Pilar didn't know her London address – Nell felt like it might be the thing to finish her off entirely. She looked at it for a long time, she looked at Pilar's face, her skin so smooth, her dress so perfectly fitting. Her husband was tall and broad and their child – it was only a few months old – was like a little kitten, its eyes squeezed shut, its fingers and toes cocooned in soft white wool. Nell went to the mirror to look at herself and again had that terrible feeling of being invisible, of being ghostly and unreal.

She found she couldn't unpack, on that trip home. She would go to her room with the intention of taking her clothes out of her bag and organizing her things for her brief stay and she would find herself sitting on the edge of the bed holding a tube of toothpaste confusedly in her hand, not knowing how long she'd been there, not knowing what it was she was supposed to do next. She couldn't find it in her to put Pilar's Christmas card in the bin so she put it under the bed, and then it kept poking out from under the bed, its sharp corners catching her unawares when she came into the room. And then she felt the pull of madness again – a sudden, terrible urge to stuff the card into her mouth, to tear it to pieces with her teeth. She knew she had to go back to London and stay there.

She doesn't tell Adrienne or Madeleine about that. But she tells them about falling for Pilar and in the telling, she sees that it was her feelings for Pilar that had propelled her to take the steps that led to the steps that led to the pregnancy. She sees that she had been trying to do the right thing, that she had been led by fear into bad decisions, she sees that the bad things came from falseness. She had not seen things quite like that before and it makes her feel a little better. She re-lives those days in Spain and she feels for the first time a tenderness for the girl she'd been, the girl first falling in love. She hadn't quite realized what a beautiful story it was and she tells it almost entirely truthfully.

It takes a few weeks to tell it all and some sessions are missed, so it's May by the time she's got it straight with them, got it straight with herself. Summer is arriving and the city is simmering and Adrienne is in the full thrust of her pregnancy. Her cheeks are full and the baby, a boy they now know, is kicking. One day, lying on the couch in the warmth of late afternoon, Nell says, 'Adi, can you take some time off in July?'

It will be Adrienne's first time in Ireland. Nell smiles resolutely as she books the flights. She inputs their passport details and thinks about how many bags to bring.

15

Ireland, 2002

The sex was the clarifying act. After it happened, Nell realized it was not something she wanted. Afterwards, she realized she was strong enough to say no to it, to say no to him. Afterwards, she realized how ludicrous it was for it to be such a big deal. She was not scared of anyone calling her a frigid any more, not because she wasn't one, but because the very idea of it in the first place seemed utterly irrelevant to her now. She was beyond it. She was beyond frigidity, she was beyond virginity. She was also beyond being a slut which was what someone could conceivably call her now, because having drunken sex at a party was, in fairness, quite a slutty thing to do.

She had other things to think about, it was almost time for Fifth Year, and then for the Leaving Cert, and then for college. She had to get her act together. She broke up with Daniel shortly after the party and he was sweetly shocked and upset, and she felt bad, but also brisk. She felt she was taking care of business, she felt she had emerged from a period of lunacy, and it was time to comb her hair and get back to work.

★ ★ ★

In one of the sessions, Adrienne asks about the morning-after pill. Nell feels embarrassed about that – about why she had not taken it. She tells Adrienne that at that time, the morning-after pill was held by some people, by many people, to be on a par with abortion. She sees that Adrienne and Madeleine then assume that's why she hadn't gone to get it. She sees them thinking, *what a terrible place, what a stupid people.*

At that time, spring 2002, another referendum was being held. The proposed amendment to the constitution was an attempt to rule out the availability of abortion in Ireland on mental health grounds, to stop women pretending to be crazy in order to get abortions. This same amendment also sought to protect the right to the morning-after pill, which had already been available for a while, but no one quite knew whether it was supposed to be. At the same time, this amendment sought to protect the right of women to travel to obtain abortions elsewhere, should they wish to do so.

It was, then, the kind of thing that anyone with a vested interest in the whole topic could say was in service of their interests, or diametrically opposed to them. It was, then, the kind of thing that left most ordinary people scratching their heads and not wanting to talk about it.

Fiona and Nell had a fight about it.

Fiona said that the morning-after pill was the same as abortion.

Nell said that was ridiculous.

Fiona said the morning-after pill makes you have your period. It forces out whatever is in your womb, including, if it's there, a fertilized egg.

Nell said a fertilized egg is not a baby.

Fiona said when does it become a baby then?

Nell said not then, anyway. Not the morning after you have sex.

Fiona said it was all or nothing. She said you had to draw a line or else nothing was sacred, nothing was safe.

Nell could see her point, but she still thought she was wrong. She let the subject drop. She didn't want to fall out with Fiona again.

It was down to Dolores that Nell understood her position. They discussed it, Dolores told her what she thought. She told Nell that she'd once been involved with pro-choice campaigners, and that's when her views were formed. She said she loved babies, she loved being a mother, but that sometimes, abortion was necessary. She said she did fear what would happen in a world that treated pregnant women as a problem to be solved, she said that some societies forced women to have abortions when they didn't want to, she said that sometimes women changed their minds. She said the whole thing was messy but that a total ban was inhuman. Nell asked her why she wasn't doing anything about it then. Dolores said her days as an activist were over and she smiled very gently at her daughter, she looked a little sad. Previously Nell would have made some sarcastic comment about how pathetic it was just to do nothing about these things, to just accept how things were. But she didn't, that time.

And that was maybe because she secretly found something attractive, not in Fiona's flinty defensiveness, but in Martina's approach to this issue. During the hermanas meetings that happened over the course of the referendum campaign, they didn't talk about abortion directly at all. Instead, Martina talked about playing the long game. She referred a few times to St Augustine and the rapture he displayed in his writing about having received the blessings of God after a misspent youth. She said this showed how all things happen in time and that if we listen, we will hear God when the time is right for us. She said that was true of the individual and that it was true of the world too. It was not our place to persuade, she said, it was our place to listen and to live accordingly. The charisma of the word of God would shine out and speak for itself.

Nell liked this idea of thinking of life in historic perspective. Maybe the world would stay turned away from God throughout her lifetime but that was okay, she had no control over that. All she had to do was listen, to observe, to let herself get dragged along by that beautiful undercurrent, to dissolve herself and her own desires within it.

It was like being drunk, sometimes, the sleepy blissfulness she felt after the hermanas meetings. She knew it was wrong, what she was doing, moving between these different ways of being, she knew she had to find a way to knit it all together, she knew she needed to make up her mind. She kept remembering, suddenly, in those meetings, that she'd had sex, that she wasn't a good girl any more, that she probably shouldn't come to the meetings or that perhaps she should go to Confession. But the sex itself felt so trivial, so unimportant. To even call it a sin seemed like an act of self-importance.

And that was the reason she didn't get a morning-after pill. But she doesn't go into all of that with Madeleine and Adrienne. It's easier to let the bigger story of her country's idiocy take the blame. And so she does.

16

At the time, she let that idiocy, which was in fact all hers, carry her through the first months of the pregnancy in an almost complete state of blissful ignorance. She was at least twelve weeks gone before she bought a test. That meant it was the second week of June because the sex that had made it happen had happened around St Patrick's Day, but of course you had to remember that the first two weeks were not actually real weeks – you counted from the first day of your last period, at which point, bleeding into your knickers, you were not, actually, pregnant.

To not know you didn't get your period in April was perfectly legitimate; to not know you didn't get it in May, less so. To be staring down the barrel of June in a blissful state of unknowing all the while your body multiplied the cells of this new organism faster than it had multiplied anything since it had started multiplying itself – this was far less conceivable and yet, she managed. She didn't have a boyfriend any more, she was a virgin, practically, she even went to Mass (literally no one went to Mass any more unless their parents made them and their parents mostly didn't). There was no way she could be, it was preposterous. She was a good girl, top of her class, well behaved, successful theatre director, going places, going good successful places. It was impossible.

She realized that she'd been praying that it could not be true before she consciously admitted to herself the possibility that it could be. One day she found herself whispering *no, no, no*; the word fell from her lips into the world as if coming from a hitherto unknown part of her consciousness, a part that was growing impatient with being ignored.

Pregnant and not pregnant, knowing and not knowing. There were thresholds between all of those states but it's impossible to pinpoint the moment they were crossed – all the legislators in the land couldn't do it, so how could they have expected her to. For years and years and years she could not understand why she didn't go to her mother. Her mother would have brought her to England, no questions asked, at five, six, eight weeks, when it was okay, when it was respectable, when it was routine. Dolores wouldn't even have been angry.

But Nell didn't do that. Instead, she waited and waited and then when the bulge on her stomach became too big to deny to herself any more, and when she finally figured out how she was going to buy a test – the next town, the Boots there – it felt like those actions were going to make this real rather than the thing that had happened many weeks ago in a room she could not properly describe even if someone promised her this situation would magically resolve itself if she could.

★ ★ ★

This is why she sat on the test for a further few weeks, until it was July and there was no more stalling. And then of course there was the deniability of the truth of her own eyes – the plus sign, that terrible, insistent bulge, not soft like she'd imagined it would be, but hard, hard and bold – that got her through to the beginning of August. And then she was, count them, twenty weeks, which was almost, but not quite, too late, but certainly too late for her, a girl who was soon supposed to be getting her school uniform and textbooks sorted for the first year of the senior cycle of her education at an Irish convent school.

And it was too late, even if it had been allowed. Because by then, it was a baby, a child and it was hers. She felt this somewhat before she went to tell Martina and she felt it absolutely after she had told her. On the bus on the way home from Martina's office, she sat up straight and looked out the window at the fields swimming past. She felt that Martina had behaved in a way that was undignified, but she didn't want to think about it, because it was painful to witness a lack of dignity in someone for whom she had respect. After their conversation, she realized that she did not need Martina's blessing, that the baby was coming whether she had it or not. And that realization gave her a startling feeling of power. She felt as if she were part of something greater, as if some force she did not understand, that no one understood, were propelling her forward, and that to acknowledge her lack of control over this power, this force, was the only way, now, to keep going, to survive. And it was okay! It was startling to realize that it was okay.

★ ★ ★

She told her mother. She saw her mother seeing her in a totally new way and she was bewildered.

'But Nell,' Dolores said, her eyes wild. 'You don't even like boys!'

And Nell fell into her arms and sobbed and Dolores hugged her like she hadn't hugged her since she'd been a child. Nell never knew how much her mother knew about how she'd ended up pregnant. She didn't know enough then to know that Dolores, or any mother, can tell when a child is lying to themselves, if they watch closely enough, and Dolores always watched closely enough.

Back then it was enough to know that her mother wasn't angry, not even for a second. She stood next to her when they told Liam. Liam was more conventionally upset by it; he was not ashamed or angry, but she could see he was thinking – what about fucken college, what about Honours maths, what about everything she was going to achieve. Liam had to go for a long walk, he had to go for a few drinks.

Jenny was delighted – she'd always wanted a younger sibling – and Liam was not happy about that at all. He told Nell sternly that she was not to try and make this seem glamorous, she was not to encourage her sister in the same behaviour. Nell was devastated by that comment, she wept her heart out at the thought of being a bad example to her sister, at the thought of her father thinking she was a source of contamination in the family. She went to him and begged him to say that he didn't despise her, and he looked shocked and cried then too, and said that he would never think badly of her, that he loved her, that this changed nothing. She begged him to forgive her, he said there was nothing to forgive. He said that these things happened. He said that they would cope.

She lay in Jenny's bed, she told her not to ever, ever have sex with a boy unless she was on the pill and he had a condom on. Jenny was thirteen, she said it was too gross to even think about, Nell said it was really gross to actually do it, and to not do it.

'I'm going to be an auntie and Mam's going to be a granny and Daddy is going to be a grandad,' Jenny said, smiling, and Nell felt briefly like some kind of god, changing the nature and substance of everything she touched. And she realized again that there was power in her situation and she understood why her father wanted to contain it.

'And Daniel is going to be a daddy,' Jenny said. She had only met him once, he had been very nice to her.

Nell shuddered. She felt like he was not a part of this story now. She wished she didn't have to tell him.

There was no question of her leaving school. In fact, the school did everything it could to keep its pregnant students in attendance; it offered alternative Leaving Certificate programmes, it accommodated short absences for antenatal appointments, it let the girls wear tracksuit bottoms instead of the usual long, heavy skirts. But Nell was not doing any watered-down version of her exams, absolutely not, and Mr Egan, the principal, seemed amused at her determination in this regard. The future was far off, no one was saying much about college but she and Dolores had talked and talked and decided between them that the first thing to tackle was passing her exams – and then other things could be organized from there. Nell felt guilty, realizing her mother was in essence signing up to be a childminder, but Dolores seemed energized by what was happening, she was not wasting any time in guilt or recriminations. In the meeting with Mr Egan, they discussed the fact that the baby was due around the time of her Fifth Year Christmas exams – which were a serious affair – and Mr Egan said that she could skip them and see how things went but to aim to be back in school as early into the spring as she could manage, even if on a part-time basis only.

'You'll manage, Nell,' he said to her on the way out. 'You know that you will.'

And she felt that she did know that she would. She felt strong and young and strange. She held her head high and walked out the door into the damp August evening.

The hardest thing was the telling of him. He lived near a village outside the town, her mother drove her out there to see him. she had texted him to make sure he was home. They hadn't been in touch for months and her stomach wrenched when she read the subtext of joy in his reply to her message. It didn't occur to him to ask what was going on – her mother had dropped her out to his house a few times when they had been 'going out' and she assumed that he assumed that she wanted to reignite their friendship in the hope of 'getting back together'.

Dolores stayed in the car while she called to the door. It had been decided that she, Nell, would go in and tell him first, and then her mother would come in too, if that felt like the right thing to do next, and talk to his mother about the situation. But when he came to the door, he was all set to go for a walk, wearing a light rain jacket and old trainers, and he said that he was dying to get out, would she come with him.

She said that she would, and she stopped by the car to tell her mam that they were going for a walk down the fields, and would be back in a while. He didn't seem troubled by this – country children were used to townies making special arrangements to accommodate them in their social lives – and he led her down a lane to what he called the back fields. It had been raining incessantly the previous few days but it had stopped and the countryside was wet and pulsing. He reached out to take her hand, it was warm, but she dropped it.

Daniel's home – a nice dormer bungalow – was built close to the river. A small ruin of a castle stood nearby and they had once before in their relationship walked towards it and back, and that's what they did that evening too. The air was so sweet that Nell wanted for a moment to take her clothes off and charge into the river, maybe that would have been the way to tell him, it was easy to hide the bulge beneath her baggy raincoat but when she was naked, it rose from her thin body, proud, prominent and undeniable.

Instead, she told him in language as plain as possible when they reached the ruin of the castle and were standing inside, sheltering from the slight drizzle which had started up again and which misted like perfume against their faces. This ruin was the site of drinking parties which Daniel had in the past shyly boasted of attending. Squashed cans of Budweiser and Dutch Gold littered the ground like pressed flowers, and cigarette butts were poked into the crevices of the moss-covered stone. She realized she had not drunk in months, she realized she did not miss it at all. Once she had faced the fact of her pregnancy, she felt the baby itself stir into life as it moved inside her and any activities that would put it in jeopardy suddenly seemed repellent to her.

She felt so sorry for him as the shock of what she was saying registered on his face. She let it roar through him, this shock, which was quickly followed by panic which she saw threatened to overwhelm him. She held out her hand to him and told him that it was fine, it was under control, that she had told her parents, the school, that she was on top of it. He looked like he was drowning and she tried to find a way to draw him back in to safety.

'You don't have to do anything,' she said. 'It's my mistake. All mine. And I'll be the one to deal with it.'

'But,' he said. 'But . . . but . . .' He looked like a caught fish, gasping and ridiculous.

'It's fine,' she said again, and she realized that she wanted to laugh, and she felt bad. It was like seeing what she had gone through over a course of months crash over him in seconds.

'I'm sorry,' he said. 'I'm sorry, I'm so sorry, I'm so sorry.' Tears were now rolling down his cheeks, and she stopped smiling. She was witnessing the end of someone's childhood and it was horrible. She wanted to look away.

'We were both drunk,' she said. 'So, so drunk.' He shook his head as if to shake the knowledge away, he looked like he could not breathe.

They trudged back through the fields to tell his mother. When they reached his driveway, Dolores got out of the car and looked at him, all sorry and red-eyed. She laughed.

'It's all right,' she said. 'It'll be all right.'

His mother knew what was coming. She was sharp-eyed and no nonsense. She could see by the shape of Nell as she came in the front door, she wasn't born yesterday.

'So,' she said, before anyone else could speak. She had led them into the front room, it was large and bright and clean. 'Dolores. Is it what I think it is?'

'I'm afraid so, Connie, I'm afraid so.' Nell didn't know they knew each other's names and the sense of comradeship that suddenly seemed to come into being between them surprised her.

His mother shook her head. She looked at her son, he was sitting on the couch beside her, his head was buried in his hands. She raised her hand and for a moment Nell thought she was going to belt him across the back of the head. She did not. Instead she put her hand on his back. She had short blonde hair, she was about Dolores's age.

'You are just two babies yourselves,' Connie said. 'What were you thinking at all?'

'I've talked to the school,' Dolores said. 'They've been very good about it. Very accommodating.'

'They'd want to be,' Connie said. 'They've enough experience of it at this stage. Is it the fashion, among you young ones, to get into this situation?' she said, addressing Nell for the first time. 'I see more of you and more of you, and I don't know what is going on. Are you thick or what? Dolores, in our day we didn't have anything, did we? And you – you have it all! And you still manage to get yourselves in this situation.'

She raised her eyes to the ceiling of her living room. Her

son squirmed beside her on the soft corduroy couch — it looked new, it looked expensive. They were doing well, this family, they had been doing well. Connie worked at a travel agency, and her husband did some sort of work for the council. She was freshly tanned and her nails were shiny and polished.

Nell flushed. She wanted to say that they had used a condom but she didn't want them to find out how drunk she'd been — she was afraid of getting into trouble for drinking so much. Her mother trusted her to go drinking because she thought she was sensible about it. She didn't want her to know how stupid she'd been. The only person who knew how drunk she'd been was Martina. And Daniel.

Dolores cleared her throat. 'You're right, Connie, but what's done is done. And it's too late, too late to do anything about it now.'

And Nell saw Dolores and Connie look each other straight in the eye, and she knew what they were saying to one another — about England. And that seemed to clear something between them, and the tension eased a little bit.

After some more talk — about dates, mainly — Connie and Daniel walked them out. The mothers dropped back to talk in the shelter of the porch, Nell and Daniel continued towards the car. She looked at him, his hair was damp and glistening, soft hair grew on his upper lip.

'I missed you,' he said. She felt the charge of truth in what he was saying. 'I missed you when we broke up.'

She smiled. It was nice, after all this, to have someone be kind to her.

'I missed you too,' she said, though this was not at all true.

He reached out and touched her hair, which was damp and curling in the rain. 'You look amazing,' he said. 'I don't know what it is, like. But you look unreal.'

Again, she knew this was true. Her hair was thick and strong, her skin clear and shining. In the soft light of the early evening, she felt herself glow on the freshly tarmacked driveway.

'Thanks,' she said. 'But . . .' And she wanted to say, *this doesn't mean anything, we're not back together, I'm not in love with you, actually I don't even fancy you and I never really did*. But how on earth could she say that to him, and he standing there before her with his life blown wide open and his mother about to tear his head off the minute they were gone?

So she stumbled forward into his arms, and he embraced her tightly. She smelled his teenage-boy sweat and his teenage-boy aftershave and she again tried to turn the tenderness all of that evoked into something stronger, something enduring, something real, something more.

17

Nell likes to remember that day, the day she told Daniel. It's one of the few memories that she can hold on to, it's a very real, tangible one. She likes to remember how she felt, standing there on his driveway, while he looked at her. She has a photo or two from those days, the days of her pregnancy, and she really was radiant. She glowed like an unrepentant princess, she shone with ill-gotten glory. It was a very real, true feeling, it couldn't be squashed or forced into hiding, it was life or nature or God or whatever making itself felt through her and no one could do anything about it. She realized that day that no matter how angry Connie got or how ashamed people made her feel when they saw her belly under her school uniform, they could not do anything about the charge of electricity, the buzzing, the thundering forward of life that she represented, standing there in the white August day, glowing and humming, more alive than anything ever would be.

She remembers how she kissed him on the cheek and how she went home and ate a hearty dinner.

★ ★ ★

But that's why it all fell apart. It was very hard to remember that day, without thinking that what happened next was punishment for it. Her exuberance was too great. She'd no right to it. She should have been sadder, she should have been more ashamed, she should not have rejoiced. If she'd been more downtrodden, more apologetic and cowed, then maybe God wouldn't have noticed her. Maybe he would have left her alone. She knew it was absolute madness to think like that but mad is what she was. After what happened next, mad is all she could be.

Her mother decided it for her and for that she was grateful. Her brain was in pieces, she pictured it in two great lumps, unconnected, severed. There was no way to decide.

The baby had died inside her and the first thing to figure out was how to get it out.

The baby was lost at twenty-nine weeks, on 28 September, a lovely, treacly, autumn day. But no. The baby had already been lost by then, they didn't know when exactly, but it was taken from her body on that day, via Caesarean section, which Dolores had insisted upon even though the doctor said it was better to deliver. Dolores said there is no way she is going through that, there is no way.

The scan, a few days before, was routine. Dolores came with her – she came to all her appointments with her and she had gone white as a ghost and wept, she had wept as Nell herself, her brain sliced in two, just sat there, agape, uncomprehending.

Nell didn't remember feeling anything – until after her belly had been sliced open and the baby removed. She felt then that she had to hold it, she had to look at it. The doctor had told her beforehand that she didn't have to, that lots of women didn't and there was no shame in it. Nell had just nodded, mute, sundered. But when the baby was lifted out, her mouth opened and her mouth said, 'I want to hold him.' She hadn't known it was a boy until after they found out he was dead; it was not the fashion to know the sex in those days, it was thought bad luck. The doctor had told her after they realized that his heart had stopped beating – the bad luck had come anyway, fate had no more secrets to withhold from them.

She was not at all afraid – she had thought she would be – but she was not. She felt nothing but the desire to hold him, to see him. The nurses wrapped him in a blanket and brought him to her and she looked closely at him.

He was very small. He was very perfect. He was very still.

Daniel wept silently at her side. Dolores held on to Liam. Nell looked at the baby, and at all of them. She felt like some great cosmic trick had been played upon her. Everything was wrong with this. There was no sense – what was the connection between these people standing around her, and her? The baby dazzled her with its perfection, but it was dead. The only thing that held all of this together was shortly to be taken away, to be removed from her, the only person he had ever known, for ever.

The thing that had blown her life apart was the thing that held her together was the thing that was taken away. There were too many pieces. It was incoherent. It was wrong.

Because it was a stillbirth, not a miscarriage, there were so many questions – what had caused it, what did she want to do for a funeral, what was going to happen next – and she couldn't answer any of them. There was to be a post-mortem and by that point she wanted to tell them, *Don't bother, it was all because of my wrongness, all of this, that's why it died*, but if she said that out loud then they would think she was crazy, so she didn't say anything. She didn't say a word – not to Daniel and not to her parents – she just got wheeled back out to the recovery area and then spent a night in the hospital with Dolores sitting bolt upright, rigid, white, shell-shocked, on the chair beside her.

Daniel went home, his mother came to collect him. She didn't even come up to see her on the ward, Nell could not blame her, and she was relieved. She felt that Connie knew, that Connie alone knew the terrible thing she had done (had sex with her son when she didn't really want to have sex with her son) and that she had hurt him in this stupid, needless way when she should have known better, if only she had known better, she could never forgive herself for not knowing better.

But she also couldn't quite wish she had never done it because she couldn't quite bring herself to wish she had never been pregnant. It had been the most profound thing that had ever happened to her – to be handed that perfect child that had come from her body – and it was beyond her to wish it had not happened. She did not know what to wish, she did not know what to say, she did not know what to be.

18

London before Adrienne, 2008–2015

The desire for transcendence is the same as the desire for God. That is what Martina taught her.

Nell did not allow herself to want transcendence for a long time after the loss.

But then she came to London.

The air was thicker, life was denser.

More people, more sounds, more stuff.

One night, she found herself at an all-night party in a large building near Angel. She was with her flatmates and her friends, they barely knew each other and they were all a little frightened. But the good thing about Nell, the best thing about her in those years, was her powerful scorn, her hard-worn contempt. It would take more than some mere party to disturb that. Amanda from Cardiff – working as a temp in a lettings agency, trying to get into telly (producing), red hair, gummy smile, veteran vodka-drinker, chain-smoker, ketamine enthusiast – even Amanda was nervous that night, the place had a different atmosphere, an art-school frisson, people who pronounced the word *year* like you could drive a truck right through it, talking about who they knew from drama school in the smoking area.

Nell didn't give a fuck about any of that.

She had lost so much, she felt like the clothes hangers in her wardrobe, her clothes fell off of them onto the floor and the hangers hung there emptily defiant, and that was her. She never pretended to know about things she didn't know about – and she didn't know about much. For these reasons – her honesty, her swagger, her hard-won humour – people were drawn to her, thought her mysterious with her pageboy haircut and nose ring and liking for video games and cooking. She was a good housemate, she emitted a pulsing, steady energy that made it okay to talk or not talk in her presence and she found herself best suited to the company of ever-so-slightly off-the-rails straight girls, newish to the city and beside themselves with poorly concealed self-loathing and the desire to not be like their mothers. It didn't matter if such girls were posh – like Vanessa, her first one, or not so posh, like Amanda, her most enduring one – their energy was basically the same.

She very much enjoyed denying her national identity at this time. Her people and its artists like to emphasize and expound upon the particularities of their nature, which Nell enjoyed denying existed at all, if it ever came up, which it rarely did. She deliberately avoided anyone from there and her accent changed and morphed and no one noticed or cared, it blended with the thick dense polluted choked padded sense of the city. That was what London gave her, a sense of melding, of disappearing into a thickness, a thickness of the crowd, of noise, of life, she felt cocooned and never, ever afraid.

Okay, maybe sometimes afraid, but never while *out*, never while walking the streets or never in a place like this. The only time she felt afraid was when she was alone, and then she was frequently terrified, frequently sick with loneliness which is a terror of the self, so hence the partying, hence the job – a kitchen is never not full of people – hence the straight girls who always wanted to talk, who always wanted to watch TV together, who never let her down. She became excellent at friendship; she was quietly devoted, but also careful to never become dependent, never controlling, and for this she was loved and cared for by many people. Her friends liked her, her friends needed her.

As Amanda did that night, in the smoking area, her skin warm with chemical heat. Amanda grabbed Nell and told her she'd stolen something, a handbag, an exquisite purple handbag that belonged to a girl called Peony who worked alongside her at the lettings place but who was posh and had gotten a job, one that Amanda had killed herself preparing for, at a production company, answering phones, but she won't be answering phones for long, Amanda said, bitterly, and anyway, Peony was *here*, drinking Red Stripe from a can and pretending that was normal for her. Peony had seen her before she had time to hide the bag and what was going to happen now?

Nell lifted her face to the starry night, there was a delicious smell of roasting meat on the air, and she told Amanda not to worry, that she'd deal with it, just go find her. But she didn't need to do, Peony emerged then from the building, seven feet tall, wearing feathers and little else, her skin like honey and teeth like mini-fridges and she looked at the two of them and Nell saw what she saw – a short, angrily androgynous woman with a ring round her nostril, and a thieving Welsh girl with a honking laugh and a thick accent – and Nell knew *she* was afraid.

Nell approached her, and beckoned her away and told her Amanda was so sorry about the bag, she was intimidated by her, and Peony from her great height blushed in acknowledgement of this inevitability, her tiny boobs visible and peeking upwards towards the moonlight. (Peony was destined to appear in front of the camera, a presenter on a property show, and later, much later, an Insta-mum with enough followers to render her one of North Londoners' top micro-influencers.) And Nell said, 'We'll give you back the bag, and some of our drugs, let's be friends,' and she did, and they were, and they created Jesus-in-the-midst in that warehouse and over McDonald's in the morning and all the way home on the bus to Kennington where Nell had found a flat in 2008 that she did not leave.

Nell especially loved London in the early mornings, which she experienced from both ends. She worked in kitchens mainly in Soho and around the Charlotte Street area north of Oxford Street, only a short twenty-minute cycle distance from her home south of the river. And she enjoyed the journey, gliding through the almost empty streets, her hands cold, her cheeks still soft with sleep. Food service was an obvious one for her – her mother's sandwich business meant she could chop efficiently and work methodically, but she never aspired to anything beyond sous-chef level, she distrusted ambition, she didn't want it, didn't need it and the fact that she eschewed it while being good and efficient enough to do whatever she wanted within that context earned her respect and trust.

There was plenty of work, even in the early recession days, and she benefited from the fact that she was competing against workers who did not speak English. She could move jobs when she wanted – and she did, often – and her out-of-hours lifestyle, at-work meals and preferred transport method meant she spent little money and after a while, even on her barely above-minimum-wage jobs, she found she was saving a lot – and then the saving of this money became the way she accounted for herself on this earth.

She did not have a career. She did not have love. She did not have a dream. She did not have a god. She just had this moment-to-moment existence in London and her slowly accruing ISA, every couple of hundred pounds saved proof to herself that she existed, that she was real, and that was all she really needed in those days.

She bought her food in Aldi and at the market in Lewisham, her clothes at Primark and at the stalls on the Walworth Road. She liked white T-shirts, jeans and trainers. She wore jewellery, gold chains, lots of rings which she bought in the Cash-for-Gold shops or in Claire's Accessories so it didn't matter if she lost them. She took drugs but never in a way that was going to interfere with her ability to keep her shit together. She had a very strong sense of the need to keep her shit together. She was organized. She was popular, in a weird way, with weird people – the kind of people working in kitchens were hard to sum up, but most of them had that streak of contained, thumping, controlled hedonism that powered Nell herself in those years. Many of them were transient, most of them were a bit broken, their cultures were difficult to parse, their countries newly constituted, their politics wacky and sometimes offensive.

They understood each other, though, and they understood Nell. She felt that cities were made for and by people like her – people who didn't want to explain themselves, people who liked to be at the very heart of things, but to remain quiet while there. She was a behind-the-scenes girl in a city full of performers, but what people don't realize is that there are ten to twenty to a thousand like her, all working busily, quietly together, to prop up any single star. And the behind-the-scenes people get to enjoy all the pulsing energy of that dementedly inventive city without any of the soul-sucking desire for recognition that warps those in the spotlight – be it for singing, acting, cooking, writing, whatever, it was all the same, Nell thought, people who wanted recognition were fundamentally all the same, and she was not one of them, she wanted nothing more than serene invisibility, to be drowned out by other people's noise.

She felt no need to change. Sometimes, cycling through the dark on her way to or from work, she felt so rapturously happy that she removed her headphones and howled. London didn't flinch. London could contain her, and her howling, and she loved it more than she had ever loved anything, more than herself, more than her family, more than God.

She avoided any scene that related directly to her sexuality – she didn't even call it that, even in her own mind, the word made her cringe, she didn't want to call it anything. At first it was mainly because she didn't need to, her life was full enough because of the kind of work she did and the kind of people she chose to live with. And as time went on it became a decision, it became a horror of groups, of identities, of clubs, of organizing, of belonging. She wanted to be free. She wanted to be of no one and from nowhere, when people asked where she was from, she said Kennington, her accent gone, her pupils flickering and avoidant. She was almost celibate during those years, falling in craven lust with someone every once in a while, falling deep into a few weeks of intense, mind-altering activity that made her feel delirious and then sick. So she scarpered – that's the word she used, such a silly word, such an English word, but she'd tell Amanda, 'I've scarpered,' and Amanda would shake her head and say, 'What did those nuns do to you?'

> To have no ego.
> To have no self.
> To love first.
> To love always.

Nell was following those commandments in her London life, much as she tried to pretend she was not. She loved her friends carefully. She planned little and did not wish for much for herself. She covered Amanda's rent when she needed it, she always had a little extra money, like Martina always said she would if she trusted God to provide. It was only back home that she found herself unable to love, unable to be anything but that furious teenage girl, unable to feel anything but hate for anyone she saw from her former life, the girls walking down town after school in the same uniform she had worn, their silly laughter, their shrill, unbearable politicking.

So she stopped going home. She had no home. She was free.

19

Ireland, autumn 2002

After, she went back into school, back into Fifth Year. Her parents didn't want her to do that, they thought it would be too much pressure. They wanted her to take some time off; she could defer her exams, it would all be okay.

But Nell wanted pressure. She wanted work and study. She wanted Honours maths and four hours of homework every evening. She wanted the teachers telling them it was time to focus, girls, they were seniors now, no more messing around. She wanted the tension she felt when she looked at the stacks of books on her desk, a tension that made her brain feel dense and full, a tension that helped to block everything else out.

She chose chemistry, biology, history and French which she studied alongside the compulsory English, Irish and maths. It was an unusual choice – very hard, altogether, people said. But she needed the two sciences to do medicine and she needed history because she needed to figure out what everything that had ever happened meant – and then she could relax and understand what she meant, what she was in the world.

Dr Ellen Larkin. Dr Nell. Dr Larkin would be strong and powerful. Dr Larkin would understand her place in the world. Dr Larkin would not feel full of guilt about the fact of her existence because Dr Larkin would understand the context in which everything had to exist. Science plus history meant full understanding of the world, she reckoned, and she was excellent at both.

It was the best thing for her, she heard her father say to her mother only a few months after, at the time of her Fifth Year Christmas exams, which were serious, which determined whether you were going to be able for the subject load you'd chosen, whether you needed to drop down to Pass in anything. Nell aced them, she calculated that if she maintained her grades, she'd get medicine, no hassle. It was the best thing for her. And slowly, everyone agreed.

To get medicine required at least 550 points, which meant A1s and A2s and maybe a B1, but only one. The teachers knew what she was aiming for, and as the months went on, she felt like they were all part of a team, rowing hard in the same direction. She felt very sorry for and quite contemptuous of any girl who didn't know what she wanted to do – how did they live with themselves, she wondered, particularly baffled by any of her fellow brainiacs who wanted to study fluffier things like business, or, worst of all, arts. She was herself very good at English; her writing style was pointed and crisp, she always selected a discursive essay rather than a story, she worked through the set texts they were to analyse with efficiency, always selecting the easiest 'theme and issue' (the role of women, it was so easy to write what was expected of one on that subject), always dissecting the poems she was set with clarity. She didn't really get the point of it all – she didn't read for pleasure any more, she who had been such a bookworm, she didn't have time, she was too tired from studying, she had to be strategic about all of this.

One day, an English teacher, a newbie, fresh out of college and full of shiny ideals (bit of a hogareña vibe, actually) asked to speak to her after class. The teacher said she felt like she could give more, like she was holding back. The teacher said she was impressed by the clarity of her voice, that she thought she could write interesting prose, that she'd love for her to experiment a bit more.

'But I only need a B1 in this,' Nell said, deliberately misunderstanding her. 'I don't need to experiment, I haven't gotten less than a B1 in anything. Ever.'

The teacher looked hurt.

'It's not about *grades*,' she said. 'English is a place you can explore. Why not write something from the heart? I think you'd be surprised at what you might find there.'

Nell didn't say anything, she just looked at the teacher with her face straight and plain. Eventually the teacher blushed, and she looked down at the attendance journal on her desk.

Nell figured she could leave and was turning around to do so when the teacher spoke, in a clearer voice this time.

'I know what you've been through,' she said. 'I know how hard it's been. I mean, I can only imagine how hard it's been.'

'I'm going to do medicine,' Nell said. 'I have my plan and it's working. I don't see the point in making problems where there aren't any.'

The teacher shrugged and began to gather her things, the

blush still on her cheeks. Nell wondered what it was that made people feel like they had to impress their way of being on others.

It was a time during which Nell was finding the power of silence. People said so many strange things to her and because her new anger prevented her from rushing in with the need to placate them, the need to smooth things over, she mostly just didn't say anything in response. And then she saw how uncomfortable people were with that and how quickly they would leave her alone. It was almost like discovering some kind of magical trick. You didn't have to talk if you didn't want to. The less you said, the better, in almost all cases.

Her mother had forbidden her to see Martina or go to any meetings. Fiona was no longer her friend – she had never gotten over the shock of the pregnancy in the first place and afterwards, it was as if everything that happened was a mountain between them, too immense for either one of them to scale. They were doing different subjects; they did not share any classes. Nell saw her move through the corridors the same as ever and she noticed that she held herself a little straighter than before. She saw that Fiona had pictured a future and was working towards it, and that Nell – and all of the chaos she represented – was only something that could get in her way. Nell heard from someone that the hermana unit in town no longer met up, that Fiona and Rebecca now travelled to Dublin for meetings, that Ursula had stopped attending.

She stopped going out drinking too. She stopped going out altogether. She didn't want to see anyone who had seen her do the things she had done in the time leading up to her pregnancy. She feared, greatly, what they thought, what they all said. She tried to avoid being in town altogether, she imagined people whispering about her in corners, she felt strange shapes looming in the shadows of the narrow alleyways.

She coped with all this by building on her great silence. It started to cocoon her; it was like her own padded invisible cell, with herself as the nucleus, and everyone else safely on the outside. She studied calmly, ferociously and always with this sense of two parts of herself: the part that was taking in the necessary information, writing down notes, getting the grades, and then this other part, this part that was teeming and roiling underneath. And later, when it all went wrong, again, she wondered if it was because of this separateness, this feeling that she was not whole, that she was not one. (One what? One with Jesus, is what Martina would have said.) She could not shake the feeling that she was not intact or whole or *real*.

To avoid that feeling, she studied and she thought of the future. In her mind, and in her mother's mind, and in her father's mind too, a doctor represented the fullest of what a person could be – someone who was competent at the most important work anyone could do (easing suffering), and not only competent but essential, and not only essential but financially secure, and not only financially secure, but *safe*. No matter what happened, people would need doctors; no matter what happened, people would *pay* doctors. Nell often felt it was too good to be true, that all she had to do was get these grades, which she was more than capable of, and then study some more, and then she would be there. Up there. Dr Larkin. A doctor in the family changed everything, for generations. And even though Nell knew she would never have another child herself – she was never again going to have sex with a boy so she was never going to have a baby – it was pleasing to her to think of creating a legacy anyway, for whoever it might be. Thinking about all of that made her feel stable, it was the only thing that made her feel stable, it calmed her like a drug.

It could be for Jenny, this legacy. The little sister she had long ignored emerged back into her life around this time, floating back into the picture, trailing her long silvery hair and completely ridiculous notions and making Nell laugh and shake her head in utter bewilderment at the thought that they could have come from the same source.

Jenny was doing her Junior Cert and she couldn't care less about it, she still dotted her i's with hearts, she read the *Cliff Notes* versions of her set texts, her maths book was covered in doodles. She only liked fiction that featured magical creatures, she lived for her Saturday afternoons at drama club. The only subject she did well at was art, the only job she ever murmured any interest in was childcare provision. In the aftermath of Nell's loss, the honest, broken-hearted grief her sister exhibited not just at the notion of the abstract loss of a baby, but the real actual loss of a nephew – this honest simple suffering was one of the few straightforward things that Nell could understand, and hold on to. And she loved her for it.

20

It was very predictable, what happened to Nell when she started at UCD. It was almost time-honoured, the experience that the top student at the humble country school feels when she joins dozens of other top students from other similar schools – and then the ones from schools that were not so humble. It was a double blow to her ego, to find out she was not so special in her intellect after all, but then to understand how important this status of specialness had in fact been to her ego. Nell had always been of the opinion that her scholastic ability was something she inherited and was not, therefore, something she should take any pride in – it was like being proud of being taller or blonder or prettier than average and she would not hesitate to heap scorn upon anyone who took pride in having been bestowed with those (far inferior, in her opinion) gifts.

But it turned out to be massively destabilizing to find herself middling, average, not the best. And it was mortifying to find that so many of the other students she encountered at Belfield had, unlike her, partied their way through Fifth and Sixth

Year, on their polished brown limbs (why was everyone so much more tanned here) and it was that partying that they mainly wanted to talk about. She had done nothing for two years, she had barely been to a nightclub, she had rarely drunk, she didn't even go to her own graduation party. So she had nothing, nothing at all to say to these husky-voiced Dublin 4 types who all knew each other, who all hung around in big groups with boys who were doing engineering or law or accountancy.

Dolores drove her up to her campus accommodation, and on the way in, they drove past groups of students walking by in little packs, looking happy, looking purposeful, looking connected. Nell was suddenly shaken by a terrible wave of fear. It was impossible that she would join these people; there was no way she could walk around like that, with an Adidas backpack and O'Neill's tracksuit bottoms folded down at the front so you could see a glimpse of belly, so that you could show that you were both cool and sexy. It was not going to be possible for Nell to do that, absolutely not, no way, no never. She felt as if everyone here would be able to see her for what she really was and that thought made her heart seize up in her chest.

Dolores helped her take her stuff from the car to the room. Her parents were paying for her to have her own single room, and she felt guilty about that — she had not worked a part-time job in Fifth or Sixth Year like most of her classmates had, partly because it was agreed that if she was aiming for medicine then she needed all her focus to be on her schoolwork; partly because her classmates only really worked so they had money to go out drinking and Nell never went out drinking. Her family were now weirdly rich, or at least that's how it felt to Nell who remembered her mother holding her breath when she input her number at the ATM.

There were no university fees to pay because they had been abolished. There was so much work available that it was possible to get a job just by walking into a cafe and looking vaguely respectable. Flights to Europe sometimes cost less than ten euro. Nell knew all of this was historically weird because she had studied and because her mother sometimes talked to her about her own time in Dublin twenty years ago and it was almost like hearing someone talk about a land before time itself. It added to Nell's sense of unease, her understanding of how profoundly things had changed. She was aware that she should be very grateful, that she should be very happy. This sense that she should be grateful sat on top of the bedrock of misery her exam success had not erased.

After everything had been unloaded into the room, Dolores turned to hug her daughter. She saw that silent tears were rolling down her pale cheeks. Nell was short for her age, and flat-chested. She didn't usually look younger than she was because of the defiant tilt of her chin, but she did now. She looked like she was about twelve years old.

'I'm not sure, Mam,' Nell said. 'I'm not sure about this now.' She laughed, as if she were cracking a joke.

And Dolores laughed too, because it was kind of funny. The whole family had been working towards this for years now, all of them so focused, so relieved to have something to direct all their confused pain and buried grief towards. So it was comical to admit uncertainty into the process once the finish line had been crossed, like shrugging when you won an Olympic gold.

'It's going to be fantastic,' Dolores said, determinedly. 'You've worked so hard. You deserve it all.' She thought of all the things a university offered. She thought of the fun Nell could have now. She privately didn't even much care how she got on with her studies, she just wanted her girl to taste something of the world, to find a way back to being excited about the world.

Nell said nothing.

'You have the numbers of the others,' Dolores said, meaning the girls from the convent who were also starting at UCD that term. Dolores had referred to them often in the past couple of weeks, Nell had ignored her every time. Dolores could not understand why Nell had ditched her friends. She had always been the type to form close friendships, she had always been the type to fall head over heels for new people, to be excited by new people. After what had happened, she understood that Nell felt some trepidation at reconnecting but she did not understand why she had hidden herself away like she had. She could not comprehend why Nell seemed so determined to keep punishing herself.

'Text them, meet them. Don't be alone,' Dolores said, finally breaking, finally letting her own tears come. 'Don't be alone so much.'

She suddenly felt panicked. She realized that in all their focus on helping Nell recover and study for her exams, and the careful way they kept the home so quiet and cosy, and in the meticulous researching of the different medicine courses and the analysis of the accommodation in various cities, and in the transport links to and from the cities to home, and in the final careful selection of the order on the CAO form, and in the utter overwhelming relief in her success, and then in the fierce, massive pride in the *huge* success – she got top in her year, she got her first choice, she was, Dolores calculated based on information in the *Irish Times*, in the top half-percentage of students in the *country* that year – in the focus on all of this, she had forgotten to show her how to live day-to-day life.

They had babied her, these last two years, Dolores admitted this to herself now. She had called Fiona's mother once, in the aftermath, to see if they could find a way to get the girls to reconnect but she – Ita – had been less than keen and Dolores was furious. How fucken dare she, stuck in the dark ages with her medieval view of sex and pregnancy and unclean women, no doubt, so she stopped trying. Fiona barely scraped the points for primary school teaching – she was going to have to get in the back door through doing theology ('sure she'd only love that, little god-botherer that she is,' Dolores said darkly when Nell told her) and Dolores allowed herself a moment of delicious *Schadenfreude* in this regard. In fact, it was a moment of absolute glory for Dolores, the whole town knew who got the top points in the year and the fact that it was *her* girl, who had been through what she'd been through with all of its attendant judgements (softened, certainly, from what it would have been in Dolores's time, but still certainly present) and who came from a family that didn't have a college degree between them – it was absolutely delicious.

So it was easy, in the pursuit and then the glory of this triumph, to lose sight of the girl at the centre of it all. The girl who had no friends any more. The girl who had a teen-agehood that had gone all awry. The girl whose only close friends were her younger sister and an American living thousands of miles away and who, Dolores feared, would never love her in the way Nell wanted her to love her.

Dolores knew about Nell before she knew herself. Nell knew that she knew – and it was one of the things that connected them in these hard years, that this truth could exist so gently and unspoken between them. But Dolores now wished she had spoken it. She wished she could say, frankly and clearly to her daughter, that day she stood before her looking so young and afraid in her spartan little room, she wished she had said to her, go find the gays. They'll look out for you.

But she didn't. Because she wasn't entirely sure that they would. Because she had learned, like Nell was learning now, that groups and communities and cliques and societies had their own agendas. And even though Dolores was old enough now, in her early forties, to understand that the essential dichotomy in this life was between love and freedom, her understanding did not yet go beyond just realizing this dichotomy existed. She had no clue yet how to live within it. She doubted anyone did.

Dolores felt weary with the uselessness of her wisdom. So she said nothing other than, 'I love you, I'm proud of you, ring me any time, day or night. Come home if you need to.'

The parties were endless, they went on for days. The only way to get through them was to re-learn how to drink. Nell was way out of practice but with the help of her flatmate – a nice, polished girl from the posh bit of Cork, called, god love her, Pádraigín, aka Podge, a comically ugly name for the caramel-haired beauty that she was — with Podge's help, she quickly caught up. The alcohol, Nell learned, was the way to deal with it all. Of course it was.

Everyone drank, all of the time.

Before what had happened, she drank only because it was cool and then after, she stopped because she didn't care about being cool any more. She didn't care about being cool now either, which meant that her connection to alcohol was much deeper and more meaningful. She learned that alcohol made the pain inside her melt away. In fact, through the power of its blissful dissolution, alcohol made her realize that in fact she *was* carrying pain inside of her — because of the way the pain returned, like a prodigal son, when she woke up. In that respect, there was almost something healthy about the way she was drinking.

But everyone else drank like maniacs too, and they had not all been pregnant and lost babies and their faith and all of their friends before their seventeenth birthday. She and Podge would go to Lidl to buy vodka for pre-drinking, then continue with spirits and mixers while out, and then finish on the cheap Lidl beers at the after parties. Medicine was basically just science for the first year so therefore it was more than acceptable, indeed it was expected, that med students would drink as much as anyone in their first year. More, even, as they knew serious things lay ahead of them and the opportunity for abandon was limited and hence more intense.

Podge was a precursor to the London straights that Nell would later live with but Nell was too unpractised in the art of adult friendship for it to run as smoothly as those later relationships did. She vacillated between cool distance and judgemental froideur at what she considered Podge's faults (obsession with clothes, boys, make-up, reality TV) and overwhelming neediness for Podge's warmth, good humour, friendliness and the shield of her massive popularity. Podge was doing commerce and hung around with girls she knew from home and some Dublin girls she knew from playing hockey, which meant her dance card was frequently full and there were many nights that she was too busy to remain where Nell wished she would – glued to her side at the pub and then the nightclub. Nell had no damn idea how to fit in in those places – she didn't know how to dress, how to stand, how to dance. Podge and her crew wore backless tops and jeans or backless tops and skirts or backless dresses and see-through tights. Nell looked comical dressed like that, she once tried on some of Podge's clothes and they had both rolled around the place laughing, so Nell instead just wore jeans and vaguely girlie tops that she got in Dunnes, but they didn't suit her, and she only ever felt good when wearing plainer, more masculine things but dressing like that while going to the places that Podge and her crew went to made her stand out like a clown at a funeral.

She considered going to the LGBT group. She also considered – for a wild moment – going to the Christian group. The fact that she had these two instincts made her feel it was a bad idea to go to either. Anyway, she had Podge now, she had her studies, she had her alcohol, it was enough for anyone. She went home every weekend, to hide away for a bit, to sleep off the drinking, to see Jenny. She had her first ever email account and she and Pilar wrote to each other semi-regularly. She told Pilar about all of the drinking she was doing and Pilar said that she had several friends *in recovery* and that she should be careful. Nell laughed at what self-important lightweights Americans were, though she didn't say anything to Pilar. It was different over there.

The shock of realizing how ordinary she was intellectually compared to other people on her course lasted through the first months at UCD. There was a boy who ranked internationally at chess. There was a girl who had won the Young Scientist Competition when only fourteen and had patented some kind of chemical that Nell couldn't even understand. Every second person had Grade 8 piano, and someone had written a detective novel that a publisher was interested in.

All Nell had to show for her teenage years was familiarity with the Bible and her C-section scar, two things she was not at all interested in sharing with anyone. She was, she realized with a shock, an extremely dull person. When her classmates in medicine talked to her they quickly found she had not much to say – no hobbies, no wild stories from back home, no boyfriend. It was always a relief to get back to the flat and to feel almost intellectual in front of the afternoon telly Podge liked to watch, the two of them chatting amiably and chain-smoking until it was time to get ready to go out.

Podge's friends didn't like her. And she didn't like them either. Podge by herself was sweet-natured and relaxed but with her friends, their collective vapidity was undeniable and overwhelming to Nell, and she couldn't deny her distaste for it.

A girl called Aoife, Podge's closest friend, was the worst of them all. They had met at the Gaeltacht, and the only reason they didn't live together was because Aoife was from Dublin and lived at home with her parents. Or at least in theory she did – she ended up crashed out on their couch more often than not as the term went on.

Nell found it impossible to talk to Aoife – somehow the words between them crumpled like lit fire paper whenever she tried. Aoife was beady-eyed and had a flat, square face and a turned-up nose, and she liked to get the measure of people. Nell was hard to categorize, she was a country girl, but without the GAA vibe; she was doing medicine but wasn't a starry over-achiever. She was tight-lipped and evasive about her past and didn't seem to have any friends from home. Aoife didn't understand it, and she didn't like what she didn't understand. Nell felt her meagre little eyes all over her, trying to pin her down, and she hated her for it, she despised her, she once dreamt of slapping the vile pale square of her face. She drank more than ever when Aoife was around.

One night, after the Christmas exams, the last hurrah before everyone went home for the holidays, she overheard Podge and Aoife talking about her. She had gone to bed, but hadn't yet fallen asleep. It was around two in the morning, early for them to be back from town, but they were travelling home the next day and had not yet packed. Nell was feeling less dreadful than usual, the waves of misery had intensified with the stress of the end-of-term exams and the deepening darkness of the year, but the high of finishing them and the release of the post-exam partying had swept through the class and lent even her a gentle feeling of being okay, maybe, for a while. She'd gone to the pub with the med students, she usually avoided socializing with them, but she went that day, and people were nice to her and she played some pool with a couple of the boys – and it was fun. She declined to go out with them in town, instead she met Podge and Aoife and the rest of their friends, and she felt alive and bright, and she just watched people dance. She reached a stage of beyond drunk without actually feeling that drunk, a stage she later grew familiar with, a stage she later strived to achieve – a combination of alcohol, adrenaline, exhaustion and release. Together, all of this brought on a really nice state of watchfulness, of contained energy, of almost spiritual calm. She felt almost nothing, like her very insides were clear as vodka.

Podge came over to where she stood, leaning against the bar, and dragged her into a crowd to do some shots, tequila, her favourite. It was the first year of the smoking ban, which she enjoyed; it was nice to have an excuse to go outside and stand there alone and maybe chat to someone for a moment before having the excuse of having to go back inside. Podge was sick that night, rare for her, she could usually handle herself, and Nell was very happy to hold back her hair while she vomited and then to supply her with chewing gums from the array of sprays, make-up and sundries provided by the establishment on a tray and guarded by an African woman of around their mothers' age. Podge often tried to make apologetic small talk with these women, it was always excruciating. *I hope they are at least getting the minimum wage*, Podge said that night, her hands draping down inside the toilet, her high heels in a clatter on the floor behind her, dropping a tenner in the tip jar on the way out.

They returned to the flat after Podge was finished vomiting, all in high spirits, not too drunk. Nell wanted to sit at her window and smoke on her own, so she left the others in the kitchen. She had avoided time alone as much as she could throughout this term, but that night she felt strong and in need of peace. Because of this avoidance of solitude, she didn't know it was possible to hear everything that was said in the kitchen from her bedroom.

The ugliness of Aoife's tone was shocking. Nell had never heard anyone speak in pure hate before. When she told Amanda about it years later Amanda said it was probably because Aoife was gay herself and was afraid of what she saw. Nell had never considered this but Amanda insisted on pointing out how statistically unlikely it was that only one girl of all the girls Nell had known as a teenager was gay (that one being herself).

But that was much later. At the time, Nell was not thinking about that. She had decided – not in any conscious way, it was like her soul decided – that she was going to ignore anything to do with that part of herself for as long as possible. It was like something heavy on an upper shelf – she didn't yet have the upper-body strength to take it down without causing herself an injury. She did feel on occasion an overwhelming desire – for what, for intimacy, she supposed, for touch – but she let it ring through her, she let it pass.

Podge probably knew about Nell – in fact, in later years when they spoke it was like it had always been known. But even as a drunken eighteen-year-old, Podge understood that you shouldn't make people account for themselves, that you should just let people be.

Aoife knew no such thing. She was angry, that night, a

low, drunk, vehement anger. *She's a fucken dyke and she's always perving on you, Podge. I dunno how you put up with it.*

A short silence followed and then Nell heard someone cross the room and fill the kettle. The sound of the water boiling didn't hide any words of denial, any loyalty, any defence.

At home, over Christmas that year, Nell went to a very dark place. The walls of the house were too tight. Her mother was too watchful. Her sister too tentative. Her father too cheerful. She smoked a lot of weed, a new habit she'd picked up from one of the boys in her med class, the only real friend she'd made there – a soul so similarly lost that they couldn't bear to be around each other too much. She hadn't smoked with Podge because Podge was too straight for that so when she got home she got started in earnest. Her parents ignored it and Jenny didn't even recognize the smell.

The psychologist at the hospital was very keen on categories. It was what made Nell distrust her so much. What was the difference between a depressive episode and depression? What even was depression? Was it just this feeling of heavy limbs? Was it just this emptiness of energy, this devoidness, this hopeless nothing? How could that be anything medical? Her sadness was caused by what had happened, all that had happened, and what had happened wasn't a disease, it was just – what had happened. But maybe it had happened because of something more intrinsically wrong with her, which was maybe related to this thing they called depression. And so forth, her thoughts.

She let the psychologist talk to Dolores who talked to the

university who talked back to the psychologist who talked to Dolores. There were many words said about her, and the words seem to build up an edifice of their own and then understanding this edifice seemed to be what they were all trying to do – rather than understanding Nell herself, who was behind it. Sometimes she felt that if she could just go to Spain and see Pilar and be in a place where things were separate and distinct and real – then she would be fine. She thought of the colour blue a lot, the blue of the sky, the blue of Pilar's dress. Her memory of this time is of living through grey, trying to find blue.

She didn't go back to UCD after Christmas, after her stay at the hospital, but everyone agreed she'd be fine by September. She could start fresh then, the college allowed it. There was the small issue of having to pay fees for the year (education was free up to a point) but her parents said not to worry about it, it was a small price to pay for her being better. She went back in September and after a few weeks she was home again, worse than last time. This time the depression had the edge of mania to it, a feeling of choking. Because if she dropped out again that was two years' worth of fees to pay. If she dropped out again, that was more explaining to do to people she met down town, to people she met when she eventually restarted her course. She smoked hash to take the edge off the paranoia but that just created its own more throbbing paranoia and messed up her sleep. She went back for another week to the nice hospital; she came home again.

But once you stopped caring, really properly caring about what people thought – then you were in a strange kind of trouble. You had no tether, no hook. You'd get up at three in the afternoon and eat nothing but Weetabix all day. You never got your hair cut, you never bought any clothes. You didn't say hello to people who called in to see your mother, you went days without saying a word to your sister who was doing her Leaving Cert herself now because somehow two and a half years had passed since you did yours.

She didn't know when everyone stopped thinking she'd go back to college. She didn't know when everyone stopped believing she'd be Dr Larkin. But once she found out that they had given up on this – the grief of it was dreadful. It crashed over and through her like nothing had crashed over and through her since the loss.

It was another overheard conversation, the bookend to the one between Aoife and Podge. It was her father, saying to Dolores, 'She's not able for it, Doll, she's not. We have to help her let go of it.'

Not able for it.

The humiliation of it. The panic of it. She wondered if her whole life she was destined to reach for ways of being that would float away: she'd wanted to be a normal girl who liked boys – gone. She'd wanted to be a good girl who loved Jesus – gone. She'd wanted to be a brainy girl who'd become a doctor – now also gone. She'd wanted to be a mother, for five minutes that was all she'd wanted – gone, gone, gone. Now she was really nothing, a stinking recluse, a source of constant worry to the people she loved, a burden.

21

Ireland, 2006

Liam wanted them to invest in property abroad, like many people were doing. But Dolores was unenthusiastic.

'What business have we, buying a flat in a country we can barely find on a map?' Dolores said.

Liam's arguments were sound – these countries were new, there was no reason to think they wouldn't thrive like their own was doing, no reason whatsoever that these newly minted EU member states wouldn't go stratospheric, and when that happens, Ireland will be in second or fifth or thirteenth place, he said.

'And then we'll only be kicking ourselves. No one is looking after us, Dolores,' he said. 'We have to look after ourselves.'

'People who can risk losing their money have a lot more in the bank than we do.'

'We have the house,' Liam said. He looked around it, as if to double-check. It was nothing special, and she could see him thinking that. But it was warm, it was safe, it was clean. It was a three-bed semi in an estate built in the 1980s, it had a garage they had converted into an extra sitting room, it was always a little cool in there. The kitchen cabinets were a dark wood, the window frames dark brown, there was a green outside on which kids used to play, most of those kids were now grown up. The mortgage was almost fully paid off and it was now worth something like three to four times what they'd paid for it twenty years before. All of this, to Dolores, was calming. Sometimes she could not believe her luck. Sometimes, she felt relaxed enough to feel safe, to feel she could count on shelter, on warmth, for the rest of her days. She hid this feeling from Liam. Such gratitude, such peasant gratitude, would irritate him.

'Whatever happens, we won't lose our house,' he said. He was boyish in those moments, and full of excitement. Liam was the type for whom even the loss of the house would have come with something of a thrill.

Dolores never thought they deserved what they had in the first place, and that was something that made life between her and Liam hard for a time. She was skittish with money; he accused her of preferring being broke, and that had hurt because it was in some ways true. She was used to squirrelling money away, she was used to the pound in her chest when she input her PIN. He couldn't bear that. He wanted to live a bigger, more expansive life. When times were good, she forced herself to buy new clothes, just to make him smile.

Still, it was surprising to find how little emotional impact having money had on her. She'd imagined, all her life, that if she'd had money then things would have been different, she could have expected more of herself. But then when the money came, she felt nothing much other than relief. Liam earned very well from the late nineties through to the mid-noughties and they did up the house, they went on foreign holidays, they bought things for the girls, they ate out, and they saved. It was nice to be able to do all that but it didn't change the fabric of things. Dolores still worked her job of making sandwiches in the morning and then selling them in the girls' secondary school. She still worried about the future.

But she was implacable about the foreign property venture. She just didn't think it was right. She couldn't bring herself to callously slap down money on land she knew nothing about, and charge people to live in their own homeland while they built an extension they didn't need. She said that given their history, she didn't know how he could do it either. She said it was bad karma; he said to get over her hippy nonsense. He said that none of the foreign lads he worked with on building sites would have any such qualms if the roles were reversed, he said it was simply business.

'You think it's about good guys and bad guys,' he said. 'When actually it's about winners and losers.'

'It's not my dream to be an absentee landlord,' she said and he didn't talk to her for a week.

In order to show him, to show herself that she wasn't completely unable to enjoy their good fortune, she allowed herself to go on a shopping trip to New York with some of her women friends, early the following year, early 2007. The shock of Nell's pregnancy and what had happened afterwards still reverberated through her body; she felt she had aged twenty years since it happened. After dropping out of college, Nell had spent a month in a private psychiatric hospital in

Dublin, it had eaten up a chunk of their savings. Dolores felt grateful for the fact that they had this money, but it was also a reminder of how the money was so easily spent, so easily gone. She had stopped spending after that and Liam had gotten annoyed with her. So she went to New York. To show him, to show herself.

Manhattan was just like it was on the TV and she couldn't shake the feeling that the fronts of the buildings were fake, they were just propped-up facades that might fall down on top of her at any moment. The air was still and vaguely sweet-smelling; people were forthright and strident and occasionally sentimental when they heard her accent. She walked the streets of the Lower East Side alone while the other women took a bus to an outlet mall somewhere on the outskirts of the city. She felt that she should buy things, so she picked up a knock-off designer handbag for Jenny in a shop in Chinatown. She did not like to do things she had seen being done many times before on TV – such as go shopping in New York – she felt an uncanny fake sense, as if she were performing rather than just doing.

Back at the hotel, she waited for her friends to come back. She stood on the balcony and watched the city move beneath her and she thought of Annie and those days in Dublin – the only time she'd spent any time living in a city, though this city she was now standing in made a mockery of the very idea of Dublin as anything at all. A feeling of intense home-sickness rocked her suddenly – it was like not being able to breathe properly, like she'd been locked in a dark cupboard. And then a second little punch of shame. She was, in essence, a provincial woman frightened of the big city. How Annie would have laughed at her, Annie who was now an academic in Trinity, married to another academic, still fighting the good fight, but in a more subdued manner now, so subdued that it was very possible to go many years without hearing her name.

Geraldine, her friend, came into the room with two fistfuls of shopping bags. She unpacked the things she had bought, folded them carefully and put them on the empty shelves of the wardrobe, which Dolores thought silly as they only had two nights left. Geraldine was always bustling about, organizing things, straightening things. Her children were all hale and hearty and getting through college and doing great, and even though she spoke about them often and at great length, Dolores could never remember what any of them were doing because nothing ever went wrong in their lives.

The women were going on the *Sex and the City* bus tour that evening and Dolores did not want to go. But she had gone alone to the Met the day before and she did not want to seem diffident and aloof, she was not usually diffident and aloof. None of the women actually watched *Sex and the City* but it had been offered as part of the flights-and-hotel deal and Joan, the organizer of the trip, felt it would be a good way to get a bus tour of the city, and if you were to pay separately it would have cost much more. Plus there was a sense among these women that they would not be mocked or cowed by anything this city could offer them – and even though their daughters shrieked with laughter when they found out about the *Sex and the City* tour, that only made the women even more determined to go and have a good time and to enjoy the complimentary cupcake and cocktail you got as part of it.

The man who provided the commentary was performing a campness Dolores suspected was entirely fake, and his act involved a contemptuous hauteur towards the women which they were obliged to find hilarious and which they duly and obediently did. Dolores thought of the episode she had caught on TV late one night in which the characters discussed how many abortions they'd had, and she wondered how Joan who used to go around with the baby-feet pin in her jumper would feel about that if she knew – or maybe she did know, and she was, like Dolores, just going along on this trip, and just laughing along with the jokes, because she was lonely and wanted to belong to the group, and this option had presented itself to the group via the holiday booking form, and now here they were.

After the dinner, which wasn't bad, and the cocktails, which were strong, they got cabs back to the hotel and drank more in the lobby. They finally found a barman who would chat to them; he had a soft, old, face; he had stories of drunk celebrities and washed-up politicians; he paid due regard to their national identity.

On the way up to her room with Geraldine, Joan came up behind them in the corridor, her footsteps muffled by the carpet, her high-heeled shoes clutched in her hands, saying that she wanted to see what Geraldine had gotten out at the outlet mall. She said the word *mall* easily and without embarrassment. Joan then made yet another comment about how she couldn't understand why Dolores had skipped the trip to the mall – *it was great, such brilliant value* – and Dolores resented the implication she was making which was that she, Dolores, was too thick or too poor or too *controlled* to be able to treat herself properly. When they got back into the room, she went straight to the mini-bar and helped herself to a miniature bottle of whiskey, demonstrating to Joan that she couldn't care less how much it cost.

Joan may have sensed this mutiny from Dolores because she mellowed, lying back on the pillows of Geraldine's bed and talking with sudden frankness about how she was both jealous of and delighted for her children to be growing up taking trips abroad for granted, and how hard it was not to spoil them nowadays, and how she never knew if she was doing the right thing by them at all.

The women all knew about the general shape of the ins and outs of Nell's troubles, and they didn't ask much about it, but were also careful to not *not* ask about it either. Dolores then felt guilty for judging them and suddenly grateful to them for including her – she wasn't really part of this gang, she wasn't from town like these women were. Dolores had her hippy side, Liam said she'd caught it in England that time and had never entirely shaken it off. She had an interest in spirituality, she once went to a meditation retreat in Kerry, she was glad that Ireland was shaking off its stultifying conservatism but she also felt there was much that they were losing too. She was discomfited by the material excess of the Boom years, she disliked shopping centres and felt suffocated by all of the things people now had. She knew about the whole thing with the climate but she could never bring herself to join in with any of the groups who organized around that issue. She'd tried, once or twice, but found them utterly divorced from everyday reality and was depressed at how eager they were to tell people what to do, to tell people how to live. It was Annie, all over again, and she couldn't bear it. She preferred to be with women like Geraldine, like Joan, women who would make fun of her, women who thought she was a bit different, a bit odd, but women who would always be there for her, no matter what her children put her through.

Joan then suggested they go out on the slim balcony of the hotel room to take a photo of the skyline and themselves against it to mark their last night. She fiddled with the controls on her new digital camera, finally managing to get it in what they would later call selfie mode and the three women squinted into its flash. They took a number of photographs, laughing at themselves, with Joan getting so carried away at one moment that she hit her wrist against the side of the balcony shattering the cheap clasp on the watch she had also bought at the outlet mall. The watch plunged suddenly and brokenly down to the stagnant alleyway beneath them. Joan lunged for it and she dropped her camera too. Dolores reached out and caught it at the last moment. It felt solid in her hands, cool and reassuring and hefty.

Joan thanked her, she was almost tearful as she thanked her. The camera had cost over three hundred dollars, it would have been a terrible thing to have lost it, she seemed frightened and shaken by the idea of it. The women returned to the room, and drank some more whiskey and they talked late into the night.

Dolores felt peaceful on the plane home the next day, and she figured that it was because she was starting to remember how to have a good time. She used to know how but she had forgotten, the terrible events of the last few years had made her forget. This made her feel ashamed, because there was something dreadful about being miserable. Brigid had always managed to have a good time, to have a laugh, to hold on to some part of herself, within herself, something that made it possible to get through day after day of monotonous work, of unceasing sameness. And Brigid held a special contempt for those people – especially those women – who seemed unable to do that. Brigid had always preferred the company of men; she was quick to judge any woman who spent too long at the bar while it took a huge amount of drunkenness for her to look at a man with anything other than affectionate disapproval.

Brigid should have lived to one hundred and three. She could have withstood regime change, culture clash, economic boom and bust, family estrangement, reconciliation, tragedy, success, riches, bankruptcy and everything in between. She was just that type. It made no sense for her to die so young. She wasn't the type to die young.

And she wasn't the type to curry unhappiness. Which is why, Dolores figured, as the plane turned east towards dawn and home, she suddenly found herself thinking about her so much. Brigid would have greatly approved of this jaunt across the ocean. She would have preferred if the husbands had gone too, and she would have liked to have had drinks with them in a sports bar, maybe, and talked business with the local bar staff, trying to figure out how much they took in on a good day. She would have gone to the outlet mall, Dolores thought; she wouldn't have wandered around the streets alone, the way she had, trying to feel some kind of essence of the city, trying not to wish she was twenty years younger. Her mother was not one for wishing things that couldn't be. Dolores recalled how she had stood in front of a painting at the Met and felt something in relation to the colours, something big and hypnotic and expansive. But then she couldn't remember what the painting was called, what the artist was called. She wondered if that meant that these places were not for her.

The women got the early bus home from the airport, arriving in to town at around ten in the morning. Liam was there to collect her in their new car. She sat across from him at the table in the kitchen while he made tea and asked her how it had been. Jenny got up when she heard her and demanded to know if she'd been brought anything – Dolores had copied Joan and grabbed some cosmetics and make-up at the airport, Jenny squealed in delight and surprise as she presented it all to her inside the Chinatown handbag. Dolores watched her and smiled. She felt a weird kind of sadness, she tried to shake it off.

Nell got up a little while later, and she saw in Dolores what the others hadn't. Nell always saw her too clearly. That's why things were so hard between them at that time.

'I went to the Met,' Dolores said to Nell. 'It was too big altogether. I needed someone to show me what to look at.'

Nell understood she was saying that she needed *her* to tell her what to look at. But at that moment in her life, she was unable to recognize that she had any worth at all. So she took this gentle compliment as babying condescension. It sat on her like a weight on top of all the other weights. Dolores saw that she had said the wrong thing and felt an even deeper despair.

'Liam,' she said, suddenly. 'Liam, I think you're right about this house. It's too small. It's time to move.'

Those words felt like a rope she was pulling herself up with.

Liam came in from the living room, looking wary and startled and tentatively pleased.

'Was it Joan put this notion in your head?' he said.

Dolores shrugged. 'Does it matter?'

But it was too late. By the time they had found somewhere they wanted to buy – a place not too far from town but with enough space to extend, with a garden that Dolores told herself she'd definitely learn how to tend, how to enjoy – by the time they had their own place valued, by the time all of that happened, it was early 2008 and the bottom was falling out of the building trade and hence their world.

Dolores was heartbroken for Liam but there was something in that small crisis (they were ultimately fine, they hadn't taken out stupid loans, their house *was* almost paid off, and paid off at its original, eighties price which had to be more akin to its intrinsic price though everything they and the country were learning at this time pointed to the fact that nothing had any intrinsic value whatsoever), they found themselves again. Liam stopped resenting her because her carefulness was vindicated – but it was not only that. He stopped scheming and stopped feeling like he had something to prove. No one had anything to prove any more. He signed on the dole and read the paper in the mornings, spread carefully and neatly out on the kitchen table, a tea with two sugars to go with it. Dolores was taking in a few hundred a week, which did drop a little as people were inclined to send their kids to school with their own lunches when money was tight, but her prices had always been reasonable – too reasonable, Liam said — so the impact was not as great as it might otherwise have been.

They went on holiday together, they went to Italy. They'd never been to Italy — people like them went to Spain — but Liam said, fuckit let's go to Italy, they had savings, what were they waiting for? Dolores was nervous about leaving Nell, but Liam said that was ridiculous. They were forty-five years old and they looked younger. Dolores's hair was shiny, his was thick and curly. In Florence they saw all of the art and it made Dolores weak in the knees and Liam loved to see how it made her weak in the knees, and she forgot to worry about not knowing enough about it. They held hands and walked around and one day they stayed in bed all afternoon. It was very hard to see each other properly after so many years but on that holiday they tried hard and here and there they did.

22

Nell got up one day in early 2008, and she stood alongside her mother. It was 9.30 a.m. and Dolores was laying out slices of bread on the high countertop in the kitchen. The slices looked like clean white pages, and Nell felt peaceful looking at them. She picked up a knife and slid it gently over the surface of the big square box of butter, it was perfectly soft. She buttered the slices of bread as Dolores stood back and leaned against the sink and watched her. After all the slices were done, Nell washed her hands, and took a packet of ham from the fridge and put the meat carefully on the bread. Her mother told her when she'd done enough ham ones, and when to start on the cheese.

The sandwich business saved them, that year. It wasn't so much the money – although with Liam out of work it certainly helped – but the feeling of having something to get up for, something to deliver. Liam drove Dolores up to the school, he collected her afterwards, he didn't have anything else to do. Nell began to bake cakes and buns and cookies, they sold them too. Nell thought about the money she had cost her parents, the college fees, the college accommodation, the psychiatric hospital, and she saw each sandwich she made, each cake she sold, as a repayment towards that debt. She figured out how to make the perfect Bakewell bun with thick pastry at the bottom, she even made her own jam. They sold for two euro each, the staff bought them all before the students got near them. Nell leaned against the oven as the cakes rose in the early morning, she felt her heart thunder in her chest. Her mother made coffee. They spoke little in the winter blackness, they spoke a bit more as the spring began to break through.

Nell told her mother not to tell the staff at the school that she was helping with the business. She couldn't bear the way they'd say, *oh, that's great, so it is, we're delighted to hear that*, when she knew what they'd all be thinking: *Nell Larkin still at home at twenty-two, not a doctor, not anything, just helping her mammy in the kitchen, how the mighty have fallen, wasn't she all on track to do medicine? I suppose she wasn't able for it, well, I suppose it's not surprising, after everything.*

The knowledge that she wasn't going back to UCD, not that year, not next year, not any year ever, had sunk into her bones. And she realized that though this knowledge hurt, still she breathed, still she was there. She used to feel so desperately sorry for anyone who didn't want to be a doctor, for anyone who couldn't be a doctor – and now there she was among them, all the non-doctors, the drop-outs, the losers, the sandwich-makers, the order-takers, the unemployed builders, and still she breathed.

The world went on, and she with it. All she had now was

her body, this home, and the work that was to be done. She thought of Martina, who tended to the thing that was in front of her – and that is what she did.

23

When Nell met Adrienne in around the middle of 2015, she had been starting to feel as if the way she was living was going to have to change in some fashion, but she was ignoring that feeling because she could not face it. She heard of someone, a woman known to Amanda through a friend of a friend, about a decade older than they were, who had come to London to work in finance in the nineties. She had bought an apartment in Islington, this woman had, for like, literally nothing, you can imagine, and as time went on this person, this woman, realized she could live on the money she made by simply moving out of her Islington flat, and renting a room in another, cheaper flat in another, less fashionable district – and the difference between the money she earned in rent and the money she paid in rent plus her mortgage was just about wide enough to mean that as long as she lived quietly, as long as she lived humbly, she need never work again. And so that is what this woman did.

Rotherhithe, Amanda thinks, is where she lived then, in 2015, edging further and further out as the years went on and more and more parts of the city were eaten up by waves of gourmet coffee and six-quid loaves of sourdough bread. Nell listened with fascination to the story of this woman's life, her increasingly hermetic habits, her inclination towards conspiracy – who *really* runs things, that was the question she dedicated her now ample free time to – her deepening suspicion of anyone who lived, as did this friend of a friend of Amanda's, cheerfully and well.

And Nell figured then, as she came up to thirty, that it was not at all hard to become a shut-in, to become a crank – and the cold feeling around her heart when she realized that made any activity related to ensuring this did not happen feel totally impossible for her to embark upon. It wasn't as if she didn't have money. She didn't have an Islington flat, but she had close to fifteen grand stashed away now – a result of her frugal and yes, slightly crankish ways – and she knew Liam and Dolores (which is how she referred to them to her friends, always in an ironical tone, always rolling her eyes for some reason) would be only delighted to lend her more if she wanted to go back to university or buy a place or do anything, anything at all. But their efforts to broach the idea of any such projects with her were always met with impatience, evasion and an ever broadening of the great expanses of time during which she did not call.

She still worked in kitchens, still in and around Soho, and she was thus occasionally adjacent to the celebrity culture and cultural celebrity that ran through the veins of the city. Nell abhorred celebrities on principle but then she kept bumping into them – reality stars and TV chefs in the main – and she couldn't help herself from often kind of liking them. And because of the way this affectionate truculence prevented her from behaving with the obsequiousness that so irritated the celeb class (she once, for example, saw a food editor curtsy like a peasant when introduced to Jamie Oliver), she was not infrequently asked to work behind the scenes at various vaguely celebrity events – helping out at a cooking demonstration at an expo in Earl's Court, for example, or assisting at the photo shoot for a starry and over-priced recipe book.

It was at a latter such event that she first met Adrienne, food stylist and sometime chef, who was, unlike Nell, not at all shy about her abilities to work with the food elect and her desire to perhaps one day join them. Adrienne was similarly un-dazzled by fame but she displayed this in a different way to Nell; she was loud and bossy with her shining charges, she told them what to do and teased them when they didn't do it, she understood exactly where to draw the line between professional camaraderie and inappropriate chumminess. Nell was dazzled by her, rendered speechless by her, the phrase that came to her was, weirdly, from the idiom of mid-century America: *what a knockout*. Adrienne did have a bit of a 1950s vibe – she wore bright floral dresses (from Liberty if she was flush, H&M if not) that flared at the waist, high wedged sandals on her soft, tanned feet, and her brow was often caused to furrow in a stern, disappointed, maternal way by the antics of suddenly famous wellness blogger/*Bake Off* contestant/uppity pastry chef struggling to prove they knew the first thing about anything at all.

Adrienne was also wild fun once the work was done – gossipy, friendly and madly profligate at the bar. Nell hadn't been smitten like this in as long as she could remember.

At first, in the early, heady, heaven-sent days, Nell thought that Adrienne had fully shattered the ice inside of her and made it possible for her to live again, to reach beyond the mere existing she had been doing and really actually live, whatever that meant. Nell had this sense of herself as someone who did not fully inhabit her body, she dreamt often of frostbite. She countered this feeling through a lot of exercise — she cycled to work, she ran in the park, she did weights — but still her lean, tough body felt, from the inside of it, as if its blood did not fully circulate around it. When she fell in love with Adrienne — and it was exactly like that, *falling* — her body tingled with aliveness, with awareness, with the full bold flush of life itself.

Adrienne was out to her family, not very long but they were cautiously okay with it and then totally okay with it after a few family meals with Nell and the realization that they bickered flirtatiously and held hands and went to Ikea to get laundry baskets and fold-away beds like everyone else. Adrienne's family lived in one of the outer southern boroughs of the city, suburban, diverse, not too expensive, a pain to get to after dark, lots of chain restaurants beloved by Adi's mum, scorned by Adi herself. Adrienne had moved back home to save for a deposit, and so their relationship was accelerated by the convenience of spending nights together in Nell's Kennington flat where they drank coffee on the back step of the overgrown shared garden, slept off their hangovers and invited friends round for long, messy and unnecessarily elaborate meals.

Previous to Adrienne, Nell had considered what other people called love nothing more than an evolutionary by-product, a toxic, potentially flammable substance that should be handled with extreme care, if at all. She was vindicated in this world view by the culture of that moment with its sex apps and its valorization of individual achievement: people wanted sex to procreate, people wanted status to protect the results of that procreation, love was therefore unnecessary and could only bring pain. But then the love she had unexpectedly found shattered all of that from its core – they could not procreate, could they – so what on earth was all this incredible happiness *for*? It was wonderful not to have an answer to that question and she spent the best part of two years floating in its hot, light-filled (it felt like summer for two years straight) mystery.

But slowly, inexorably, like an antidepressant losing its efficacy, she started to come down to earth, and things started to go grey at the edges. She initially liked to think of this as triggered by Adrienne's desire to have a baby – how lovely it is to blame – but she knew really it wasn't that. Her fingers were starting to curl up and blacken, she felt her soul-goblin, which had been swinging from the rafters, shrink and turn green inside her. Adrienne knew a little bit of what had happened to her – the scar just above her pubic line begged a question – and she also knew it was, though apparently long-healed and faded, in actuality tender and untouchably raw.

They never went to Ireland together. At first, Adrienne didn't notice that Nell hadn't been home, but as their first Christmas as a couple rolled around, she of course asked and was startled to learn that Nell couldn't remember the last time she'd been back. Adrienne talked to her mother every day, short, often barked phone conversations punctuated by crossness, silences and laughter.

Adrienne's family were disappointed to find she had only one sibling ('That's not like the Irish, Adi, is it,' her father said, chuckling, his massive belly wobbling), and then a little sad to learn she didn't speak to them much. Lydia, Adrienne's mother, was good at containing her inquisitiveness but it showed in the bright directness of the way she looked at Nell. Adrienne had two older brothers, a lawyer and car mechanic, and they were sweet and gruff and not that curious about the woman their little sister brought home, though pleased to learn that she didn't want to engage them in chatter and was passably knowledgeable about weightlifting. A normal family, in short – or as close as it got – and it forced Nell to think about her own. She knew Dolores would give anything to have the kind of relationship that involved quick, informal phone calls about what one was having for dinner, she also knew that it was beyond her power to initiate those. Adrienne could not understand it: at first she tiptoed around it, assuming Dolores had forced Nell to go through with a pregnancy she didn't want, and then she was confused, and then very cross when she learned – due to conversations that were, in Nell's view, thrust upon them by the increase in discussion around abortion in Ireland that was happening even in the British media then – that Dolores had in fact been involved in the campaign *against* the introduction of the (increasingly infamous) Eighth Amendment back in 1983, and therefore the loss Nell had suffered had not been due to the traditional intransigence of the Irish Mother.

Through this conversation, which she did not want, Nell

saw the image of Dolores as some fussy old granny with a well-worn set of rosary beads dissolve in Adrienne's imagination and, with nothing to replace it, Nell felt she had to show her a photo. She felt an odd surge of pride as Adrienne said, incredulously, '*This* is Dolores?' and Nell blushed, proud for perhaps the first time in her adulthood to be the daughter of the fine-looking, dark-haired woman in her early fifties.

'So your mother got involved when she was at uni?' Adrienne said. 'That's cool.'

'No, she wasn't at uni. She didn't go to uni.'

'Well, that's even better.'

'Is it?'

'Yeah,' Adrienne said. 'It's only students who can afford to have principles, usually, isn't it? That's why everyone hates them.' Adrienne possessed a third-class degree in media studies from Kingston, she liked to boast that she forgot to go to the graduation and most of the final year.

Nell shrugged.

Adrienne waited for more, more was not forthcoming. They were sitting outside a pub, it was early in the spring of 2017, Nell was rolling a cigarette, it was still quite cold.

'What happened after? After her side lost, I mean.'

Nell shrugged again. 'I don't know. She didn't stick to it. She didn't talk about it much.'

'Were her family pro-choice too?'

Nell laughed, Adrienne frowned.

'No. There was no such thing,' Nell said. 'No one talked about that stuff. Not when I was young, and definitely not when Dolores was young.'

Nell was starting to feel herself go red. She felt a little

panicky. She felt guilty, constantly, for not thinking or feeling the thing you were supposed to think or feel about this issue. She was never happier not to be living in Ireland as she was at that time.

'So she went against her family? That's incredibly brave, Nell,' Adrienne said. She took a stern sip of her by-now warm white wine.

Nell looked at her, feeling that she loved the way she got so irate about things. She reached out her hand to brush her fingers against Adrienne's plump wrist; she noticed there was a little hollow in the bone just below her thumb.

Adrienne pulled her hand away.

'I want to meet her,' she said. 'I won't understand you until I meet her.'

As time went on, Adrienne's unstoppable ambition also caused troubles for the couple. She wanted to build her own food-styling brand, she wanted to be the go-to behind-the-scenes person for any new food entrepreneur, the person who made those Instagram images look so invitingly dishevelled. At first Nell much admired her pragmatic approach to celebrity and fame – Adrienne had zero interest in being the kind of person who was stopped in the street and she treated her social media as part of her work, not as part of her *self* – and she seemed to understand, way before anyone else did, how damaging, how embarrassing it was to confuse one's own private self for one's online persona. In essence, she seemed to be careful about drawing lines between things and this was attractive and comforting to Nell, who never stopped feeling borderless and permeable, so much so that she didn't even have a Facebook profile any more – it demanded far too much – let alone a Twitter or Instagram account.

Of course, Nell couldn't resist taking something of a superior attitude towards those who did let social media dictate the shape of their thinking, and given the circles they increasingly moved within, it wasn't long before Adrienne spotted and scrutinized this attitude and diagnosed it, more correctly, as a site of great insecurity and fear. Upon so doing, Adrienne felt prompted to explore what the hell Nell was doing with her life, anyway. To Nell, this was a startling turn of events – she had not had to explain herself to anyone about anything more contentious than when the rent might be due, for the best part of a decade – and she had no words with which to defend herself. So she attacked Adrienne for being materialistic and shallow, for caring only about her profile, for being fame-obsessed, for basing her life around things that were flimsy and worthless and dumb. And here of course she struck a little too close to a truth – Adrienne *did* love the lifestyle that went along with being associated with those known to the public, she *did* follow a lot of ridiculously ostentatious interior decorating accounts, she *would* have given her right arm for a three-storey town house in Primrose Hill or – let us be realistic, even in our dreams – on one of the fancier streets in Peckham.

'You are a *stylist* for *celebrity food-bloggers*,' Nell said, at the drunken tail end of one of these most vicious of rows. 'You don't get to lecture *anyone* on their choices.'

'*Choices?* What *choices?*' Adrienne returned, furious, cheeks aflame, sweaty. 'You haven't made a single choice in your entire life. You are a *child*.'

'Well, isn't that what you're looking for?' Nell returned, coldly, horribly, humourlessly. Adrienne had at that point barely broached the topic but it was there, it was in the atmosphere, the idea of this baby, terrifying, diffuse, gestative, and Nell, by pointing to it, by scorning it, humiliated Adrienne in a way that felt shocking and unforgivable.

This led to a cooling-off period of some weeks, during which Adrienne stayed with her parents out in New Malden and Nell paced the flat alone, feeling like she was drowning in her own company. Her last flatmate had moved out without her really noticing, she and Adrienne had at that point been living together for around a year, using the spare room as a home office for Adrienne. It was a truism of that time that it was good to *talk about it*, that there was no shame in struggling with one's mental health, and Nell thought that if she had to listen to another hot blonde TV presenter talk about her struggles with anxiety she might – ironically – kill herself. In truth, she was terrified of telling Adrienne about the time she had spent in psychiatric care; in truth, she was absolutely petrified of what might happen to her if she opened the box where she stored all of the memories of what had happened. She felt an urge to bite into something hard, like the edge of the table, or to tear her own fingernails off.

Those few weeks without Adrienne were a living nightmare – she had never felt anything like it in her life. She had never been properly in love before – unless Pilar counted, and she found it difficult, then, to admit that she did – and so she had never felt this most mainstream kind of heartbreak. She'd felt so many other kinds of it, but not this, its most celebrated iteration. She barely slept and walked around in a wordless stupor. At work — she was then working in a Mexican restaurant close to Covent Garden — she went through the motions of prepping, chopping, assembling with the sense that she was outside of her body, watching it with a flat disinterest. At the end of her shift, she sat and drank with the staff, feeling the alcohol numb her in the way that it always did, in the way that she had to be so cautious of. She'd never given up the booze but she did keep an eye on it — she loved drinking too much to lose it — but now for the first time in years, she let it all go, she drank and drank and drank until she fell into bed and pissed herself.

The temptation of the gutter, the temptation of the life of a committed drunk. There was a dignity in refusing to strive, in refusing the farce that was the performance of day-to-day life, and it was appealing to her. She left her phone on the Tube on one of those days — she was riding the Tube mindlessly in the hours before work started, she didn't have anywhere to go or anything to do — and in the kerfuffle of losing it and then finding it again with the assistance of a softly spoken TFL worker, she started quietly weeping, and the man, the TFL man, said to her, 'I am so sorry for all of your troubles.' It made her laugh, just the cadence of his voice, the poetry in his phrasing, and it made her recognize that her troubles were indeed just that — troubles — and as such negotiable in some way, and she got to work and was all right again for a few hours.

Presently, Adrienne came back to her and they were reconciled, and in the relief and joy of all of that, the issues at the heart of the disagreement were forgotten, but of course they did not go away. Adrienne wanted a biography – she wanted to know what had happened and when and in what order. It was difficult to resist Adrienne's instinct to wrap it all up in an, *oh that was just Ireland, oh so backward, oh so Catholic*; Nell was vaguely offended by this but also relieved. How could she explain that in fact she had sought out the Catholicism, that the normal thing for someone of her age to do was to reject it, to ignore it, to laugh at it? That it had been all her fault for falling for that ridiculous mumbo-jumbo, that no one had shamed her or forced her or scared her into it? That every single one of the terrible things that had happened had been entirely her fault?

Adrienne knew enough, Nell reckoned. But then, she decided, they decided, to try for a baby. And this decision brought a steely clarity to Adrienne's view of their world. It was not right, she said, to bring a child into a family home full of skeletons in the closet and unspoken secrets and all of that nonsense. It was unnecessary, the suffering it led to, the misunderstandings it bred. Adrienne had done therapy herself, years before, and she was a great advocate of its efficacy. Nell defensively said that she'd done some too, but she didn't want to say anything more about it – therapy was one thing; sedation and nervous breakdowns were another.

Adrienne said that being an unconventional family as they were, it was even more important and with this, Nell could not argue. Privately, she had thought it would take for ever for Adrienne to get pregnant, privately she thought she could just go along with it and it would turn out to be too financially and emotionally ruinous, and they could get back to their own life. But it happened on their second cycle and Nell's reaction – absolute terror – was one that she could not fully hide. What the cause of this fear was, Adrienne was determined to find out.

24

It's a beautiful day when Nell finally comes home. A blazing hot July day in London, the heat pumping out of the brick and the concrete, she often at this time of year likes to stop and place her palm against the heat of the structures around her, it makes her feel calm. But they are in a rush that day, they are lugging bags down the stairs and onto their backs and onto the Tube to London Bridge and then the train to East Croydon and then on to Gatwick where they arrive amid throngs of holidaymakers – flip-flops, tiny shorts, kids riding wheeled suitcases shaped like animals.

'We should have got an Uber,' Nell says when they arrive and Adrienne harrumphs, indeed they should have, it had not occurred to Nell and then she feels guilty – what kind of woman is too cheap to get a cab for her pregnant girlfriend? She is supposed to be gallant, she supposes, but she forgets. She hasn't been conditioned in gallantry, has she? She feels bad about the way her tendency to float away, to not-listen, to extract herself mentally from wherever she physically is makes life hard for the people around her – for the person around her, Adrienne, her partner, her lover, her (and she will never say this because she can never think it) *wife*.

Adrienne wants them to get married. Nell is torn between the relief she feels in having found someone who wants to remain with her, tethered to her, and the fear – 'The fear of what?' Adrienne asks, and asks, and asks, and Nell cannot really say. But the fear that by tying herself to so hardy, so weighty a set of ideas as *married*, as *wife*, that she would expose a flimsiness that Nell feels inherent to the condition of her being her. She still feels that she is, at the bottom of her soul, nothing. And that's why she can't marry Adrienne, that's why she can't even stay present with her in the bustle and thrum of the airport as they go to see if they can unload their carry-on luggage at check-in.

Nell has not travelled much in her life. She went on a few Ibiza trips with some of her wilder friends back in her wilder days, and was persuaded on a trip to New York with Jenny once which had been fun, kind of, but she avoids travel overall. There's too much pressure to have a good time. She doesn't even like getting out of the city – the English countryside holds no interest for her, she loathes the cute little towns that you have to stay in in order to access it, and besides, she can't drive and train tickets cost a fortune.

What she doesn't say is that being outside London makes her feel exposed, makes her feel visible. It makes her feel like the only person standing in a great yawning expanse. The city is full of nooks and crannies, the city is full of places to hide.

Adrienne, upon discovering Nell's travel reticence, is initially highly amused by it and then gets them on a rotation of city breaks – Paris on the Eurostar, Lisbon, Florence, and Brussels, randomly, to see a friend, the food so bad they talk about it for years afterwards. Nell finds that walking around a beautiful city with someone you love, when the business of that someone is to know the best and most lovely things, well, she finds that travel can actually be quite bearable after all. And now, finally, they are getting on a flight to, in Nell's opinion, the least interesting of the foreign capitals close to them, the city where she enjoyed her most ordinary failures.

'You could still be a doctor if you wanted,' Adrienne would say. 'But it doesn't matter to me. It won't make you a better person.'

Adrienne should have been a politician, she is a charismatic speaker with the ability to make her listener – Nell – feel both *seen* (as the culture was beginning to say) but also challenged, emboldened, *empowered* (as it had been saying for ages, when would it stop?). The trouble is, these feelings don't last and the trouble is, if you listen to those kinds of speeches all of the time, they just become background noise, and the foreground noise becomes what it always is – *you're shit, you're crap, you're wrong, you're nothing*. That's the tune that never goes away and Adrienne's speechifying is starting to make her seem like some kind of frenzied kids' entertainer, trying to distract the inconsolable child who just wants its mother.

She thinks she'd gotten to the bottom of it, Adrienne does. They have done the therapy, Nell has told her what happened, she's told her almost everything. Adrienne had already known about the loss of the baby, but she hadn't known how she'd gotten herself pregnant, she hadn't known about Pilar. She hadn't known about the breakdown during the UCD years. Nell feels proud of herself, for all that she has given Adrienne.

The telling of it all opened up new depths of understanding between them. Nell feels grateful to Adrienne for understanding her attraction to the movement, she doesn't think it's stupid or pathetic to have been interested in a more spiritual way of life, to have gone towards things everyone else was moving away from. Adrienne in fact seemed to think that was kind of lovely. She tells Jacob about it, and they all discuss it together, and he tells Nell how it felt for him, to come from the strict Christian world he came from, and to accept his feelings around his sexuality but to also know that he could never cut loose from the faith of his family and culture. He says he is glad that Nell has a spiritual side, he said he thinks it important that they have values in common, given how unconventional their arrangement is. All of this bonds the three of them together, Madeleine is very pleased about it when they tell her.

Liam is picking them up at the airport. Nell feels grumpy as she gets off the plane, her skin prickling in protest against the always-ten-degrees-below-whatever-it-is-in-London temperature. In arrivals, she feels a thump of love as her eyes settle on her dad – he is waiting for them, starched, upright, trim; he's probably been there half an hour already though their flight landed on time. He is of average height, her father, with a thrumming, energetic presence. He does triathlons and still sometimes works on building sites, though these days he mainly services boilers.

He likes Adrienne very much. They are temperamentally

alike: pragmatic, organized, fun-loving, more or less immune to anxiety that isn't related to immediate material threat. This is only the second time they've met but they greet each other like old friends. Nell is surprised to see what she thinks are tears in his eyes as he says something about Adrienne's growing bump – she is seven months now, it is there, it is happening.

Adrienne sits in the front as she is prone to car sickness and Nell shuts her eyes and tries to doze as they chat and Adrienne talks about Jacob, saying that he is a Londoner like her and so he would be around because Londoners didn't leave London, but he wouldn't be around too much because it took at least an hour to get anywhere in London and he didn't live locally to them, he lived in a part of the city that would for ever be far too expensive for them to live in. Liam laughs, and says, 'Well, this is the world we live in, and it's great, isn't it.' Nell senses from him an unease that she feels in herself and she wishes for the millionth time in her life that she wasn't the way that she is. And then she feels guilty for that wish, it's not an acceptable one to have in this new land of shamrocks and rainbows.

But it is impossible not to be joyful in the presence of a woman expecting a baby and this joy that bounces between Liam and Dolores and Jenny when they arrive home bounces off Nell too, and she feels, for a while, that she could be happy, actually, she really could. Adrienne is very good at being pregnant; she has the shiny hair, the nice skin, and the ailments – heartburn, some insomnia – are minor enough to cause smiles rather than concern. Nell tells herself that if she can just continue like this, it will be okay.

Before dinner, Nell suggests that they take a nap, it has

been a long day and Adrienne is surely tired. 'I'm not actually,' Adrienne says. 'I want to see the town. Can we go for a walk?'

Nell feels an old dread. She tries to ignore it, she tries to say, yes, let's go. But then Jenny steps in and says, 'Let me take Adrienne, Nell, if you're tired.' Her sister is a beautician now, she is tall and strong and engaged to a strapping young man from out the country. They are building a house on his family's land, Nell has seen the plans, it's enormous, in the middle of nowhere. She pictures it like a castle and Jenny its long-haired princess. It makes her anxious, the thought of it, it makes her own self seem so meagre in comparison. But she can never imagine being so bold, being so sure, as to build a house like that.

Nell lies in her room, she tries to sleep. Her parents have thoughtfully replaced her single bed with a double. The room feels entirely different, it's been repainted, it feels bland, neutral. She thinks about what Jenny will be talking to Adrienne about, she figures it will be a nice chat about TV and celebrities and restaurants. She thinks it would be hard to broach anything beyond that.

The next day is sunny, and Nell thinks maybe she and Adrienne could go to the beach for the day, it's not that far. When she suggests this, Adrienne looks at her like she's crazy. 'We've come to see your family,' she says.

It's a Monday and Jenny and Liam are working, though both say they will finish early, that they will all go out to eat together later. Nell and Adrienne eat a late breakfast and afterwards Dolores brings them tea. She is trying to give them space, Nell notices, but she wants to be close to them. Adrienne must notice this too because she invites her to sit with them. Adrienne talks about how nice the town is, how she enjoyed seeing it. She says she likes to imagine Nell there as a young person growing up.

'I kept thinking about you and your friends in your movement,' she says. 'It's so cute to think of you all.'

'So you know about all that, Adrienne?' Dolores says. 'Nell told you?'

'Yes,' Adrienne says. 'It took a while but she did tell me.'

'About Daniel too?' Dolores says. Nell looks at her. She feels, for a moment, bewildered. She feels for a moment that she doesn't know what her mother is talking about.

'Nell's boyfriend?' Adrienne says. 'Yes, but actually I don't know what happened to him. Are you still in touch with him, Nell? He probably has other kids by now.' She reddens a little then, for having referred so casually to the lost baby, Nell thinks. She is so thoughtful, Adi is. She genuinely cares about people.

Dolores is still watching Nell. Her face looks clear, it looks open. It reminds Nell of how it looked when she told her about the pregnancy, all those years ago. For a moment, Nell hates her mother, for all her honesty, for all her innocence.

'And Martina? Did you tell Adrienne what's happened to her?' Dolores says. Her tone is hard and Nell is surprised at this. Her mother never gets angry at her. Nell doesn't feel defensive, she doesn't feel anything. Except again this confusion, this unravelling. Why have they come here? she thinks, mildly.

'Martina's been very unwell,' Dolores says, moving her gaze

to Adrienne. 'She's been in and out of the psychiatric unit at the hospital. I think she's at home at the moment, but she's not working or anything. Her mother and sister are looking after her.'

'Isn't the movement taking care of her?' Adrienne asks. 'I thought it was like being in a convent or something.'

'She left it,' Dolores says shortly.

There's a silence. Nell feels as if she is on the edge of a large hollow.

'Why not go and see her, Nell?' Adrienne said. 'While we're here? It might help her. She must feel very alone. It was her whole life, that organization, wasn't it?'

Nell watches Dolores. She feels as if they are playing a game here. But she doesn't know what side she's on, she doesn't know what the point of it all is. She feels a pressure in her head, she sees a foot slipping in the mud.

'Why would I?' Nell says and her voice is throaty. 'I haven't seen her since I was a teenager. She probably doesn't even remember me.'

Dolores laughs then. It is a horrible, angry laugh. 'For fuck's sake, Nell. You know that's not true. I told you that she wanted to see you. I told you that she keeps asking for you.'

Adrienne looks from one to the other again.

'I always have this feeling that Nell is keeping something from me, Dolores,' she says. Her voice sounds clear and English and uncontaminated. 'She told me about the movement, and about losing the baby. And about falling in love with Pilar, and dropping out of uni. But there's something else too, isn't there, Dolores?'

'Daniel,' Dolores says, and suddenly there are tears on her

cheeks. 'You didn't tell her about Daniel? Why wouldn't you tell her that? Nell, why wouldn't you tell her that?'

Nell puts her head on the table.

'I can't,' she says. 'You tell her.'

After his death, Nell dreamt often of the play.

He took the role of Demetrius, the one who is twice fooled. At the beginning of the play, Demetrius is in love with and betrothed to Hermia, but she is in love with Lysander and he with her. Demetrius is pursued by Helena, but he is indifferent to her. After the fairies do their meddling, Demetrius finds himself in love with Helena, but Lysander is now in love with her too, also due to the meddling. Helena thinks they are making fun of her and that they both still really love Hermia.

This is the best part of the play. Everyone understands what it's like to suspect you are being made a fool of. Everyone knows there is nothing worse than someone pretending to be in love with you in order to humiliate you. In Nell's production, they cut back whole chunks of dialogue from other parts (no one cares, frankly, about Titania and Oberon) but this part, they follow to the letter. It thrilled Nell to direct this part — she felt so clever, understanding Shakespeare, telling her mother how playful Shakespeare was, saying that he probably had people their age in mind when he wrote Helena and Hermia. Nell especially liked the part where Hermia talks about what good friends she and Helena were at school.

Daniel was good as Demetrius. The boy who played Lysander was more dashing, more strutting — so Nell got Daniel to be gentler, humbler. It bothered her though, the asymmetry of the ending. Lysander and Hermia end up together because the natural order is restored but Helena and Demetrius find their joy only through artificial, fairy means. It never felt quite right to her, it feels off-balance, half-finished, the stability implied by the triumphant ending not quite restored. But who is she to argue with Shakespeare?

And so, after Daniel's death, she dreamt of him moving through an afterlife, a forest, for ever searching for the real love implied but not delivered by the play. She told Martina that and Martina told her that he was in heaven, he was with God and so whatever love he was searching for he surely found. And Nell said, didn't Catholics think suicide means you don't get to go to heaven? Martina said, no, it didn't, of course it didn't, they didn't say that, not any more. And Nell said, well, it didn't matter because she didn't believe in anything any more anyway. There was no heaven and he was not there.

25

'Did you really think she was never going to find out?' Dolores says. 'Did you really think that?' They are driving out to Michaela's farmhouse and she is talking rapidly, rhetorically. The scene the day before has unleashed something in her. She seems unbound. She has not mentioned Daniel in over a decade and now she is referring to him and all that happened as if they talk about it all the time. Nell looks out the window of the passenger seat. She does not answer her mother. She is hungover, and her body feels weak and uninhabited.

Adrienne was very upset, and very angry after Dolores told her about Daniel the morning before. The rest of the day was awkward and tense. It occurred to Nell that going to see Martina might stabilize things. She suggested it to her mother, her mother called Michaela, and Nell went to tell Adrienne that it had all been arranged for the next day. As she looked at her, she felt like a child, bringing some pathetic token to her parents for praise. Adrienne looked confused for a moment but then she nodded and said, it's a good idea, it's the right thing to do. She spoke vaguely; she looked beyond Nell as she spoke.

Michaela's farmhouse smells like turf and old bread. It hits Nell in the heart as she walks in and it reminds her of the smell of a tiny corner shop near her flat in Kennington, the kind of shop that sells shrivelled bananas and doesn't take card. Michaela welcomes them with a grasping of their hands – Nell remembers that she actually had met her once before at a Mass, and she is briefly shocked to see how old she is now. Her hands shake, she walks uncertainly, her skin hangs from her face, she wears scarlet lipstick, a long flowing black skirt, a purple shawl.

They sit at the kitchen table while Dolores and Michaela chat. The kitchen is at the back of the house and dark; there are flush green trees outside the window, big empty fields beyond it. Dolores knows exactly how to talk to an old lady like this, and Nell feels like an adolescent as she listens. She thinks that these people are her people, this is the kind of place she belongs, the kind of place she should belong. The farm is run on a part-time basis by Lucy's husband, Michaela tells them, and it's grand, so it is – Lucy is in to her every day, and her grandkids too.

'I'm feeling well in myself despite me oul face,' Michaela says, 'and sure I can hardly see it so what does it matter.'

Michaela is interested to hear Nell's tales of London, she says she'd been once herself, a great town, lovely people, the English, once you got to know them. Dolores tells Michaela that Nell's girlfriend is having a baby, that they were expecting it in the autumn, through a sperm donor.

'A sperm donor, would you believe, Michaela,' Dolores repeats loudly, to ensure the old lady hears. Michaela grins widely in a display of neat grey teeth and holds out a shaking hand to Nell.

'You'll never forget the days your babies are small,' Michaela says and Dolores murmurs a gentle acquiescence. They grow quiet for a moment as if something is settling between them. Michaela then fixes her attention on Nell. Her small eyes narrow and she looks curious and shrewd.

'Martina talks about you,' she says. 'She talks about you all the time. Do you know why that is?'

Nell feels every *you* like a jabbing finger in her face. Her thoughts wheel through her brain. Various images arise in her mind, they have no connection to where she is, or what question she has been asked. She looks back at Michaela and she feels that on her face she has an expression of confusion, and that this expression is an appropriate response to the question.

She nods when Michaela asks her if she'd like to go upstairs to see her.

Martina's bedroom faces the front of the house, and it is full of light and trembling shadows from a big tree outside her window. The bed is high and old-fashioned, the bedlinen white and fresh and well worn. At the foot of the bed, there is a chest of drawers with a framed photograph of Martina with some young children – her nieces and nephews, perhaps. The window is open, the clouds outside are stirring. The breeze outside and the bluster of the clouds give Nell a sense of being at the still heart of some kind of turbulence, she feels like she can't quite hear properly.

Martina herself is sitting on a chair at the foot of the bed.

She does not get up when Nell enters the room, though she responded with a clear *Yes, come in* to her knock. She looks at the younger woman and a flicker of confusion passes over her face, and then one of apprehension. Nell feels herself strong and powerful suddenly. She feels like a bully, come to loom over a smaller, weaker child. Martina is tiny, she notices. Shorter than her, and very thin. Was she always so thin?

'Hi, Martina,' she says. 'It's good to see you.'

She looks almost exactly the same, except her dark hair is now almost fully grey and her eyes, once so full of certainty, are now faltering and vague. They do not rest on her face as she responds to her. Her pupils are large and dark. Her face is blurrier, it has lost its elfin look, its darting, nimble quality.

'Hello,' Martina says. 'It's good to see you too.' There is a terrible poignancy in how she speaks, Nell can feel a dignity trying to assert itself, but one that doesn't quite believe in itself.

Nell sits on the end of the bed.

'How are you feeling?' she says. 'Your mother tells me you haven't been very well.'

'That's true,' Martina says. 'I've been in a bit of a state, they tell me.' There is humour in her voice and Nell feels a flicker of relief.

'You look the same,' she says.

'I never change,' Martina says. 'Sure he won't let me.'

'What?' Nell says. She doesn't understand what she means. But she starts to feel the blood gather in her brain, she starts to feel as if the outside world is disappearing around her.

'He's always there,' Martina says. 'Always by my side. Even when I don't want him.' She laughs then, a wistful little sound. 'I mean, of course it's not that I'd ever not want him.'

Nell says nothing. The bed beneath her is soft, she has a sudden sense of sinking into it, of being buried in it.

'He's still the same too. Not that I ever really knew him. That was the whole point, that I didn't *know* him. I feel like I do now though, Nell.'

It's the first time she's said her name. It strikes an odd note of clarity. It sounds clear as a bell.

'He forgives me, by the way,' she says. 'At least, I think he does.'

She is still sitting on the chair, she is speaking very calmly. But she's not looking at Nell any more, she's looking out the window, out at the trees. Beyond the farm there is a small woodland, Nell walked it once years ago, it had been spring, it had been full of bluebells and tiny white flowers shaped like stars.

'What are you talking about, Martina?' Nell says. The sound of her own voice makes her flinch but the harshness in it calms her a little, it brings her back into the room, it brings her out of the sense of sinking, of burial.

Martina turns from the window and smiles very gently at her. She looks at her like she used to years ago, when Nell was struggling with some facet of life and she was standing above her, showing her how everything was all right, how everything was possible.

'He told me that he forgives you too,' Martina says.

Dolores was getting her hair done in town the day Daniel's body was found. She saw the woman who took the calls and the appointments answer the phone, she saw her hand touch her chest, she heard her ugly gasp and then her frail, broken cry. The woman was the boy's aunt, Connie's sister, Dolores realized later. The word spread around the salon quickly and Dolores went cold. No one seemed to know about her connection with the family or if they did they were too shocked to think of it. She told the girl drying her hair that she had to go, the girl was blinking absently into the middle distance, Dolores dropped cash on the counter and left.

It had barely been two months since they had told him about the pregnancy. After the initial meeting with his mother, Dolores had tried to create some distance between her family and theirs. She understood that Nell didn't want to reignite their relationship and Dolores had – she now realized – begun to think of him as something of a nuisance, a complicating factor in an already complicated situation. Once she had gotten over the shock of Nell's pregnancy, she had surprised herself at how quickly she had adapted to the new reality, how easy it had been to go into practical mode. She had not given much thought to the boy at all.

And then, when the baby died, Daniel seemed even more like a jigsaw piece that didn't fit. She knew he was bothering Nell, trying to get in contact with her, and she knew Nell didn't want that.

Dolores stood outside the hair salon feeling the world sway. She felt, she tasted, for a terrible second, the bewilderment and hurt he must have felt. How could she have just brushed him aside like that, how could she have omitted him from all of the many permutations of ideas and feelings and thoughts that had wheeled through her mind in the last few months?

Nell had only just returned to school. After the loss of the baby, she stayed at home for two weeks, and then, before

Liam or Dolores dared suggest it, she appeared one morning in the kitchen, her uniform on, her face scrubbed and defiant and hopeful. She did not enter back into any other realm of her life, she returned home promptly every day and stayed in her room until dinnertime. She said she had loads to catch up on, she said she was fine. None of her friends called to the house, she did not go to theirs.

Dolores drove towards the girls' school. She had not returned to her work there that term because she had thought she was going to be looking after the baby. At the office reception, she asked that Nell might be allowed home, she didn't offer an excuse. Some small talk was attempted – she knew the office staff well, of course – but she rebuffed it.

After a few moments, her daughter appeared and Dolores's heart swelled as she watched her approach her down the corridor. Nell smiled at her mother, which was a surprise, she had not smiled in weeks, a heartbreakingly unexpected little moment of love, it destabilized her for a moment, it sent her reeling, for a second. But there was no time. She had to tell her fast, before she heard it from one of her friends, the kids spread news on their phones like wildfire.

So she told her in the car park of the shopping centre across the road from the school. She just couldn't risk the short time it would take to drive home. It felt like the greatest urgency in the world, to tell her before anyone else did, and once she had done it, she felt relieved, for a second. But then rushed in the next feeling which was anguish on behalf of Connie. She watched Nell, but she thought of Connie. She couldn't fathom what her daughter was feeling. She could feel all too vividly what Connie was feeling.

Nell sat very still in the front seat. She turned to her mother with a look of confusion. She said she didn't understand. She said it simply, as if she were saying no to something. Dolores looked out the window and thought that she could in some universe be angry with Daniel for doing this. She often felt anger, when she heard stories of when kids did this. They had no idea what they were doing; they had no idea, none at all, of the kind of torment they were leaving behind. But she did not feel anger.

The atmosphere in the car was thick and rigid. Dolores tried to see her daughter, tried to feel her way towards her. She reached out her hand to her and stroked her hair. Nell watched her. There was a blankness in the moment. Dolores longed for a rush of tears. Nell's eyes were dry and staring.

'What did we do?' Nell whispered eventually. Her voice cracked, Dolores's face itched. She shook her head. She wanted to pretend she didn't know what Nell meant.

26

After Nell and Adrienne go back to London, Dolores is filled with a sense of dread. She had hoped that something had changed in Nell, that her relationship with Adrienne and the impending baby were such huge, momentous, wonderful, life-affirming changes it had to mean that Nell herself was healed, and had overcome whatever it was that was hurting her. But it hasn't, Dolores can see that, and it frightens her. She has this terrible feeling that something is amiss. Liam and Jenny, who are over the moon, who adore Adrienne, who just can't stop talking about the impending arrival, are irritated by her apprehension, which she does not articulate but which they recognize as well as they recognize their own faces in the mirror.

She does not tell them that Nell had not told Adrienne about Daniel. It's such incontrovertible evidence that things are not right, and she needs Liam and Jenny to believe things are okay. She can't face them knowing the full story – because she herself does not know what that full story is.

Dolores has changed her own life in some modest ways

since Nell went to London. In 2010, a few years into the uncertainty of the post-boom times, she heard someone on the radio talk about how going to therapy had helped them deal with the shame they endured as a result of losing all their money. Dolores had never considered anything like therapy or counselling before; she felt that she was fine, she'd always been fine, who was she to indulge in such a thing. But after hearing that interview, she realized she was bored to death of her own thoughts and that if she were going to live another thirty or so years – which was likely, given that she was only forty-eight and had long given up smoking – well, she might as well try and see if she could think of some new ones.

She had recently stopped selling sandwiches at the girls' school. After Nell went to London, it felt lonely and boring without her, she felt she'd done it long enough. She took some other bits and pieces of work – a hotel receptionist for a while, a cafe manager when a friend was on holiday – but there was not much work going, the town was quiet and bleak. Liam did any kind of work that could be found – cash in hand, generally – and they were okay, and so the forty euro per week she spent on the therapy felt like a permissible expense. What she wanted most of all was newness – she wanted someone to help her picture the future.

It was therefore a matter of some surprise to her that she spent most of the sessions with tears rolling down her cheeks talking about the past – her mother, her mother's death, the subsequent falling out with her sisters, the tentative reachings towards reconciliation, the loss of her brother Walter, the death of her father. All of these things had happened, she had let them wash over and through her; all these things happened to people all of the time, they were just to be borne, they were not to be discussed. She didn't know that they could be discussed. She inclined always towards effacement – *worse things happen to people*, she kept saying, *I have so much to be grateful for*.

'This is not what I was supposed to be talking about,' she said, after most sessions, and the therapist – a man, amazingly, called Diarmuid, from Cork, lovely accent, former teacher, bald in an endearing way – said that was a good sign and she said, 'Well, Diarmuid, you would say that, wouldn't you?'

She had to stop herself flirting with him, he was around five years younger than she was and very careful and wise.

She briefly considered trying to find another, less wonderful therapist (because she knew from American TV that falling in love with your therapist was something that happened and what a load of hassle that would have been) but she also knew good ones were hard to find, so she managed to control that part of her feelings. And it wasn't too hard, so interesting was she finding the new or maybe not new, maybe just buried, self Diarmuid was helping her to see.

He was very efficient. After a few sessions, she found that she had let go of some of the heaviness around her feelings towards her mother, and she made a determined effort to speak more regularly with her sisters, who, to her surprise, were receptive, who appreciated it. She had remained close to James, always, and Declan, somewhat, and she found that forgiving herself – *for what! For putting a tea towel over my head thirty years ago!* – she found that so doing, quietly, in her own mind, opened up the possibility of connection with her brothers and sisters in ways she could not have thought possible before. She threw a big party for her fiftieth birthday, they all came. They cried over Walter, as they had not done in years, as they had not done since it happened. They formed a new WhatsApp group, and they even used it.

And so then she tried to fix Nell. But that was not possible, Diarmuid said, because she could not control how Nell behaved or what Nell did.

'I just want her to let it go, to let herself be free of whatever it is that is tormenting her,' Dolores said. 'I just want to take it from her, I would give anything to do that, I want to rip it out of her hands.'

She stopped then, surprised at her own vehemence. And Diarmuid smiled the maddening, weary smile of someone who has to tell people every day that they must live with the pain of not being able to control the actions of those they love.

Despite this, after a year of seeing Diarmuid, her brain felt light and rearranged and it suggested to her that there was no reason she might not avail herself of one of the newly cheap commercial units in town and maybe try her hand at a more interesting kind of catering than anything she had done before. She had learned a lot from Nell's stories of London's kitchens over the years, and she surmised that you had to be careful not to scare people too much with what you thought they should be eating, but if you kept that carefulness in mind, then you could do new things.

She also learned that having a focus was a way to stand out. Nell snorted derisively at Irish menus that offered steak and lasagne and curry – what kind of cuisine is that, she'd say, and Jenny would make fun of her for being such a snob.

Dolores was not what anyone would think of as a foodie but it was a satisfying kind of puzzle, to try and think of a type of place that would be interesting to run and also make some money. So she briefly set up a fancy but not too fancy sandwich and coffee place on one of the small streets off the main street and it didn't work because no one had any money – it was a recession, for God's sake – but it was worth it for the energy she felt around it, and for the total lack of shame she felt when it didn't succeed.

That was exhilarating. 'Sure what was I thinking?' she said, beaming, to people who asked her about it and they blinked, unsure how to react, the sympathy they had on standby rendered redundant. It was of course a performance in some respects, she *was* anxious about what she was going to do next, she *did* worry that they wouldn't have enough money to help the girls get on the property ladder. Liam's new specialism – boiler-fixing – was proving stable and increasingly lucrative, so they were all right really, the house was paid off. But there was not much of a cushion and she had nothing much pension-wise at all.

She started a module on women's literature that was run through an offshoot of one of the universities newly located on the grounds of the boys' school, and it was enjoyable, kind of, but ultimately she found it quite depressing. So much writing about how boring being a woman was and how the mere fact of being female could drive you to madness. It was not what Dolores needed and she found the lecturer increasingly irritating in her determination to discover women's suffering everywhere she looked. She could not help but think about what Brigid would have to say about that way of looking at the world. She was also intimidated by some of the other people on the course, they could speak more fluently about theme and structure and meaning than she could, and she was reminded for the first time in years of what it had felt like to be around Annie and her friends and those days, and that was painful.

Interestingly and strangely, just when she was reminded of Annie, she appeared on the news again as the campaign around repealing the Eighth Amendment started to take over the airwaves. Dolores couldn't bear to listen to her, it was so painful and excruciating she almost went back to Diarmuid the therapist to talk about it. Annie was an academic at one of the universities and she was still the same, still exactly the same, except greyer, still with long hair and a wistful affect and a dreamy humour that was kind of endearing if you didn't know her but kind of unbearable if you did. She wasn't one of the main talking heads – she was too old, for one thing, the TV coverage seemed mostly interested in the younger, prettier campaigners, the ones who liked to boast about how they hadn't *even been born* when this amendment had been thrust upon them – but she did occasionally appear and it made it almost impossible for Dolores to engage with the issue itself.

She did eventually, in her own way. She saw that it was happening mainly online and she stayed away from that side of it. But she had to do her bit for the cause – and there was so much harping on about how they all had to do their bit for the cause. She joined in with a local group and that suited her much better, the kind of people who were brave enough to go knocking on doors and talking kindly to old ladies with

Sacred Heart icons in their hallways were the kind of people she could deal with, the kind of people she enjoyed being around. They were a nice crew, a couple of sweet-faced girls from the convent, a gay sixteen-year-old boy, and a few hardy matrons like herself. They had a lot of fun and the day itself came and went, and they won, hurray, historic, a new day, new Ireland, new future, etc. And all of that was good, as far as Dolores was concerned.

And what was also good around that time was the news from London. Dolores tried not to get too attached to the notion of Adrienne and then, after she met her on a short trip over with Liam, she tried not to get too attached to the reality of her and as time went on and she and Nell endured, she tried not to hope too much.

Because Dolores wakes up every day of her life with a feeling of worry around Nell, the pain is like a muscle that aches with overuse. It is, at this juncture, more than thirty years into being Nell's mother, basically impossible to try and see the relationship for what it is – it's too big to hold and examine, she can't gain a foothold in it, she can't climb to the top of it and see what the hell she is standing on. She knows that Nell is angry at her in some deep foundational way, and she wants to atone, she would get on her knees and stay there for as long as is needed but she doesn't know what she is atoning for and maybe that's it. The not-knowing is what is unacceptable to Nell, she feels, and to confess is to imply a knowledge of what the sin itself actually is and so she can't confess and so she can't be forgiven.

So this state of ostensible, provisional, nervy contrition is the one she found herself operating from in relation to her eldest daughter, until Adrienne came, and then Nell was so happy that her anger seemed to have gone away and contrition was thus unnecessary. And that was wonderful, but it was too wonderful, and Dolores sees, on the girls' first trip home together, that the anger has started to seep back into Nell and that the imminent baby is not the cause of it but might – oh god, let her not think this, how could she let herself think it – but the imminent baby might be the one to suffer the most from it. A cold, angry parent, a parent tyrannical in their unhappiness – these are not things children can endure, Dolores knows this, she feels a panic in her knowing of this.

This thought chills her heart. As she drives back from Michaela's farmhouse that day in July with Nell lying on the back seat hungover, white-faced, shaken by something, shaken by whatever it is that's driven Martina Power mad, Dolores lets herself flood with that same old fear and that same old dread.

27

Martina is forty-seven that year. Her birthday is 1 January, and she's always loved it; it feels like a hushed, special time, just after the shortest day of the year, just as the light starts to grow again.

That birthday is the first in twenty-five years she has not spent with her hogareñas. She had been living at home in her mother's farmhouse for around nine months by then, trying to figure out what she was going to do with the rest of her life, trying to figure out what was going to happen to her, trying desperately to hear the voice of God within her, the voice she used to feel so overwhelmingly, so clearly. It had gone quiet and all she felt was an emptiness so dense that it sat in her stomach and made it hard for her to eat properly and sometimes even breathe.

That was maybe what had started the panic, the feeling that she was being choked from within. And then, the build-up to the referendum and the relentless talk on the radio and the TV began. Women and pain and the way they had to kill their babies in order to protect themselves, in order to be free. All of that coming from outside of her, building up on top of her, burying her, it sometimes flashed in her mind – that vision of Johnny falling on top of her like a tree. So these two forces, the dense emptiness within and the burying from without, meant that days went by and she did not eat anything. She could not eat anything. No one noticed, her poor mother was too short-sighted to notice anything much at all.

And so Martina felt herself float. Squeezed out between these two sources of pressure, all that was left was a tiny slip of being, a scrap of spirit, an almost nonentity. She lay day after day in her room watching the light crack over the fields at dawn and at the chokingly early dusk and it was all fine, all she had to do was witness things, wasn't it? That's all she was here for, after all. When she slept, her dreams were bonkers, sometimes vividly sexual, sometimes broken and jagged, and then, full of Nell and the boy. She remembered how Nell had told her that she dreamt of him after he died, of him being in a forest. Martina then found herself in that forest alongside him, both of them exiled, walking through an endless spring.

It was Lucy who saved her, Lucy who said to her, *Martina, Martina, when did you last eat something, Mammy, what the fuck is going on here?* Lucy who brought her into the hospital where a bed was found and where she was found to be suffering a nervous breakdown and where she was sedated wonderfully and blissfully and where she resumed her acquaintance with the boy. He was so beautiful to her, he had sandy hair and brown eyes, and he was mischievous and full of messing.

She knew what he looked like from the funeral, from the photograph that had been displayed by the closed coffin. She had attended, she'd sat at the back. Nell had been there, she'd sat with her parents. Nell had seen her, she had looked through her. Martina had felt nothing that day. She couldn't.

Afterwards, she went to the head of the movement in Ireland and said they had to send her away. She went to Spain and worked in a centre belonging to the movement there, she felt tough and resolute, she felt God was on her side. God did not approve of the modern world, nor did she. They could hide, in the clear blue mountain town, she, and God, and her faith. But year after year after year, her toughness wore down, until she realized – God was not with her at all. She was a shell, protecting something that was not there.

Eating was the main problem, back in her mother's house, back in Ireland. She couldn't eat more than a few mouthfuls. She was told by one of the nurses that the anorexics were the most difficult of all the patients they had to deal with, and if she didn't watch it she was going to end up like them, and because she associated anorexia with a desire to be thin and since she had never cared about fat or thin or anything, she figured it would be very confusing for everyone if she were to be grouped in with them. So, she forced herself to eat while secretly in her mind she couldn't think or focus on anything except her endless thoughts about the boy. She wished she knew someone who had known him, she wanted to talk about him the way she used to want to talk about Jesus.

She gained enough strength, enough weight, enough grip on reality to go back home to the farmhouse. There, she teeters on the edge of her sanity. The weeks pass, the months pass, and the day of the referendum comes and goes, there's weeping on the streets, herself and her mother watch it together on the TV and Michaela says, 'Well, it's about time.' Martina didn't even vote, though Lucy came to the house to bring them both to the polling station — Michaela can no longer drive and Martina does not have a car, everything she once owned belongs to the movement. Martina declined and because they all know what her position on the subject is likely to be, they didn't push it. They don't argue with her either.

She feels them feeling sorry for her. She knows that they know she doesn't belong to this time, that she isn't of this time. They don't mind that about her; in some ways they love that about her. They love her the way she loves Niall, her brother, who spends most of his days living in a carefully run facility for people like him, he comes home only twice a month for the weekend, he speaks less and less. She finds it a comfort to be with him. She feels grateful to her family, and a glimmer of the old love, the old solid, sane love stirs within her. Lucy brings her books of puzzles from the local pharmacy, she says they'll help calm her thoughts.

She doesn't feel upset any more, about the way the world is going. She is beyond feeling anything ordinary like offence or anger or disappointment. She begins to feels curious, to feel detached, almost. The kind of language that the women on the news use and the kind of emotion they express and the kind of sisterhood they proclaim — it is an insight into a way of being that while alien to her in its detail is in fact not all that different when you zoom out a bit. She figures this is what it must have been like for her family when she first encountered the movement, when they first heard her use words like *Jesus in the midst* and *hermanas* and *my life with God*. But because she has left behind that idiom and because she will never be accepted by this new tribe, *bodily autonomy*, *choice* and *freedom* are notions as alien to her as the language of a different species – what is there for her now? Just her empty room, she supposes, and this sweet and terrible haunting.

She begins to talk again of Nell. She spoke of her before – back before she went into hospital, back before the thoughts of the boy took over. And she knows that she shouldn't, but she needs to stay away from talk of the boy, that's the most important thing. In the evenings, she and her mother play cards – it helped so much to have something solid to hold on to, something to do with her hands and to engage her brain with – and she talks about Nell. She asks Michaela if she ever sees Dolores around town. She has to stop herself from talking about her too much, it is evident to her that she's at risk of falling into the thick of another madness, and that surprises her. She had always supposed that the mad didn't know they were mad. But she knows she's losing it, she knows that reality is henceforth something she is going to have to struggle to remain immersed within.

Which is why she is unable to talk to Nell that day she finally arrives at the door of her bedroom. She wants to tell her that she feels that the boy forgives them, that in the quiet of the forest she meets him in, he seems peaceful, he seems joyful. She bites back those words because she doesn't want to frighten her away, she tries her best not to say them. But then she realizes she has said them, and that she has frightened the girl – the woman, the young woman, in the thick of her life, looking as driven and intense and unflinching as ever. She says those crazy, unsayable words and she frightens her away.

28

Timing is everything. This is true of the serving of food and it's true of love. Adrienne arrived in Nell's life when she was ready for her and that's why it felt possible, that's why it is possible. These are some of the lies Nell tells herself as the pregnancy progresses. Everything happens in time, everything happens for a reason.

When you are not reconciled to your existence, the way you live is by making as little impact on the world as possible. That's how she has survived: a person of little import is a person of little impact is a person who is safe, is a person from whom the world is safe. But that's not allowed any more. She is shortly to make a huge impact on the world by making a huge impact on a child.

She sees children, everywhere there are children. And everywhere there are their mothers. One day in the playground in the park opposite her flat she lets herself watch the mothers, watching their children. She notices how the mothers smile and talk to one another; she notices the way their glances flicker across to the play equipment; she realizes that no one sees the world as it is, in its own way, everyone sees it as enlivened by the thing, the person, they care most about. And no one cares more about anything, she can see that, than those mothers care about those children.

She knows she can love like that. That's not the problem.

At a rooftop bar in Peckham is where Nell feels at her lowest, at her emptiest, at her drunkest and it's where she tells Amanda, the only soul she can trust, that she doesn't want the baby, that she's terrified of the baby, that she feels she doesn't deserve the baby. Amanda shakes her head, she is not surprised. She could sense it, she's not an idiot. But she's not sympathetic, Nell can see that, and why would she be.

Amanda tells her that it's too late now, she needs to cop herself on – a phrase she, of course, got from Nell – and man up and be there for her family. Nell is happy to hear her say that, it's better than fake sympathy, but the words just slide off her. She gets home late and drunk and Adrienne doesn't even bother getting annoyed. Nell feels herself slipping away, she wonders if she'll be able to do anything to stop it. She feels she is watching Adrienne too, waiting to see what happens next.

29

The small church near Michaela's farmhouse offers weekday Mass at 9.15 a.m. Part of the church was built in the 1300s, before the dissolution of the monasteries, before Cromwell, before O'Connell, before the Famine, before Independence, before – what's the next thing – before Repeal, Martina supposes. She thinks about that word a lot, it is everywhere, on T-shirts and tote bags and books and TV programmes. She thinks about it like a peeling back of layers of history, layers of days and weeks and years in the hope of finding something truer, something real.

On a cool rainy day in August, she goes to one of those morning Masses. There's just her and a few elderly people and a young woman she does not recognize. After the service, which is short, no sermon, she leaves without taking Communion and walks around the back of the church to the small garden. She touches the dark grey stone of the church, it is in shadow, it is very cold.

She cannot take Communion any more. That is because she has never confessed her sin, which is her original sin involving Nell and the boy, and then the countless times after that she had taken Communion without having confessed fully, without having confessed to that awful sin. She doesn't think she even believes in God any more but still she cannot not let go of the enormity of all she has done wrong. So she comes to Mass in a state of suffering without any expectation of redemption, she comes to Mass out of habit, she comes to Mass out of a lack of anything else to do.

It is not possible, at this time, to attend Mass at that small church every day without being noticed by the parish. One day, the priest, a middle-aged Polish man, calls to the farmhouse. He asks if she might be interested in training to be a Minister of the Eucharist. Martina tells him she is not. He asks if there is anything she would like to talk to him about. She tells him there is not.

She wonders if her mother has spoken to him, she would be annoyed if she could still feel feelings like that. Mostly she feels nothing, just a floating alienation, punctuated by occasional flashes of terror that this feeling of floating will lead her back to madness. She recalls the way cartoon characters float towards roasting hunks of meat in old-fashioned cartoons, led by the smell. That's how tempting this feeling is, how strong the pull. She tries her best to resist but it is delicious; and she is only human, which is to say, she now supposes, only animal.

Her mother says to her one day, 'Martina, would you not get a bit involved with the parish here? It might help you feel better. And they're not as intense as that other crowd.'

That other crowd is how Michaela now refers to the movement. Martina is brushing her mother's hair in the dark back kitchen. It is brittle and white. She uses one of those soft-bristled brushes that people use for babies, Lucy dropped it in.

'I can't, Ma,' Martina says. 'I don't believe any more. And I can't be involved in the Church if I don't believe that Jesus Christ is the son of God.'

'Sure what's that got to do with it?' Michaela says and she shrugs her slim, still elegant shoulders. 'I don't see what that's got to do with anything at all.'

Martina laughs at this. Her mother says that she's serious.

'It's all just words, Martina,' Michaela says. 'It doesn't have to be anything more than that.' Martina stiffens. It hurts, to hear her mother dismiss her whole life in this way, even if she herself can't defend it any more either.

Michaela turns around in the chair and looks up at her daughter. 'You have goodness in you, Martina. There's nothing you need to do, except let it be what it is.'

30

Nell tells Adrienne the full truth. She tells her one evening in August. She tells her because there is no more hiding and because the future is taking its shape around them, and if she doesn't try and grab on, it will pass her by. She tells her because there is a baby on the way.

They are sitting outside, on the back step in the summer dusk. The city hums around them, the air thick with sirens and pollution and the thump of far-off music. Nell couldn't tell her in any other place. It has to be here, in her flat, in this place she had found and made her own, and in which she sometimes manages to grow some parched herbs and a few straggly geraniums. This flat amounts to everything she has achieved. She doesn't own it, but that doesn't matter. It is an achievement, for her, to have stayed in the same place this long, to have held things together this long. She has a sense of things about to disintegrate but even if she does, she realizes, she has still managed to get here, to come this far. And she feels another surge of love then, for this city, the place that saved her.

Her head is heavy. It keeps lolling forward, towards her chest, and eventually she just holds it there. She tries to speak as clearly as she can from this folded, penitent position.

'It was a week or two after I lost the baby. I was still at home. I hadn't gone back to school yet. There was this terrible feeling in the house. No one knew how to feel or what to say. Jenny kept crying all the time.'

'And he kept texting me. Daniel did.

'He kept saying, are you okay? I'm worried about you.

'But I didn't want to talk to him.

'I couldn't look at him.

'It was everything I had to hide from. I had made this huge mess and I felt so guilty. And he wanted me to comfort him, and let him comfort me and maybe even get back together with him.

'When do you ever hear of a teenage boy grieving the loss of a baby he didn't even want? Where was he to go with that? What was he to do with all of that?'

She stops talking and tries to remember him as he had been. His friends barely out of their Lego. They wore football shirts as their Sunday best and talked only in traded insults. She lets herself remember that, she gathers the pain it causes, she starts talking again.

'And his mother. His mother was so angry with me, and I think with him too probably, I don't know.

'He kept ringing and texting and eventually he came to the house. And I was so angry when I saw him because he was so hurt!'

She pauses then, remembering that. Her feelings had been bound up in irritation as well as pain. It is shameful to remember how such a trivial feeling could have attended that moment also.

'I didn't want him to be hurt, Adi. But not for good reasons, not for kind reasons. I only wanted *me* to be hurt, I only wanted *me* to be sad. I couldn't cope with having made anyone else sad.

'He came into the house, we were in the front room. I remember how still it felt, but off-kilter. He said he loved me. He said he was heartbroken about what had happened to me and to the baby. He said he thought if we could just be there for each other then we could be okay.'

Nell looks up then and across Adrienne, as if through her, to another space.

'And then I just got angry. I thought about the sex and how drunk I'd been and how I hadn't wanted it. And then I said it. This is what I said, Adrienne. I said, you took advantage of me when I was drunk, you made me pregnant, this is all your fault. I said, our baby was made from you violating me and that's why it died. I said, our baby came from your violation and that is why it died.'

Nell stops speaking. She feels the need to gulp something, like air, like water. But she doesn't want to move.

'Adi, I said that. I said all of that and I said it, and it wasn't true. It wasn't true.

'He did not violate me. I violated *him* by pretending to care about him. I used him. I used him to get things that I wanted. I used him and misled him, I pretended to him that I cared for him. It was all lies and it was all in the service of my own agenda, my own desires.

'And not only did I do that, but then I went and said to him that he had violated me. I piled lie upon lie upon lie.

That's what I did, Adi. That's what I did, and no one knows. No one except Martina and now you. And it's what's driven Martina mad, and I think it might drive me the same way some day. That's what I'm afraid of. That's why I'm afraid about the baby. I'm afraid I deserve to be punished and something terrible is going to happen again, and that it will be about the baby. Our baby.'

Adrienne does not say anything. Nell knew that she wouldn't. Another person would rush in with comfort and excuses, but she knows Adi will not. That's why she loves her, and that's why she is going to lose her.

'Martina used that word when I told her I was pregnant,' Nell says. 'She was the first person I told about the pregnancy and she said I had been violated. I took that word from her. I didn't mean to but I did. I should have been brave enough to say, no Martina, it wasn't, it was my choice to do what I did. But I let her give me this word, this lie, and I took it. I didn't mean to use it but then it was there, I had it in my possession like a bad penny, and then I went and used it.

'Then I told him to leave me alone. I told him he wasn't wanted. I literally said those words, *you are not wanted*. Can you imagine being told that? *Not wanted*.'

She stops and lets herself feel that.

'And so he did. He did leave me alone, and then he went and left everyone alone.'

Nell looks at Adrienne. Her face is passive, as if she is thinking about something else. She reaches out her hand and strokes Nell's arm. She says that they should both get some rest.

★ ★ ★

Nell lies in the dark, looking at the ceiling. She senses from Adi a withdrawing. She feels that Adi has lost patience with her, she senses a terrible indifference from her. Maybe her secret, her lie, her shame – maybe it doesn't actually matter all that much to Adi. Maybe what will push her away is not the lie she told, but her impatience at Nell for not being able to get over this lie. Which maybe Adi thinks is trivial.

She realizes then that the idea of it being meaningless is worse than it being shameful. If it is meaningless, what she did, then nothing means anything. If it is meaningless, then any life that exists is also meaningless. She does not know how to hold on to reality in that kind of void. She thinks of Martina. She senses that there is a whole other level to this misery, and the fears deepen around her in the dark of the room.

The night goes on terribly. She senses Adi tense in the bed beside her, so she goes into the living room and sits on the couch. Her knees are knobbly and pale in the moonlight, she feels as if she is a very weak and small thing.

She thinks of the time after Daniel's death. It's another sliver of a moment, another crush of feeling and confusion. After she found out, after her mother told her, she went into a frozen state. She had to go to the funeral and she couldn't get a grip on what role she was supposed to play, how people were supposed to feel towards her. The drama of it all – the pregnancy, the loss of the baby, the death of Daniel – had happened so fast in the lives of her peers and many of them didn't know the full story, and so rumour was rampant and people looked at her with confusion and something she could not identify at first but then quickly realized was suspicion. There was also some pity – some people thought they were still together as a couple – and when those people spoke words of comfort and sympathy to her, she did not correct them, because she could not quite get a grasp on what it was they thought.

Then a rumour developed that she had pretended that she and Daniel were still together in order to *get attention*. This rumour thickened the existing brew of speculation around her – *Were they together when she got pregnant? Wasn't she part of some group that banned sex anyway? What happened after the baby died to make Daniel so sad? Did she get pregnant to keep him and then change her mind?* She felt all of these questions swirling around her, they seemed to form an impenetrable storm around her. In the days after the funeral, there was a drinking party at the house of one of his friends, she was not invited. She heard talk of it at school, she felt the talk designed and pitched to be heard by her.

Fiona was officially not-talking to her now. She wondered what it was that cemented their separation, the entombment of their friendship – was it the sex, the pregnancy, the loss, the suicide? She watched her take her books from her locker and march off to her classes and she wondered did she feel any sadness, any anything in relation to her?

She lost the hermanas entirely. Her mother would not let her go back after Daniel, she did not want to go back after Daniel. Martina came to see her one terrible day, the day after the funeral, and Nell saw in her eyes a look of pleading and she was disgusted. It frightened her to see her rendered so weak. They sat in the front room and Nell had the unbearable sense of them sharing something. That they had passed the lie between them was something they never said, it didn't need to be said, they both knew. Instead she told her about the dream she kept having of Daniel; she told Martina in order to punish her, she told her because it was true, she told her to scare her away. Then Dolores came into the room and told Martina that Nell needed to rest. And then she never saw her again.

She stopped going into town. She had spent her teenage years stalking the town, up and down the high street, through the back alleys, up into the housing estates and back again, usually with friends, usually with Fiona. There was nothing else to do, but she tried to never go down town during the two years that passed between Daniel's death and her leaving for college. She sensed people whispering about her around corners, faces looming in shop windows.

And it was Connie she feared most of all. At the funeral, Connie had ignored her, she had stood at the top of the church, her husband holding her the whole way through the service as if she would fall apart if he let her go. She knew that Connie could see into her soul, if she wanted to. She knew Connie would only have to look at her to know that she, Nell, had killed her son.

She thinks of this now. She sees herself, in her uniform, walking down the main street. And she sees that she was just a girl. She says that aloud in the dark. *I was just a girl.* And for the first time ever, she lets herself cry, not for Daniel, not for Connie, not for the baby, but for that girl, for herself.

The next morning Nell wakes in her own bed. Adrienne is not beside her. This is unusual, Adi is usually sluggish in the mornings and when they are both off work, it is Nell's habit to bring her coffee in bed, which she drinks with extra milk during these last weeks of her pregnancy.

Nell gets up and finds Adrienne in the living room, on her laptop. The late summer sun streams around her, she is getting very big, she is wearing a wide yellow nightdress. Her dark hair curls around her face and she is frowning. She looks like a large, angry sunflower.

Nell attempts a greeting, Adrienne does not look up. She stabs at the laptop with her fingers, as if accusing it of something.

'We can't afford to stay here,' she says, without looking up. 'Do you know how much childcare costs?' She types a bit more. 'Of course you don't,' she says then, in a lower tone.

Nell stays in the doorway, watching her. She hangs her head. She hates when they argue, she always feels like a child and it likewise infuriates Adrienne to be made to feel like a parent.

'Do you actually believe in us, as a family?' Adrienne continues. 'Or are you just waiting for it all to go wrong so you can get back to drinking yourself to death? So you can get back to punishing yourself?' She looks up at Nell. Nell feels small and foolish, leaning against the door frame. When Adi gets like this, she can't figure out a way to respond, she feels like she is drowning in a torrent of her words.

Adrienne turns her attention back to the computer. She likes to use spreadsheets, she likes to list everything that has to be done. She shares these spreadsheets with Nell via Google docs, Nell hardly ever opens them. She thinks of the lists and plans and calculations sitting there, the rows and rows of the spreadsheet like a ladder, all leading somewhere, all leading to something.

'It's not easy for me either,' Adi says. 'And it does feel strange, to be having a child in this way. But I don't know what else to do. I don't know what else there is. There's only this one life, Nell, and this is what we've decided. I didn't force you. You didn't have to.'

She stops to take a breath and then continues, emboldened by the shocking thing she's just said.

'You don't have to stay.'

She says this like it's a discovery she has only just made, like it's a new option she's found, buried in her list, formulated by the spreadsheet.

'Maybe I rushed it, but you had a choice. You are not a child any more. You don't have to stay, I won't make you. It's not your—' And she stops there. She won't say, *it's not your baby anyway*, but she will say it. She'll say it soon, if she has to.

Nell sees that Adrienne is picturing the life that she and the baby will have without her. She sees that Adrienne can see herself moving back in with her parents, getting them to help. She sees her consider the fact that her parents are older – older than Nell's own by fifteen years or so – and brushing that fear aside. She sees Adrienne think about all of this, in a flicker of a second, and resolve that it will be fine. She will be fine, because she has to be. And Nell herself remembers – in a moment of piercing clarity – her own experience of this momentum, this resolve. She blinks and opens her eyes and things are clear.

'I want to call him Daniel,' Nell says.

She feels the words come out of her mouth. They amaze her with their rightness as she speaks them.

'Adi, do you think we could call him that? Would you let me call him that?' She wants to laugh for joy, for a brief moment, at the perfect beauty of this idea.

But then suddenly she is afraid. She is afraid that Adi will turn away, afraid she'll say she's crazy, that it's an insult to Daniel's family, that it's wrong, that she is wrong, that everything she does is stupid and wrong.

Adrienne stops talking. Her face crumples and tears begin to stream down it. She wipes them away, angrily.

'What you did was terrible,' she says. 'I'm not going to pretend that it wasn't. But it's not beyond forgiving.'

Nell begins to walk towards her, Adi holds up a hand to stop her.

'I need you to admit that you deserve forgiveness,' Adi says. 'And I need you to go back there again and sort things out. Once and for all, you need to sort things out.'

Nell drops to the floor. She crawls across it until she is lying at Adi's feet. She remembers her own baby, and how Daniel had looked at them both as she held him. She lets herself think about it, and she lets herself feel it. She draws her knees to her chest and she rocks her body to and fro. Adrienne sits on the couch and weeps fat, silent tears.

31

Nell goes home again in early September. She goes alone this time, for just one night. She books a flight and goes last minute, assured by Adi that the baby won't come. She gets the bus down home from the airport and walks around the town by herself for a while before going up to her parents' house. She sees familiar faces, older faces. She sees features on small children she recognizes from the faces of people she knew years ago. It is lunchtime and girls wearing the uniform she used to wear and boys wearing the uniform Daniel used to wear are spilling in and out of the shops and onto the streets.

Normally when she comes home, she spends all her time in her parents' place, hiding. But today she walks around and she sees the place anew. It isn't such a bad place, really. A few people nod and smile when they see her, she nods and smiles back.

At home, she talks to her mother. Dolores is tense and waiting for something; Nell's decision to come home suddenly has, Nell can see, made Dolores think she is bringing bad news.

She sees that Dolores thinks that she's going to say she and Adrienne are finished.

They talk about restaurants and food. They share a pragmatic outlook on all of that; Nell considers herself informed of, but undazzled by, the mores of London's food culture, she knows you earn about the same working in a Michelin-starred place as you do in a bog-standard one. And she doesn't particularly care to work extra hard in service to some nose-to-tail guru-chef whose monstrous ambition is really just an expression of an undiagnosed personality disorder. But she has picked up a thing or two along the way, and Dolores is always keen to hear about it.

Dolores tells her that lately she's had the urge to run a pub. She then starts talking about Brigid. Nell knows a bit about her grandmother, but she had not known about the rift, about Annie, about exactly what had happened around the time of the referendum. Dolores's eyes shine as she fills her in on all the details, it's a story that seems to thrill her in the telling of it. She gets a little upset when she talks about how Brigid died before they could reconcile but she says she feels that isn't really so important any more. She says she feels that Brigid would think spending a lifetime feeling guilty over one mistake an absurd thing to do.

'I saw a therapist about it,' Dolores says. 'He helped me to see it like that.'

'I've been seeing one too,' Nell says. 'With Adi.'

They sit in silence for a while. Nell senses that her mother is anxious about saying the wrong thing. And then she feels weary with herself for making everyone so anxious all the time.

'Well, you can't run a pub,' Nell says, 'because I'm an

alcoholic.' She is joking as she says this but it is also probably true.

'I had thought that,' Dolores says, carefully. 'But sure you're hardly ever home. And we won't be seeing much more of you once that baby comes.'

Nell is playing with a softened tea coaster, flipping it over and over on the smooth surface of the oil tablecloth. She senses Dolores wanting to put her hand out to stop her but she doesn't.

'You know, we could come home for a while,' Nell says, not looking at her mother. 'I could work somewhere here in town. Adi will be on maternity leave, and she can do her brand consulting stuff from anywhere.'

Dolores laughs. She feels like someone has flung a pebble at the kitchen window, she feels like she is in that moment before it caves in, struck dumb by the sudden, brilliant shattering of the glass.

'Don't say things like that to me, Nell. You'll only break my heart with hoping.'

'Are you serious about the pub?' Nell says, trying to keep her voice steady. 'Where would you get the money?'

It is a dark, poky place, located on one of the quieter back streets in town. It doesn't do food, it doesn't have the capacity to do much more than toasted sandwiches. It serves a dwindling supply of white-haired male drinkers but Dolores thinks it could attract a younger crowd, there's space for musicians at the back. It just requires a very subtle, what would Adrienne call it, yes, a very subtle rebrand. They walk down town together to check it out, they both order pints. It smells dark and solid inside, it makes Nell feel calm and somehow excited.

'Mammy, are you mad?' she says. 'You want to spend your –' she was going to say *twilight years*, but that was ridiculous, Dolores was only, what, fifty-five now and she was looking at her daughter, daring her to go on – 'You want to spend your *precious golden years* –' Dolores swats her with a beer mat – 'slaving away until the small hours dealing with drunks and barrels of beer and washing glasses and all of that?'

'Yes,' says Dolores, happily, firmly. 'That's exactly what I want to do.'

The cost of the licence is the problem, they do not have the money for that. But the family, the couple who own the pub are elderly and want it to be kept going and have no one they trust to run it for them. Their children have all become too successful and have tech jobs and consulting jobs in Dublin and Luxembourg and no interest whatsoever in coming back to this one-horse town to run a day-care for pensioners. And so the family, who know Dolores of old, are delighted to have her come in and manage it, and to take some of her compensation as a down payment on the licence which they would, in theory, pass on to her at some point in the distant or not-too-distant future. Dolores reckons she can double the takings in a year or so, she can see it – and Nell sees that she can see it.

The main thing to figure out is how to make it a bit *trendier* – Dolores puts the word in inverted commas with her fingers, 'Mam, you're mortifying,' Nell says – without scaring away the oul fellas who she would be just heartbroken to lose. She reckons if she keeps the price of Guinness unchanged while offering more craft beers alongside it, she should be okay. Nell wonders if her mother really thinks this will make her happy, and she remembers that that is not the kind of question Dolores asks of herself anyway. Dolores has, in her own quiet, steady way, always been happy. She wonders if Dolores had had more education what she might have done – her episode in Dublin as a young woman points to a curiosity about the world that must have been unfulfilled by the kind of life she ended up living. And ordinarily Nell would just sit with that question but for some reason, here on the cusp of her becoming a mother herself (kind of), she feels that she can ask things that had before now seemed unaskable.

'Mam, do you ever feel angry? That you didn't get, like, *more*?'

'Yes,' Dolores says, emphatically. 'I did feel like that. For a while. But I don't now. I feel like things change so fast that as long as I have one or two solid things I can hold on to, then I'll be grand.'

Nell nods. She looks down at her hands. She feels her mother looking at her, steadily.

'Are you serious about coming back?' Dolores says.

Nell shrugs. 'Maybe. We can't afford to stay in London. And I'd rather be here than in some commuter town where we don't know anyone. Sure we may as well be here as somewhere like that. Our savings will go further. We could maybe even have a garden.'

'What about Adrienne?' Dolores asks.

Nell shrugs again. It is all happening. And she has made it happen. She can't keep acting like all of this has nothing to do with her. She looks up at her mother, who is trying hard to seem still, who is trying hard to suppress a huge smile.

And, look it. It's Adi's egg, it's Jacob's sperm. She needs to get something of herself into that child somehow. She just has to begin to believe that there is something worthwhile in herself, something that she could share, something worth sharing. She looks at her mother, looking back at her. She thinks of her father.

'Adrienne,' she says, 'wants to do whatever's right for the baby. And we think that maybe this could be what's right.'

That evening, she tells Dolores about Daniel, the full truth. It's a bit like the telling of the pregnancy itself, all those years ago, the kind of thing that doesn't seem real, that you can pretend isn't real until you say it out loud. Seeing Martina that time, seeing that it haunts her too, that it had happened, it was real, it had mattered — strangely, oddly, incredibly, miraculously — seeing that was, after a while, a relief. A release. Because for the longest time, she has engaged in a battle with herself, telling herself that it wasn't her fault, that it didn't happen that way, that she'd imagined that conversation with him, that it was nothing to do with her, it was his decision, that she owed no debt to anyone. Half the time, she told herself that, and then the rest of the time it was, *you are nothing, you have no right, you are nothing, remember you are nothing, remember you are nothing.*

To see in Martina's eyes that haunted look, that was what she needed. She needed to see that it was real, it was something, it was a truth and it had to be faced. It mattered. Daniel had mattered. Even if their lie was not the reason, it still mattered. They had hurt him. *She* had hurt him.

★ ★ ★

Dolores reacts with anger, but the anger is directed towards herself. *I should have known, I should have asked you, I should have talked to you about it. I'm sorry, I'm sorry, I'm sorry.*

Nell begs her not to think of it this way. She begs her to help her find a way not to drown in all of this.

32

Martina doesn't become a Minister of the Eucharist. But she does get involved. She feels like a child given a toy to play with so she won't run out into traffic. But she doesn't have the energy to pretend she doesn't need the toy.

There isn't much to be done. It's pretty much a dying parish, like all of them. She polishes the pews, organizes flowers, and arranges the parish bulletins on the table in the vestibule. On Sundays, there is a passable crowd and on Communion and Confirmation days it is standing room only, the priest informs her, and mostly the young people still get married in the church and have their babies baptized. Or the other way around, he says, and laughs.

The priest calls on Martina a few times to talk to the troubled teenage daughters of some of the more desperate parishioners, girls on waiting lists for mental health therapies. These families can't afford to go private, and they have at least a folk memory – or a folk memory of their parents' folk memory – of a time when the Church might actually do something for you. Martina says yes, but she struggles with this, with the idea that she can help these girls. She barely knows what social media is – it's their whole lives, she quickly learns – and she finds she has little patience for the kind of struggles the young girls report, the same kind of petty anxieties around appearance and popularity as before, but just intensified and multiplied. She wonders if this is how it is all going to end, the ice caps melting as everyone gazes into their own private reflecting pool, stoking and feeding their own egos in order to avoid having to see anything else or care about anyone else. To be fair, some of these young girls report terror around the environment as well as this deep, tedious despair around their own attractiveness. It's all pretty glum, and Martina has no answers for them. She lets them talk and she listens and one or two of them seem to like her. She offers no solutions. She says nothing about Jesus.

Martina sees a lady in a floral summer dress, and she remembers her from the funeral. She has striking straw-like blonde hair and wide blue eyes and big splashy freckles on her face and arms that make her look young. She is a Tuesday and Wednesday Mass-goer, she stands at the back, she is known to the parish.

She asks the priest about her. He tells her that she lost a son, he tells her she comes to Mass only during the week, when it's quiet. He is buried, the son, in the big cemetery close to town but according to the priest, the woman doesn't like to go to Mass there, the church is too big, she dislikes its large emptiness, she doesn't want people she knows to see her going in.

'I know her,' Martina says. 'But she wouldn't know me.'

All through the late summer into the autumn, she wonders what God wants her to do about this. It seems too strange a coincidence, but then people here are always claiming coincidences that are not any such thing at all — it's just what happens in a place with so few people; you run into one another. She prays for direction, she prays in a way she hasn't prayed for years. She finds herself praying for an answer that she knows will come, it's a calm kind of praying, a waiting. She has a sense of things playing out in the way that they have to, and all she has to do is watch.

And go to Confession. One day, she wakes and realizes that she is ready. She tells the priest — a different one — everything. She tells him that she had a fear of sex from when she was young, it even predated her rape, somehow it seemed to have caused the rape, she says. He doesn't say anything in response to this, and she is grateful.

She tells him that she wanted to help young people find God in the way that she had. But she wanted this for herself too. There was a loneliness in being so different from everyone else in her culture, and so when she found someone who felt the same, who might have felt the same, her soul rejoiced — not just because they were going to know the joy that she knew, but also because she herself would be a little less alone.

And she saw that in Nell. She knew the other girls were not long for the movement. There was Fiona, but she didn't feel the connection with Fiona she felt with Nell — she wasn't as dazzled by Fiona, which was unfair but true.

And so when Nell told her that she was pregnant, she just couldn't bear it. She tells this to the priest, and she puts her head in her hands. She's never said that out loud before. She tells him she thought Nell above that way of being, that sordid, godless behaviour. And so she had used her influence on her to convince her that the boy had done something wrong. And she saw that Nell didn't really believe it herself, that it wasn't really the truth – they both knew it wasn't – but Nell was too ashamed to admit to Martina, whom she loved, whom she trusted, that she had had drunken sex at a party. And now that Martina knows, via Michaela, that Nell loves women, not men, she feels she understands even more fully. Or she understands even more fully how little she ever understood anything at all.

'I was trying to control her. I was trying to use her. To protect my own feelings, to protect myself from the fear of losing her. And because of that – then.'

And she tells the priest about what the boy had done.

She recalls the day, the most shameful day, at Nell's house, after the funeral. She recalls the way Nell had looked at her in naked fear, with a devouring guilt in her face, and how she had looked back, with those same feelings. She recalls how they both knew, in that moment, without having to say a word about it, what wrong they had done. There was an unbearable mortification in that moment; Martina realized that any status, any respect she had enjoyed in Nell's eyes, had been erased and was now gone for ever.

'It was my fault,' Martina says. 'She was just a girl. It was my fault.'

The priest tells her that she sinned gravely but that God would not have taken the boy's life to punish her, that a God of love didn't operate like that. Martina thanks him and leaves the confessional.

She doesn't believe the priest. She knows it is her fault.
And so still she waits.

33

It's February when they next come back. There's three of them this time.

Daniel is a top baby. Hardy feeder, fantastic sleeper, precocious smiler. He has an outrageous shock of soft black hair which points to Jacob's part-Jamaican heritage, or Adrienne's part-Italian, or maybe her Greek bit. No one can say for sure. They run their fingers through it, grinning like punch-drunk idiots.

Nell's love for him grows easily, it grows effortlessly, it grows like the grass after a rainy spring. While Adrienne was being stitched up in theatre – it was a forceps, almost an emergency section, absolutely terrifying – Nell stood in the recovery area, weeping every tear she had over the transparent plastic cot. She noted the pink skin of the soles of his feet, the desperate squeeze of his tiny fists.

The welcome parties at home feel the same. She and Adrienne are waited on like royalty. They catch up on sleep. They walk around the town in the few slender hours of winter daylight, beaming groggily. Nell sees her town with new eyes, which are partly Adrienne's eyes, and partly Daniel's eyes. She sees that Adrienne would relish the challenge of setting up shop here, she sees that she would love the attention of being the exotic London blow-in, she sees that her culture's wild, insouciant evasions would suit her wife (yes, they are engaged) just fine.

She sees that a little boy could be safe here. Or she sees that a little boy could be as safe here as he could be anywhere.

Her mother establishes contact. She drives them out, to the same house, to again talk about a baby. Dolores has seen Connie a few times over the years, she still has her number. They got drunk together once, in the back of a pub, after bumping into each other at an event at the arts festival. They didn't talk much about anything, just swapped ordinary family anecdotes and drank endless gin and tonics, Dolores never forgot the hangover.

Connie has two daughters, they stayed local, they didn't want to leave. She said to Dolores that night that she was all right, that it never went away, but that she was all right.

That was before the grandchildren arrived, all girls. Nell and Adrienne are shown photos of them, their toys are piled up in the corner of the front room, Connie looks after them for their working mothers – a hairdresser, an accountant – a couple of days a week. She is retired, her husband still works. He took it hard, he drinks too much. Dolores doesn't know how she knows this but everyone knows this.

Daniel is asleep when they arrive, strapped onto Nell via the expensive if perplexing-to-operate sling they have acquired. She mostly carries him, Adrienne has back pain and she tends to get sweaty and overheat. Nell is cold-blooded and thinwristed and she loves the warm heft of him against her in this his first winter.

Connie weeps as she holds him. She nods eagerly, intensely when they ask permission.

Nell isn't going to tell her. She isn't going to tell her because her mother told her not to. Dolores is of the opinion that the telling would do no good, would serve no purpose after all this time. She says that Nell has no way of knowing what he had been thinking, that she never would and that it would bring nothing but pain. Nell knows that this is propaganda – the forgivable propaganda a mother employs in order to convince herself that the course of action that best protects her child is the objective best course of action. But just because something is propaganda doesn't mean it isn't true, and she does think Dolores is probably right. She reckons it's better for her to carry this guilt, this pain, rather than risk causing more anguish to Connie, who seems, as she says, all right. But it is never a still thought for her. It will stay with her for ever.

34

They invite Martina and Connie to the wedding, and it is a surprise to discover on the day that they already know each other. Martina is doing all right, she's got a new job, working in admin at one of the call centres on the ring road, still living at the farm, still involved with the parish. Nell sees her semi-regularly, the farm is a fun place to take Daniel, he looks in alarm at the cows, they say that's because he is a city boy at heart.

The wedding comes at a stressful time, Jacob is having a bit of heartache and regret over letting them move away – Adrienne is furious at him, there is no question of him *letting* us do anything, she says, but Nell is sympathetic. She knows what it's like to change how you feel about a baby. She convinces Adrienne to invite him to the wedding, she says it will all work out okay.

Starting up the pub is also stressful. For a while, Dolores and Adrienne thought that Adrienne could serve food, that she could bring her Middle Eastern-influenced tastes to the town, but Nell fears the clash of personalities that would involve – they both like very much to do things their own way – and she is relieved when Adi says she'd like to take a bit more time off first. Which means Nell has to find work, which she does, at first in a hotel owned by one of the wealthy pub-owning dynasty-families in the town and then, when she gets bored of that, she starts working alongside Dolores, in her place. They end up doing sourdough pizzas, not particularly imaginative, but they are popular and there is a decent margin on them.

The rent on their small house is just about affordable, and Nell thinks she might, maybe, no promises to anyone, think about studying something, maybe getting a degree, every idiot has a degree nowadays, it wouldn't kill her to get one too. Her parents help with childcare, Liam more than Dolores, he feels that the child needs a strong male role model. Nell senses a rebuke in that and is upset, but Adrienne tells her she is imagining it, she tells her that they are blessed in what they have.

Her father and mother are changed, are different, and it's interesting to Nell to think of all they have done and been in the years she has been away. Running the pub together – Liam gets involved as it gets busier– seems to unite them, to strengthen them. But as that happens, they try, gently, to push her away from it. Her father tells her this is not her future, he reminds her what she was good at in school. He leaves university prospectuses on the kitchen table when he visits their house.

In the past, this would have irritated Nell, this would have frightened her. But now she feels that there is no path decreed for her, except one that involves Adrienne and Daniel. She feels she can do absolutely anything. She feels the world has nothing that can humiliate her, nothing that can hurt her. Any pain she has, she carries and she carries it gladly.

Amid all of that then, the wedding.

The ceremony, in October, Daniel thirteen months old. The brides walk down the aisle separately: Adrienne first, with her parents – jovial, bemused, a little shy; and then Nell with hers – thrilled, upright, beaming. Jenny and Amanda followed as bridesmaids, Jenny carries Daniel, her cheek pressed against his.

Adrienne has strong opinions about weddings, she feels there should be performance and drama and tears, so friends are called upon to sing and to read poems and it is all very sentimental and unforgettable. The weather is perfect – they stand on the lawn of the stately home hidden in the depths of the countryside, the autumn sun falls on them, everyone grinning as if in a dream. Friends of Dolores and Liam boast to their children via WhatsApp messages that they are attending a wedding between two women, small children splash about in the sodden leaves, older aunts and uncles wonder if they still serve the usual post-ceremony cup of tea at these new type of weddings. Adrienne exclaims over how deep and lush and clear the countryside is and for the first time in her life Nell feels proud of where she is from.

Later in the evening, Nell notices Martina and Connie talking to each other by the bar. She feels a twinge of pain, the one that will always be there, but it has a halo of fear around it now too. What are they talking about?

She approaches them, she is slightly tipsy – though she has tried hard to pace herself, she is working on that part of herself too – and says, merrily, a little too casually, 'I didn't know that you two knew each other.' Connie nods and Martina smiles that vague, peaceful, I'm-not-saying-anything smile that Nell remembers from a long time ago.

'I get Mass at Martina's church sometimes,' Connie says. 'During the week when it's quiet.'

'Oh, right,' Nell says. She looks at Martina and she can see that she feels the same pain, that she carries the same cross.

'Well, Martina,' Nell says. 'A wedding between two women. And the sky hasn't fallen in on us yet.'

Martina's face flinches as if Nell has scratched her, and Nell feels bad. But she is also annoyed. She isn't supposed to be feeling these feelings on her wedding day.

'You both look so beautiful,' Martina says, and she holds out her hand and puts it on Nell's arm. Her fingers are stiff and cold. Nell feels the pain of her in the way she grips her.

'I am very proud to know you both,' Martina says, and Nell is relieved to see how she sits back up and looks at her straight on with dignity.

That night, Nell and Adrienne are staying in the nicest hotel in town before leaving, with Daniel, for a holiday in Sicily the next day. Liam and Dolores are looking after the baby for them for the night, they have been supplied with bottles and dummies and detailed instructions. When they get back to their room, Nell and Adrienne remove their shoes and rub their feet and gossip about the day and fall into the big bed together.

Nell does not sleep well. She drifts between the sounds of the town beneath the bedroom window, it is a Friday night, people are out and drunk and loud. When she finally does sleep, she dreams once more of a garden, and within the dream, a sense of reaching, of grasping, comes to her. She is reaching for him, the Daniel who is her son, the Daniel who was another woman's son, and the other child, the other son, the one who'd never even had a name. The dream then dissolves and all she is left with in a space between thought and sleep is a sense that she will spend the rest of her time here trying to get at the truth, at a truth, or maybe, finally, simply, to a place where there is no truth, no untruth, no God, no god, just this bodily, sacred, limited, limitless, wholly unholy devotion.

Acknowledgements

It's been quite hard writing the acknowledgements for this book – it's difficult to put into words how grateful I am to the very many people who helped me get this done.

First and foremost, Sallyanne Sweeney, a true treasure of a human being and agent. Humour, steadfastness, loyalty, cop-on and intelligence. Thank you. Thanks also to Ivan Mulcahy for the occasional stern reminders.

And then Sophie Jonathan, who saw this book in its quite mad, inchoate state and believed that something coherent could be created. I am forever grateful for your belief in those early pages. And Orla King, who worked alongside Sophie as an editor, and brought her distinct intelligence to the book.

Thanks to Siobhan Slattery, Laura Carr, Cormac Kinsella and the wider team at Picador for making publication of *Hearts and Bones* and *The Amendments* so enjoyable, and for helping to spread the word. Thank you to the excellent copy-editor Mary Chamberlain for insight and diligence.

A special thanks is due to my dear friend and story-structure guru Mark Hennigan for that Hail Mary call back in September 2022, and for many years of talking about books and films and everything else.

Thanks to the Tyrone Guthrie Centre for a vital week in January 2023. And sincere thanks to the Arts Council of Ireland for their financial support.

Thanks to the community of writers at London Writers' Salon for sharing their experiences of perseverance and fortitude. And thanks always to Parul Bavishi.

Thanks to Anne Murray, once again, for her support and sensitivity. And to Sorcha Wakely for asking the question that made this book begin. And of course to Sheena Dempsey, for ongoing creative solidarity, I don't know what I'd do without it.

Thanks to the readers, booksellers, reviewers and authors who enjoyed and supported *Hearts and Bones*.

Thanks to my sister, Rosemary, for insight and inimitable wit. To Thomas, for enduring many re-readings and many other writing-related torments over the years.

Thanks to my parents, Rose and Ger Mulvey, to whom this book is dedicated, who instilled in us the values of persistence and generosity and who only sometimes suggest doing something more sensible with one's career.

Thanks to my brothers, Éamonn, Brendan and Peter, for all their support and jokes. Thanks especially to Éamonn for assistance with the nomenclature.

Thanks to the Meehan family also, for their love and support.

Thanks to my children, Seán and Rosanna, for being the reason for all of this. Please don't read it for another few years.